Books by Dianne Freeman

A LADY'S GUIDE TO ETIQUETTE AND MURDER

A LADY'S GUIDE TO GOSSIP AND MURDER

A LADY'S GUIDE TO MISCHIEF AND MURDER

Published by Kensington Publishing Corporation

A Lady's Guide to Gossip and Murder

Dianne Freeman

KENSINGTON BOOKS
www.kensingtonbooks.com

KENSINGTON BOOKS are published by

Kensington Publishing Corp.
119 West 40th Street
New York, NY 10018

All Kensington titles, imprints, and distributed lines are available at special quantity discounts for bulk purchases for sales promotion, premiums, fundraising, educational, or institutional use.

Special book excerpts or customized printings can also be created to fit specific needs. For details, write or phone the office of the Kensington Sales Manager: Attn.: Sales Department. Kensington Publishing Corp., 119 West 40th Street, New York, NY 10018. Phone: 1-800-221-2647.

Kensington and the K logo Reg. U.S. Pat. & TM Off.

First Kensington Hardcover Edition: July 2019

ISBN-13: 978-1-4967-1692-7 (ebook)
ISBN-10: 1-4967-1692-2 (ebook)

ISBN-13: 978-1-4967-1691-0
ISBN-10: 1-4967-1691-4
First Kensington Trade Paperback Edition: July 2020

10 9 8 7 6 5 4 3 2

Printed in the United States of America

This book is dedicated to Dan—because I'm a very lucky lady!

Acknowledgments

Turning a manuscript into a book is the work of a dedicated and passionate team. I'd like to give thanks to everyone who was part of the Countess of Harleigh team. Melissa Edwards, my agent, for finding the perfect match for my manuscript. To John Scognamiglio for being that perfect match and for his good humor and patience in working with a new author. Thanks to the whole Kensington team for bringing this book into the world, with special thanks to Robin Cook and Pearl Saban whose eagle eyes caught every slip and typo I left them.

Many thanks to my Authors '18 family, whose support helped me navigate this treacherous debut year. To Mary Keli-ikoa, Emily Wheeler, and Bea Conti for your feedback and encouragement. And to my family and friends for your support and love.

Chapter 1

August 1899

London in late summer was really no place to be. With society thin and events like Ascot and the derby a distant memory, the few of us remaining in town were hard-pressed for entertainment. But if one were required to spend the summer in London, one could not choose a better site for an afternoon soiree than Park Lane, with Hyde Park on one side of the street, and some of the largest mansions in London on the other. One might almost imagine oneself in the country. If one were in possession of a superior imagination, that is.

Though the garden was large by London standards, there were a good forty or more of us gathered here, dispersed between the conservatory at the rear of the house and the small tables scattered across the lawn. It made for a bit of a squeeze and might have been terribly uncomfortable if the sun were not playing its usual game of hide-and-seek.

This was my first summer in town and I can't say I found it to my liking. My previous summers—in fact, most of my previous nine years in England—had been spent in the countryside of Surry where my late husband, the Earl of Harleigh, dropped me off and left me shortly after our honeymoon.

He returned to London and his bevy of mistresses.

I didn't mind the country so much as I minded the mistresses. That's where I raised our daughter, Rose. And except for annual trips to London for the Season, it's where I stayed, like the dutiful wife my mother raised me to be. You see, before I was Frances Wynn, Countess of Harleigh, I was Frances Price, American heiress. I found neither role particularly satisfying, so a year after my husband's death, I left the Wynn family home, with my young daughter in tow, and set up my household in a lovely little house on Chester Street in Belgravia. Now I was in charge of my life, and I enjoyed it immensely, though I could wish my funds allowed for trips to the country in the summer.

I stepped down from the conservatory to join the group at the nearest table for a glass of champagne—Lady Argyle had planned this soiree in a grand style. No watered-down punch for her—when I caught a glimpse of a marine blue hat perched atop a head of chestnut waves. Ah, Fiona had arrived. As she moved through the crowd toward me, I saw her ensemble was also blue, trimmed in peach and white.

Sadly, I wore mourning. Again. This time for my sister-in-law, Delia, who died three months ago under rather unfortunate circumstances—which I'd prefer to forget. She'd left behind two sons and the current Earl of Harleigh, my late husband's younger brother.

Strictly speaking, I shouldn't even be at this gathering, but my brother-in-law, with a degree of compassion I never dreamed possible, refused to plunge his young sons into deep mourning, with the requisite black armbands, silenced clocks, and attention to nothing but one's grief for the duration of a year or more. Children needed the joy of childhood, he in-

sisted, and decreed we'd all observe half mourning for no more
than six months. Social codes be damned.

I jest not. Graham, the staid and starchy Earl of Harleigh, dis-
regarded a firmly embedded social convention.

There just might be hope for him yet.

As applied to myself, Graham's decree meant I could venture
out in company and would not be forced to wear black all summer. Though I was restricted to gray and lavender, black was
decidedly worse. For this occasion, I wore a lavender confection, suitably light in weight and fashionable for the season,
topped off by a cunning wide-brimmed hat, but gad—it was
lavender. Did anyone look well in this color?

"Darling!"

Fiona had caught sight of me and raised a hand in greeting. A
parasol matching the trim on her dress dangled from a loop on
her wrist. Her path to me intersected with that of Sir Hugo Ridley, who, upon noting her destination, raised his hand in
greeting and followed in her wake.

She reached my side, bussed my cheek, then backed up to ac-
knowledge our companion. "How do you do, Ridley? It's been
an age since we've met."

I'd known Ridley for a number of years. He was a friend of
my late husband, one of the few I didn't avoid. Like Reggie, he
spent far too much time drinking, gambling, and generally
wasting his life. The effects of his habits revealed themselves in
the pallor of his skin, the slight paunch of his stomach, and the
circles under his eyes. Unlike Reggie, he was devoted to his
wife and could be amusing when he exerted himself.

He gave us a nod. "Lady Harleigh. Lady Fiona. I'm surprised to find you both in town this late in summer. Does that
mean you'll be attending our little soiree in honor of the Glorious Twelfth?"

The Glorious Twelfth referred to the twelfth of August—the

official start of the shooting season, when all—well, most members of the upper class return to their estates to shoot various varieties of fowl until February. The Ridleys, however, were Londoners through and through and never left town. Instead, they held an annual gathering on the twelfth for those who stayed.

"I've already sent my reply to Lady Ridley. My family and I will be delighted to attend."

Ridley smiled and turned to Fiona.

"As it happens, I'm on the eve of my departure to the country. Nash must shoot, you know," she said, in reference to her husband. "In truth, I'd hoped to take Lady Harleigh with me." She thrust out her lower lip in a caricature of a childish pout. "Are you sure you won't come, Frances? Nash and I would love to have you."

I caught her hand and gave it a squeeze. "Thank you for the invitation, Fiona, but that arrangement doesn't suit my houseguests." I was dejected to have to decline her offer but I could hardly accept her invitation and bring along three extra guests, and my daughter, and her nanny. "Besides, my sister is determined to stay in town to be near Mr. Kendrick."

"Young love," Ridley said. "Will they be making an announcement soon?"

A footman in black livery stepped up to offer a tray of refreshments, beads of sweat visible on his forehead. Poor man. Ridley distributed flutes of champagne among us and waved the man off. The three of us set off on a stroll across the lawn.

"They haven't yet set a date for the wedding," I replied. "I believe they'll wait until the fall to make any plans." Lily, my younger sister, had arrived from New York three months ago with the sole intention of finding and marrying a lord. Instead she found Leo Kendrick, the son of a wealthy businessman, and they'd been a couple ever since. Leo had asked for her hand in marriage and she accepted. They were eager to announce their engagement, but I urged them to wait. She was only eighteen. The same age I'd been when I rushed into a disastrous marriage.

I had no objections to Leo, but I'd had no objections to my feckless, philandering husband at the time I'd married him either. The objections came later and continued until the day he died in the bed of his lover. So, you see, I wasn't being obstructive, I simply wanted them to get to know one another before marriage.

Fiona tutted. "She's going to marry the man at some point, Frances. This delay will make no difference. You'd do better to concentrate on your little protégée. She must be starving for entertainment."

"If one is starving for entertainment in London, Lady Fiona, one has far too large an appetite." Sir Hugo raised his glass to emphasize his point. "I met the lovely Miss Deaver when you attended the theater last week. She seemed to be enjoying herself."

Charlotte Deaver, my "little protégée," as Fiona called her, was a friend of Lily's from New York. "Lottie is fascinated with everything London," I said, with a nod to Ridley. "And is quite able to entertain herself. She's just as content with a trip to the library or a museum as she is mingling with society. Actually, more so." I lowered my voice and leaned in toward my friends. "She's a bit awkward at social events."

Fiona raised her brows. "Dearest, you truly understate the case. More men have been injured dancing with her than were wounded in the Transvaal Rebellion."

I huffed. "That's unfair, Fiona. She may be somewhat lacking in grace, but she's injured none of her dance partners."

Ridley covered a laugh by clearing his throat. "Graceful or not, I found her charming, and doubt any man in London would say differently. I'm sure Evingdon finds her so." He inclined his head in the direction of the house where Lottie stumbled over three short steps leading from the conservatory to the lawn. Charles Evingdon, descending the steps himself, quickly caught her arm to stop her from falling face-first into the rose bushes. Sadly, he couldn't prevent her hat, a confection of pink bows and white plumes, from launching itself into the shrubbery.

"Oh, I wasn't expecting to see Evingdon here today."

"I don't mind seeing him," Ridley said. "It's speaking with him that rather challenges my patience."

I gave the man a cool stare. "I'll remind you, Ridley, Charles Evingdon is part of my family."

His eyes sparkled with mischief. "Cousin to your late husband, I believe. Therefore, I won't hold it against you, my dear Lady Harleigh. But I will beg you to excuse me."

With that he gave us a cheeky grin and sauntered away, my glare boring into his back. "Every time I think that man has turned over a new leaf, he reminds me of what a scoundrel he really is."

"Marriage isn't likely to make that man civil, dear," Fiona said. "But in this case, I'd say he was just being honest."

"Charles is different, I'll grant you that." He was certainly different from my other in-laws in a number of ways. Most notably, his branch of the family managed to hold on to their wealth, he didn't hold my American background against me, and in contrast to the cold austerity of my nearest in-laws, he was as friendly as a golden retriever.

I turned my attention back to the house and smiled when Charles raised a hand to gain my attention. He steadied Lottie on her feet, set her hat atop the wreckage of her hair, and headed in our direction.

"I daresay he's coming over to thank me for introducing him to Mary Archer." I tipped my head toward Fiona and preened a bit. "He seems quite taken with her. I believe I can count that match as one of my successes."

"I wouldn't say that overloud, dear." Fiona leaned in closer. "You wouldn't want anyone to think you were in the business of matchmaking. Or in business at all, for that matter."

"Of course not." I took a quick glance around to assure myself no one was close enough to hear. "I've simply made one or two discreet introductions. Can I help it if the recipients of those introductions chose to show their gratitude with a gift?"

"But I wonder if Mrs. Archer is grateful. Do you really suppose she's equally taken with Evingdon?" She wrinkled her nose. "He's rather dim-witted, don't you think?"

"You're as bad as Ridley. It's terribly uncharitable of you to say such a thing. Aside from being my relation, he's a very likable and kind man. He's also a good friend of your brother's, and George doesn't suffer fools."

Her lips compressed in a straight line. I was right and she knew it. In fact, it was George's good opinion of Charles that led me to believe the man must have a brain somewhere in his head. His actions certainly led one to think otherwise.

He approached us with a genial grin, one he wore frequently and which made him seem much younger than his thirty-six years, as did his tall, athletic frame and thick head of wheat-colored hair. He wore it slightly too long for fashion, but it suited him.

"Ladies," he said with a tip of his straw boater. "I was hoping to find you here. Well, actually I was only hoping to find you, Cousin Frances."

He paused, but as I drew breath to speak, he continued. "Not that I didn't want to find you, Lady Fiona, just that I wasn't actively seeking you, you understand? Good to find you all the same. Rather like looking for a book you'd mislaid somewhere and stumbling across another that turns out to be equally diverting. Not that I would ever stumble across you, of course. But one would have to admit you are diverting."

He finished this monologue with a show of dimples.

"It's lovely to see you too, Cousin Charles."

I glanced at Fiona. A line had worked itself between her brows. She parted her lips to speak, then seemed to think better of it.

I gave her arm a squeeze. "I'm sure Lady Nash is pleased to see you as well."

"Yes, of course," she said. "If you'll excuse me. I've yet to greet our hostess."

With that she slipped away like an animal escaping a trap. I took a breath and returned my attention to my cousin. "Did Mrs. Archer not accompany you today?"

"Ah. Mrs. Archer. Yes. Exactly why I wanted to speak with you."

"How are things progressing with the two of you?"

He brushed off his sleeves as if they were dusty, then straightened his tie. As he fidgeted, his gaze traveled in every direction but mine. "Well . . ." He finally looked me in the eye. "Actually, not well. Not well at all." He cast a suspicious glance at two young ladies nearby, their heads together in giggling conversation, and offered me his arm.

"Would you care to stroll, Cousin Frances?"

I took his arm and we set off at a leisurely pace around the perimeter of the garden. "Is there something you wish to tell me?"

"No," he said. "Well, yes. It seems we may not suit after all, Mrs. Archer and I. I thought we might. She's an excellent woman." He rubbed the back of his neck and let out a breath. "Lovely, pleasant, intelligent. Took quite a shine to her, in fact. But as it turns out, we don't. Er, suit, that is."

"I'm so sorry to hear that." Truly sorry. Mary Archer was one of the most patient and kind women of my acquaintance. I'd be hard-pressed to find another suitable lady if she wouldn't do. Though I could hardly tell him that.

"It sounds as though you've grown fond of Mrs. Archer. Are

you certain you wish to end the acquaintance? What you now view as a difficulty may, in time, become nothing."

He set his jaw and gave a slight shake of his head. "No, I don't see how I can pursue the connection. If there's someone else of your acquaintance who might be interested in an introduction," he added, his expression a mixture of hope and doubt.

"I'm sure there is, Charles. But in an effort to avoid another mistake, perhaps you could tell me why you didn't suit."

"As to that, I'm afraid it would be rather ungentlemanly to say more. I found no fault with Mrs. Archer and I do wish to marry, but we simply—"

"Didn't suit?" I raised my brows.

"Exactly!" He gave me another glimpse of his dimples. "I knew you'd understand."

I did not understand. Nor was it likely I'd gain any insight by speaking to Charles. Perhaps George could provide me with some guidance. Or Mary herself.

Yes, Mary was far more likely to provide an explanation for their rift. I'd have to pay her a visit tomorrow. "Just give me a few days, Charles. I'll let you know how I get on."

The garden party lasted only a few hours more. Storm clouds rumbled overhead as I took my leave of Fiona, forcing the stalwart Brit to endure my hugs since I likely wouldn't see her until spring. Unless, of course, I gave in to Lily's longing for a winter wedding. Fiona would certainly attend that event. I doubted I'd be able to hold Lily and Leo off much longer. The way they were saying farewell, one would think they too wouldn't see one another until spring. In fact, their parting would only be for perhaps a day.

Once they completed their farewells, the four of us—Lily, Lottie, Aunt Hetty, and I—climbed into George Hazelton's carriage. Mr. Hazelton was my neighbor, Fiona's older brother, and a wonderful friend who acted as escort to our little group when he was free and loaned us his carriage when he wasn't. Though I had funds sufficient to maintain my household, they didn't stretch to keeping a carriage and horses. Lily had traveled to England with Aunt Hetty as her chaperone. Hetty was my father's sister and shared his genius for making money, but I didn't know how long she'd be staying with me and I feared growing accustomed to living within her means.

The two young ladies took the rear-facing seats, allowing Hetty and I to face forward. She climbed in first, pulling out the newspaper she'd tucked into the seat earlier. I tutted as I seated myself beside her. "Hetty, you'll strain your eyes reading in this light."

She dismissed my concerns with a few mumbled words and folded the broadsheet to a manageable size. "Don't concern yourself with my vision, dear. It's fine."

I frowned at the paper hiding her face. "Can't you put that down? I have a dilemma and hoped to get your opinion."

"We have opinions." Lily gestured to Lottie and herself.

"Of course, but I'd like Aunt Hetty's, too." I gave her a nudge with my elbow.

"Go on, I'm listening," she said.

"I just spoke to Cousin Charles." I sighed. "He tells me he no longer wishes to pursue a connection with Mary Archer." I glanced up at my relations, hoping for some sympathy.

"And you thought they were such a good match," Lily said. "Did he say why?"

"No, just that things did not work out between them, and he'd be amenable to another introduction if I knew of someone suitable."

"He's the nice cousin, isn't he? And Hazelton's friend?" Aunt Hetty tucked a wayward strand of dark hair up into her hat. She was nearly fifty, and though her face was just beginning to show the years, her hair was still jet black. She wrinkled her nose. "The rather dim-witted one?"

"He is Mr. Hazelton's friend, but he's not dim-witted. At least I think that's rather harsh. He's such a good-hearted man, and pleasant company. Just confusing at times. Or maybe confused."

"He's very handsome," Lily offered.

"And he is his brother's heir," I said, "so one day he'll be Viscount Evingdon."

"So, he's good-hearted, handsome, and will possess a title. I don't suppose there's a chance he's wealthy in the bargain?" Hetty glanced from behind her paper, arching a dark brow.

"That part of the family is quite well off."

"Then why did he need your help in finding a match? I'd assume such a man would have women making offers of marriage to him on a daily basis." She stared at me with a confusion I fully understood. She was new to London society, quite different from New York, but even she knew a great catch when she heard of one.

"Actually, he does find it difficult to keep the ladies at bay, but he's hoping to find someone who is attracted to *him*, rather than his title and fortune."

"And his handsome face," Lily added. "Don't forget that."

I glanced across at my sister. Only eighteen years old and replete with blond-haired, blue-eyed, china doll loveliness. Indeed, she was the very image of my mother, while I was a combination of both parents—dark brown hair with blue eyes and fair skin. And like my aunt Hetty, I fairly towered over my petite sister. At twenty-seven, I was nearly a decade older as well. It came as a surprise that she would see beauty in a man almost twenty years her senior.

"I suggest you never let Leo find out you have an attraction for older men," I said, smiling as she blushed.

"I have eyes, Frances, but while I can see the man is handsome, it doesn't necessarily follow that I'm attracted to him. You know I'm completely devoted to Leo."

Indeed, I did know. This was just another of Lily's reminders that I was delaying their wedding, and for no good reason as far as she was concerned. In fact, later this week we'd be dining with Leo's family and I expected pressure to concede a few months in favor of an earlier wedding date. And ready or not, it was likely Lily would be a married woman before the new year. I dearly hoped she was ready.

She leaned forward and touched my wrist, bringing me out of my reverie. "What about Lottie as a match for Mr. Evingdon?"

I glanced over at Lottie in time to see the girl blush furiously. I should have seen this coming. Lily had invited her to visit during the next social season and allow me to introduce her to London society. Lottie's mother favored the idea, but not the timing. She'd dropped her only daughter on our doorstep three weeks ago, like a twenty-one-year-old foundling, and took herself off to Paris to have a new wardrobe designed.

Or so she claimed.

Since her forwarding address was in care of the Comte De Beaulieu, I found her cover story rather weak. The Comte was the notorious libertine British husbands considered all Frenchmen to be. And penniless in the bargain. If he had designs on anything, it was likely Mrs. Deaver's pin money. Considering the large bank draft she provided to cover her daughter's expenses, and my own of course, I suspected her pin money to be substantial, and Mr. Deaver was unlikely to miss it or his wife. If the gossip from my mother's letters was true, Mrs. Deaver so scandalized the matrons of New York, none of them would let their sons near Lottie.

Considering Mrs. Deaver's reputation across the pond, it was perhaps for the best that she moved on before she could establish one here. But while I appreciated the extra funds, I was left with the problem of what to do with Lottie. The unfortunate young lady sought an aristocratic husband during a time when the aristocrats were all tucked away at their country homes preparing to shoot red grouse as soon as the Glorious Twelfth arrived.

There were few social events this late in the summer, which meant we had her company all to ourselves for the weeks she'd been here. She was a pretty girl of medium height, slender, as fashion decreed, with an oval face framed by an abundance of russet hair. I found her to be endlessly interested in everything. As I told Sir Hugo, she was easy to entertain. She was also determined to be helpful. I learned very quickly, accepting her assistance could be dangerous.

If I allowed her to arrange the flowers, she'd only break the vase and spill the water. I'd once asked her to fetch a book from a shop just a few blocks away. She'd neglected to take a maid and, lost in thought, she wandered so far out of the neighborhood, three of us had to go out in search of her. A search that took several hours from my day and, I suspect, a few years off my life as I imagined her abducted and sold into slavery. How would I ever have explained that to her family?

She seemed always to have a spot on her dress, ink on her fingers, and a trail of destruction in her wake, but it was clear she always had the best of intentions. In fact, she was very endearing and I liked her a great deal, if only I could keep her from touching anything.

But as a match for Charles? I wasn't quite sure who would make a good match for Lottie, but I'd never have picked him. For one, his home had far too many priceless antiques to be broken. For another, though I protested Aunt Hetty's saying it, he was a bit of a dunderhead. Lottie needed someone to help her navigate the twists and turns of society. That would not be Charles.

There was one objection I could make. "It would probably be wise to find out from Mr. Evingdon why he didn't form an attachment to Mrs. Archer before I introduce him to anyone else."

"Why did you consider her a good match for Mr. Evingdon?" Lily asked.

Hmm, a good question. "In part because she's a widow and her late husband's family is rather prominent in society. They did a great deal of entertaining and Mary was quite the darling of the fashionable set. When Cousin Charles inherits, he will have to take his place in that world, take his seat in the House of Lords, and Mary would be a good helpmeet in that area."

"Well, that's very practical, I suppose." Lily sounded as if she were talking about stale bread—it could be eaten, but she'd have none of it. I chuckled as she wrinkled her nose.

"That is only part of it, of course. They had many shared interests, and Mr. Evingdon told me he was seeking a woman of some maturity and intelligence. Mary fit the bill on both fronts. She is almost thirty and is very intelligent. Her wit is rapier sharp, but she is a very kind and caring person. I feel badly that she and Charles could not make a go of it. She doesn't go out in society much these days, and I fear she may have fallen on hard times since her husband's death. She's managed to keep the home they lived in on the edge of Mayfair so perhaps she receives an allowance from her late husband's family. Her only family is a sister who lives near Oxford. So, Mary is quite alone."

Lily frowned. "Well, now I wish things had worked out between them."

"I can always try again, I suppose. In two months I'll be out of mourning and able to move about in society more. Perhaps I can find another likely match for her. From what Mr. Evingdon tells me, a match between them is impossible."

"What did you say her name was?"

I glanced up to see Hetty watching me over the turned-down corner of her newspaper.

"Mary Archer. Why?"

Hetty twisted her lips into a grimace. "It appears Mr. Eving-don is correct in this matter. Whatever divided them, he'll have no opportunity to reconcile with Mrs. Archer."

Confused, I stared at my aunt. "What are you saying?"

"I'm sorry to give you this news, Frances, but I just read about her in the paper. It appears she's been murdered."

Chapter 2

Murdered? I snatched the newspaper from Hetty's hands and spread it on my lap. "Show me where you read this."

Hetty leaned forward and ran her finger down one of the columns of newsprint, landing on Mary's name. It was one paragraph. "'Found dead in her home,'" I read. The sentence was followed by Mary's name, age, and family connections. "'No details given by the police, but foul play is suspected.'"

"If the reporter has no details, why does he suspect foul play?" Lily asked.

"I think what he means is, the police implied they suspect foul play." I crumpled the paper and stared up at my companions. "Why would anyone murder Mary?"

Lottie leaned forward in her seat and squeezed my arm. "I'm so sorry, Lady Harleigh. Was Mrs. Archer a close friend?"

Now that's the strange thing. I'd known Mary for several years and wouldn't say I knew her well. Yet I already felt her loss and regretted we hadn't been closer. I patted Lottie's gloved hand with my own. "More acquaintances, I suppose, but I liked and respected her."

I didn't notice we'd already arrived at Chester Street and drawn up in front of my house until the driver opened the carriage door. I climbed out first and waited on the pavement while he assisted the others, turning to gaze at my house. The pride of ownership still gave me a thrill. Though it was the smallest in the block of terrace houses, it was all mine.

Mary must have felt much the same about her home, as she never returned to her family after her husband's death. The thought of some criminal breaking in and murdering her made gooseflesh rise on my arms. But she lived completely alone, I reminded myself, while I had family and servants with me.

The driver turned the carriage around the corner to the mews and the four of us proceeded into the house where Mrs. Thompson, my housekeeper, waited in the foyer. Her stiff spine and crisp black dress, buttoned up to the neck, gave her the appearance of a guard.

"Inspector Delaney is here to see you, my lady," she said, shaking her salt-and-pepper head.

I took a step back. "Delaney? Whatever for?"

"He wouldn't say, ma'am, but he was insistent about waiting for you. He's been in the drawing room at least a quarter of an hour now." Her hand was unsteady when she took my hat and bag.

"I'm sure it's nothing you need trouble yourself about, Mrs. Thompson."

The housekeeper pursed her lips but stopped short of revealing her doubts. Of course, she didn't believe me. Delaney had never stopped by for nothing before. In fact, I hadn't seen him for months, since the occasion of a particularly gruesome murder in my garden. His calling on me now set butterflies off in my stomach.

Hetty laid a hand on my arm. "Perhaps he's here about Mrs. Archer."

"I can't imagine why he would come to me on that account." I took a step toward the drawing room and stopped as all three of my companions crowded behind me. "Inspector Delaney asked to see me and I'm quite capable of speaking to him on my own." I turned to Mrs. Thompson. "Please have Jenny bring in tea."

Hetty appeared ready to argue but backed down as I raised my brows. "Fine. We'll wait for you in the library."

I opened the door to the drawing room and stepped inside, no more eager to speak to the inspector than Mrs. Thompson had been. Like Hetty, I wondered if his visit had anything to do with Mary's murder.

He was seated in one of the wingback chairs by the window and stood as I walked toward him, extending my hand in greeting. Heavens, if I wasn't struck with an odd wave of affection for the man. To say he'd been kind to me in our past encounters would be a great breach of the truth. He'd been gruff and domineering, but he'd also provided me with a sense of almost parental security, though he was only perhaps a dozen years older than myself.

I noted he wore a new, shapeless suit, this one in a dark shade of gray. Delaney was a tall man, so the lack of cut made him appear rather lanky. His complexion was a warmer hue than I remembered, as if he'd just had a holiday in the sun, and his brown-gray hair and eyebrows, as usual, had a life all their own.

He returned my welcome with a warm smile, hinting that he recalled me with some affection as well.

"Inspector Delaney," I said, leading him to a conversational grouping of sofa and chairs around the tea table. "May I offer you some refreshment?"

"A cup of tea would be most welcome, my lady." He waited for me to choose a seat before folding himself into the chair next to mine.

"Excellent. It should be here momentarily. In the meantime, tell me, how have you been faring? Has the newest Delaney made his appearance yet?"

A smile broke across his face like a sunrise, crinkling the eyes beneath those bushy brows. "*She* arrived about a month ago," he said. "After two boys, my wife was hoping for a girl this time and I've never seen her happier."

It appeared to me his wife was not the only one. "My congratulations, Inspector. My own daughter has brought me nothing but joy. I hope the same is true for you."

A knock at the door warned of Jenny, my housemaid, entering with our tea. I had bribed Jenny away from my brother-in-law's household when I moved to Belgravia. A buxom, sweet-natured, country girl with more intellect and curiosity than I'd first given her credit for. After placing the tray on the table, she reached for the pot, as if to serve us. I could tell she was hoping to pick up a bit of gossip.

"Thank you, Jenny," I said firmly. "I'll take care of this."

With a bob of her head, she slipped out of the room and I poured Delaney a cup, waiting for him to tell me why he'd called.

It didn't take long. "Are you acquainted with Mrs. Mary Archer, ma'am?" Delaney asked, leaning forward to place his cup on the table.

My teacup rattled on its saucer and a tiny amount of the dark liquid slipped over the side. I quickly placed it on the table. "So, you *are* here about Mary. Yes, I am acquainted with her, and I must confess, we read of her death just a few moments ago. Is it true she was murdered?"

"I'm sorry to say she was, ma'am." Delaney flashed me a warning look. I wasn't sure I wanted any of the details of her murder, but he made it clear there'd be no point in asking for them. I waited, assuming he'd get to the point, eventually.

"How well did you know her?"

"We were friends," I said, surprised by the intensity of his gaze. "In a social way. We attended the same events, met occasionally at mutual friends' homes for a salon or afternoon tea."

"Forgive me, Lady Harleigh, but you were visibly shaken when I mentioned her name. Are you certain you didn't have more than a nodding acquaintance?"

"Heavens, Inspector, of course I was shaken. I suppose because I'd just heard of her death and had not really absorbed it yet. The murder of a friend, whether close or not, comes as a shock to me. Indeed, we had more than a nodding acquaintance. Over the course of several years, I've come to think of her quite highly, but I'd still not say we were close friends."

He leaned forward in his seat, sliding to the edge of the chair. "So, if you needed someone to confide in, share your troubles with, you would not have turned to Mrs. Archer?"

I blinked. "No, we were certainly not that close."

Delaney reached into his pocket and removed a small notebook, which he seemed to carry at all times. From the notebook he removed a folded sheet of paper. Reaching across the table he handed it to me. "Any idea how she might have come by this information?"

Curious, I took the sheet, noting the elegant writing as I first scanned the contents, then gave it a second, more thorough reading. I dropped my hand to my lap, the paper still tucked in my fingers, while my other hand drifted up to my mouth, seemingly of its own volition, likely for the purpose of containing the foul curses trembling on my tongue.

The note contained a complete summary of what I referred to as the battle of my bank account. A bitter and hard-fought battle with my brother-in-law, Graham, the Earl of Harleigh. We eventually forged a truce and Graham withdrew his suit, but the matter was of such a personal nature only my immediate family and two close friends knew of it—well, and Inspector Delaney. I lifted my gaze to find him observing me closely. "This was in Mary's possession? However did she learn of it?"

"You never told her about this dispute?"

"Of course not."

"Is there any chance that the earl did, or perhaps his late wife might have done so?"

I would have dismissed the idea but Delaney's penetrating stare forced me to give it some consideration. "Obviously I couldn't say for certain, but I can't imagine either of them sharing this information with her, or anyone else. It does not reflect well on them. I should think they'd be even more careful than I to ensure no one heard of it."

"That's rather what I thought." He let out a weary breath. "Would the earl have been careful enough to pay Mrs. Archer for her silence on the matter?"

I leaned back as if I could distance myself from such a distasteful implication. "Are you suggesting blackmail? I can't believe Mary would do such a thing." I glanced down at the paper in my hands, assailed by confusion. How had she come by this information, and why would she document it? Perhaps the inspector was correct in his assumption.

Delaney tapped his pencil against the open page of his book, waiting for an answer. Had Mary committed blackmail and been murdered for her effort? Heavens, he wasn't here to tell me of her murder; he was investigating it. I drew a breath, releasing it with a shudder. "She never approached me with the threat of exposure. Graham is a grieving widower." I raised my hands in confusion. "No one with any decency would threaten someone in that state."

Delaney reached out for the note. Much as I wanted to burn it, I handed it back. I suppose he'd need it as evidence. "I'm inclined to agree with you," he said. "But I'll have to speak to the earl before I can eliminate him as a suspect."

"As a suspect in Mary's murder? You can't be serious."

The furrows in Delaney's brow told me he was dead serious. A chill came over me as I felt a moment of doubt. Graham and I had been on opposite sides of a battle in the past. He was not an easy man to deal with when thwarted. But murder? Well, I simply couldn't imagine it. For one thing, it would require entirely too much effort on his part.

I pressed a finger against my temple as I watched him fold the page, and my secrets, back into the book. "Well, I must say

I've had far too many shocks for one day. I've just learned my friend has been murdered. You announce she may have been a blackmailer. And to top things off, I learn my brother-in-law may be a suspect. I suppose I should be relieved you don't consider me as one."

He gave me a wry smile. "I can't see you committing this crime, no. You shouldn't worry overmuch about the earl being a suspect either. He's only one of perhaps a hundred."

It took a moment for his words to register. "A hundred suspects?" I gave my head a shake in an attempt to clear it. "Are you saying you found more of these potential blackmail notes?"

He stood to take his leave and gave me a stony glare. "I'm saying nothing of the kind, and though I doubt I can keep you from sharing this information with your brother-in-law, I would greatly appreciate it if you would otherwise keep this conversation to yourself." He released a sigh that spoke of mental exhaustion. "It might take weeks to interview all the suspects, and I would prefer they have no advance warning."

Good Lord, there were other notes. "How had I misjudged her character to such a degree? Heavens, to think I was trying to make a match between Mary and my cousin." My shoulders drooped. "Well, no wonder things didn't work out."

Delaney, who had been on the point of departure, stopped and turned, regarding me with great forbearance. Oh, dear. I may have just given him suspect number one hundred and one. He lumbered back over to the chair he'd just vacated and sat down. "Lady Harleigh, when I asked how well you knew Mrs. Archer, this is the type of thing you should have told me."

I chewed on my lower lip, assessing the level of his anger. The inspector possessed a great deal of patience and I had a tendency of putting it to the test now and again. But Cousin Charles seemed an even less likely suspect than Graham. "I suppose you're right, Inspector, but I was not intentionally withholding evidence. You were speaking of blackmail earlier and that had nothing to do with Mr. Evingdon." My gaze sharpened. "Unless, of course, you found a note about him, too."

"I haven't read them all so it's possible we have one, but let's put blackmail aside for now. Perhaps it would be best if you'd just tell me what you know of this Mr. Evingdon and his relationship with Mrs. Archer, so I can decide if he should be considered as a suspect." He tipped his head to the side. "I'm assuming he did have a relationship with Mrs. Archer?"

It might be for the best, but I'd prefer to tell him nothing. I exhaled a huff of breath to show my indignation, but Delaney only raised his brows in response. Fine. "Charles Evingdon is cousin to my late husband and of course, the current earl. He's also a friend of Mr. Hazelton." Delaney knew and respected George, so I was hoping that would be a point in Charles's favor.

"He's lately been considering marriage and asked me to introduce him to a suitable lady. Considering his character, personality, and needs, Mary seemed to be a good match. I introduced them a few weeks ago, and to the best of my knowledge, they were simply becoming acquainted with one another. I heard he escorted her to a few events, but whether he was actively courting her, I couldn't say."

Delaney retrieved the notebook from his pocket and scribbled a few lines. Lovely. Charles was now a suspect.

"I can also tell you I spoke with him today. He told me he no longer wished to pursue the relationship."

"Did he now? Any reason for his change of heart?"

How to explain? "In a rambling, roundabout way he told me it would be ungentlemanly to explain their differences. He would only say they didn't suit."

Delaney didn't need to say a word. His expression was that of a miner who'd just discovered a nugget of gold. To his mind, Charles was an excellent suspect for Mary's murder. I raised a hand to slow his conclusions. "You can't imagine he murdered her simply because they did not suit, Inspector."

"Could you have imagined Mrs. Archer blackmailing people, my lady?"

"No, I suppose not," I said, admitting defeat. "I take it you intend to question him?"

"Unless you've recently introduced Mrs. Archer to a more likely suspect, he's just moved to the top of my list." Delaney tapped the stubby pencil on the notebook and slipped them both into his pocket.

"I was afraid of that."

After showing Delaney to the door, I walked back to the empty drawing room, to the card table near the front window. I gazed down at the marquetry pattern of the tabletop, wishing my thoughts were so organized. Or better still that they'd been organized before I'd spoken to Delaney.

"Is he gone?"

I turned sharply as Hetty, Lily, and Lottie slipped into the room, glancing around as if Delaney might be hiding behind a sofa.

"Just," I replied. We all gravitated to the tea table and seated ourselves on the chintz-covered chairs. Hetty leaned forward eagerly.

"Well?" she said. "Was he here about the murder?"

"Yes. And I'm afraid I may have implicated Cousin Charles in the matter."

Lottie gasped. "Mr. Evingdon?"

"Goodness, Frances! He's your cousin," Lily said.

The two girls gawked at me as if I'd accused one of them of the crime.

"It wasn't intentional, I assure you. I simply answered his questions."

Hetty, practical as always, patted my knee then rose to her

feet. "You need a drink, dear. Then you must tell us about this conversation."

While she moved to the drinks cabinet along the wall, Lily and Lottie eyed me with suspicion, waiting for my explanation. Heavens, what part had Delaney told me to keep to myself? The blackmail, wasn't it? Yes, that and the notes.

"There really isn't much to tell," I said. Hetty handed me a snifter with an inch of brandy. I noted she'd brought one for herself as well. I took a sip and as the liquid warmed me, I detailed my conversation with Delaney, at least as it pertained to Charles.

"Dearest, you've done nothing wrong," Hetty said when I'd finished. "Inspector Delaney would have learned about their relationship sooner or later anyway."

I drew a deep breath. "Do you think so? He seemed rather keen on the idea of Charles as a suspect. In fact, I got the impression he planned to question him almost immediately."

Lily leaned over the table and squeezed my arm. "I'm sure Aunt Hetty's right, Franny. Inspector Delaney will question Mr. Evingdon and find him innocent of any wrongdoing. Best to get that out of the way so he can search for the real murderer."

I imagined Charles stumbling through his answers to Delaney's questions and couldn't quite match Lily's confidence. "I hope you're right."

Hetty turned to me, narrowing one eye. "You don't believe he might have done it, do you?"

I joined in the chorus of denials from the girls while asking myself just how well I knew Cousin Charles. He was part of the Wynn family through his mother. But while the Wynns were a feckless bunch, snobs, terrible with money, and sometimes philanderers, I don't believe they ever produced a murderer.

Hetty caught the indecision in my expression. "Frances?"

I pulled my lip in between my teeth. "I can't imagine it." But could I imagine Mary Archer as a blackmailer? "It doesn't seem possible." How well did I really know him? "He's always been so kind." But did he have a temper?

"As long as you're sure, dear."

All three of them watched me closely. Then Hetty brightened. "Perhaps you should confer with Hazelton."

Of course, George. I should certainly speak with him. "Aunt Hetty, that's an excellent notion."

"Mr. Hazelton?" Lottie's brows drew together in confusion. "Is he in the legal profession?"

"He is," I said. Though I wasn't quite sure how to explain George Hazelton's profession, this would have to do. George "handled" matters for the Crown and other highly placed individuals in the government, but some of the actions he took could hardly be considered legal. Still, he had good connections, both with the police and the government, and more importantly he knew the law and what Charles might be facing.

Perhaps George could offer some clarity for my muddled thoughts. If nothing else, he could provide my cousin with some legal advice. They were friends after all. Yes, I should definitely speak with him.

Chapter 3

Pleased I'd made some sort of decision, I was eager to take action. I left the ladies in the drawing room and slipped through my library out to the back garden. Then out my back gate and in through the gate to George's garden. In this manner I avoided the front door and any chance a passing neighbor might see me calling on a single gentleman.

I caught a glimpse of George through his library window. Seated at his desk, he leaned back in the chair, as if not completely absorbed in his work, one ankle resting on the other knee in a relaxed attitude. I paused, drinking in the sight of him. George had become a very important part of my life in recent months. Longer than that, really. He came to my aid the night my husband died, well over a year ago. And his gallantry saved more than one reputation.

Since I'd moved in next door to him, he's been part guardian angel, part friend. I wasn't sure how I felt about him in an emotional sense, but there could be no doubt about my attraction to him. Watching him now, I longed to caress that rugged face or run my fingers through his dark, wavy hair. I blew out a breath and lifted the trailing curls off the back of my neck. Goodness, I must learn to curtail my imagination. Particularly since I didn't know how he felt about me.

George was an honorable man and had asked me to marry him not long ago. At least I think he did, but that's neither here nor there as his proposal, if it was one, only arose from some manly sense of duty. My late husband had married me out of his duty to fill the family coffers with my dowry. I'd rather avoid making that mistake again. Besides, I'd only just gained my independence and the single state suited me well for the time being. I rested my hand against the glass. George was far too much a gentleman to be interested in a dalliance.

Not that I was, of course. Heavens, no! My face burned as I damned my imagination.

I saw his posture stiffen seconds before he drew his gaze up to the window. I gave him a bright smile and waved my fingers. In return he gave me a look of enduring patience. He inclined his head to the left, indicating that I should meet him at the doors leading into the drawing room.

"Good afternoon, Frances," he said, holding open the French door.

"Good afternoon, George. I hope you're well?" I stepped past him and into a room so masculine in style it felt as if it belonged in a gentlemen's club rather than in a home.

"To what do I owe this surreptitious visit?"

"Well, I'm afraid I have rather bad news to report." I preceded him into his library.

"Indeed?" With a gesture, he invited me to take a seat in one of the wingback chairs near the window, then waited for me to do so before seating himself next to me.

"It's about Mr. Evingdon and Mrs. Archer."

His inquisitive expression quickly turned to a frown as his brows drew together. "Evingdon and Mrs. Archer? Why are their names linked?"

I took a deep breath and continued. "I imagine you've already heard Mary Archer has been murdered?"

"Yes, I did. Such a tragedy." He tilted his head slightly to the left. "I wasn't aware you knew her."

"As one knows anybody in society. At least I thought I did until Inspector Delaney called on me today."

His brows formed one dark line. "Frances, don't tell me she had some type of gossip about you?"

"Not gossip. She had facts—pertaining to the battle Graham and I had about my bank account." I stopped abruptly as I absorbed what George had just said. "How did you know the reason for Delaney's visit?"

George's face registered his astonishment. "How did she know about your bank account?"

"Don't change the subject. Who told you she was collecting information about people?"

"We'll get to that. First, tell me how this pertains to Evingdon."

"I introduced him to Mrs. Archer and they were becoming acquainted and keeping company for the past few weeks. Today he and I spoke at the Argyles' garden affair. He told me he no longer wished to pursue the connection."

George leaned back and rubbed his hands down his face. "And you relayed this conversation to Delaney?"

I gave him a helpless gesture. "How could I not? He asked how I knew Mary and I could hardly leave out the fact that I'd attempted to make a match between her and my cousin." I looked down at my hands, fidgeting in my lap. "I'm afraid he sees Charles as a suspect. In fact, I believe he hopes he's the murderer so he doesn't have to go through all the files of information Mary seemed to be collecting."

"I can understand that, but what Delaney doesn't know is that I will be the one going through those files."

"You?" George's lips twisted in a grimace of pain as if the thought of reading all the juicy gossip was torture to him. I, on the other hand, would be champing at the bit to get my hands on it. I sighed. So many inequities in this world. "How did that come about?"

"A friend in high places called in a favor."

I sat back and crossed my arms. "I hate when you drop tiny crumbs of information, rather than reveal the whole story. What friend?"

"I'm afraid I can't tell you that."

Undaunted, I pressed on. "How high?"

He smiled wickedly, knowing he was driving me to distraction. He leaned across the arms of our chairs until I could see the dark ring circling the lighter green of his eyes. Funny, I'd never noticed that before.

"It's a secret," he whispered, his breath tickling my lips. "I can only tell my wife."

I leaned back and gave him a scowl, pushing all thoughts of his lovely eyes from my mind. "I've warned you to be careful about that, George. Someday I may call your bluff."

With a satisfied smile, he sat back in his chair. "Then I live in hope."

"Now you're trying to distract me. At least tell me why you've been given this assignment rather than the police."

"Apparently some of the information in Mrs. Archer's possession is rather sensitive, and potentially damaging, to more than one important family or career. My friend didn't trust the police to keep that information to themselves. He used his influence to have the files reviewed by a liaison to the police." He shrugged. "That would be me."

"Considering she has personal information about me as well, I'm relieved to hear you're handling this." I gave him a narrow-eyed examination, wondering how much he'd tell me. "Based on my discussion with Delaney, the theory is she was blackmailing many people and one of them decided to end it by murdering her. You are to go through her information and determine the most likely suspect?"

"Essentially."

I frowned. I still found it hard to believe Mary would stoop to blackmail. "Is there any evidence that she'd actually black-mailed anyone? Banknotes stuffed in a drawer? Large deposits to her bank account? Has someone actually made an accusa-tion?"

George smiled. "Good questions, Frances. I'll be sure to ask them. The police were called in yesterday and I received this as-signment today. I haven't read the report yet and they can't check with her bank until tomorrow. With any luck, some fool gave her a bank draft rather than currency. But in any event, I expect the police will make note of any large deposits."

"Then the whole idea of blackmail is only a theory."

"At this point, yes." One brow crept upward as he examined me. "It sounds like you don't subscribe to that theory."

"I find it rather far-fetched to say the least. Delaney turned my world upside-down this afternoon, casting two respectable people in a very dark light."

"Two?" He took my hand from the arm of the chair. "Never say you believe Delaney's suspicions of Charles."

"Are they any more incredible than suspecting Mary of blackmail? How would she even know where to begin with such an endeavor?"

"One begins by collecting information, and to my under-standing, she certainly had that." He leaned forward in his chair. "What do you really know of Mrs. Archer? Her financial situation may have suffered since her husband's death. Perhaps she needed the money desperately and saw no other way."

"I could make an equally compelling case against Charles. Perhaps he fell in love with Mary and she scorned him. Strong emotions can turn someone to violence."

George dismissed my charges with a simple wave of our in-tertwined hands. "He and I have been friends for most of my life. He is neither quick to anger nor violent. Men of his size don't have to resort to violence. Just a glare from him is intimidating enough."

"Maybe Mary wasn't intimidated."

"Why are you making this argument? Do you really think he could be a murderer? He's your cousin, for heaven's sake."

"He's a cousin to Reggie and Graham, neither of whom are known for a surplus of integrity."

"Neither are they known for murderous inclinations. Did Delaney tell you how she was murdered?"

"No."

He leaned closer. "She was strangled, with a man's bare hands. Can you picture Evingdon becoming so angry or violent he could wring the life from someone?"

I winced and turned away. Heavens, no. Not Charles. I could not imagine him harming anyone in such a way. I returned my focus to George, shaking my head. His expression was one of relief. Perhaps I should drop this argument. At least for the present.

"So, we're back to Mary as blackmailer then. When will you delve into all her salacious memoranda?"

"I'm to pick it up tomorrow, unless of course Inspector Delaney arrests Evingdon for the murder." George dropped my hand as he stood. "I should pay him a call and make sure he survived the interview. Did Delaney march straight over there?"

"I'm sure he did." I rose to my feet and brushed the wrinkles from my skirt. "Let me go with you."

He cocked one eyebrow. "Why do you wish to go?"

"Sympathy? He may have had feelings for Mary. He may be wracked with grief."

"He'd just told you he was dropping the connection."

I lifted my chin and dared him to argue further. "Fine. Then I'm going out of guilt. I brought this trouble to his door. Not only did I introduce him to Mary, I also sent Delaney after him."

Chapter 4

As Viscount Evingdon preferred a country life, Charles lived in his brother's town house on Albemarle Street in Piccadilly. The area was home to holders of the most ancient titles but only a short trip by carriage from my home in Belgravia, on the other side of Green Park and Buckingham Palace. The ride gave me little time to quiz George about his acquaintance with Charles.

"How did the two of you come to be such great friends?"

George lifted his shoulders in a shrug. "We met at school."

"But he's several years older than you. Isn't that unusual?"

"Older boys often took us younger ones under their wings. At the age of twelve, I was not the great hulking brute you see before you now. With Charles as my mentor, I was saved a great deal of bullying."

The image he brought to mind was one I could hardly credit. For one thing, he was hardly a great hulking brute. He was tall but more fashionably lean than hulking. As for Charles taking anyone under his wing, I'd be more inclined to believe he'd accidentally smother them as protect them. School ties would have to suffice as an explanation.

"He just seems a different type than you. He is a younger son yet he has no profession. He's never married and lives at his brother's home in town. Has he no ambition?"

"He's the heir."

I waved aside his answer. "Yes, he told me that was his reason for seeking a wife. But that's only recently been determined, when the viscount and viscountess realized they were not to be blessed with a son. What were his prospects before then?" I bit my lip, awaiting George's reaction. Perhaps I was being rather hard on Cousin Charles. "I don't mean to say he's wasting his life, by any means, and it's no business of mine even if he is. I only mean since you are so constantly occupied with business or investigating, he seems to be your opposite."

George lifted his hand in a *c'est la vie* gesture. "To some degree I suppose we are, but that hardly negates friendship."

As we had arrived at the Evingdon home, I suppose that was all the answer I'd receive.

Upon presenting our cards to the butler, we were shown into a bright sitting room, decorated in the typical, tasseled style popular a decade or so ago, and accessorized with so many bits and bobbles, one could only refer to it as clutter. This was one of the older homes in the neighborhood and had clearly not been redecorated for some time. Since the current Lady Evingdon rarely came to town, I suppose care of the house belonged to Charles. Dozens of small framed pictures littered every table; books, both opened and closed, were scattered about; knickknacks and gewgaws adorned every horizontal space.

"Where is one to sit?" I whispered to George, just as our host entered the room to greet us.

"Hazelton," he said, stretching out a hand to his friend. "How good of you to call." He turned to me. "And Cousin Frances as well. Lovely to see you. Blakely should have taken you to the drawing room." His gaze took in the room. "Bit of a mess, isn't it?" He flashed his winsome smile. "But since we are here, might as well make the best of it."

He brushed past me, sweeping a few books from the divan and indicating we should be seated. Taking a seat in a chair across from us, he was clearly agitated, stacking the books on the table, shifting his gaze back and forth between us. "Would you care for some refreshment?" he asked finally.

"Not necessary," George replied. "We stopped by because we suspect you are either about to, or perhaps just had, a visit from the police."

"Ah, yes, the inspector chap. I say, have you the sight or something?" He gave George a sharp look. "Left just a few moments ago. How'd you know he'd be coming here?"

"I'm afraid I'm the one who sent him here, Cousin Charles," I said. "Well, indirectly anyway. You see, he was asking me about Mary Archer and I told him about introducing the two of you." I raised my hands in a helpless gesture. "In his mind, that rather made you a suspect."

"Ah, that explains it. I wondered how he knew I was acquainted with her."

"I take it he informed you of Mary's . . . passing?"

"Indeed, he did. With all the details. Such a wretched end for such a kind woman. I'm afraid I may have misjudged. That is to say, perhaps I was too hasty." He blew out a breath as if to compose himself. "Damn, I feel like the devil about the whole situation." His face reddened. "Oh, damn! Forgive me, cousin." He waved his hand in an agitated manner. "I mean, forgive my language. It was completely in-inappropriate. Blast!" He grimaced at the expletive and jumped to his feet. "Apologies. I believe I will order some refreshment."

Rather than ringing for a servant, he strode to the door and, pulling it open, stuck his head out. "Blakely!" he shouted. "Whiskey!"

"I don't think Lady Harleigh would care for spirits," George said, while I simply stared as the scene played out before me.

About to close the door, he leaned through the opening. "And tea," he ordered. "Bring tea as well."

George ran a hand through his hair as my cousin strode back to his seat. "Charles, are you well?"

"Not at all, thank you."

He rested his elbows on his thighs and dropped his head into his hands. "That inspector chap thinks I did it. That I murdered Mrs. Archer. He's probably off to find the rope to hang me."

"He has suspicions. There's a great distance between suspicion and conviction. And my hope is to remove you from his suspect list as soon as possible. That is, if you're willing to share with us the content of your meeting with Delaney."

Charles darted a glance at me, then locked eyes with George, who gave him a nod. I suppose I could understand why he would question my trustworthiness.

"I did not intentionally point the police in your direction, and as soon as I knew Delaney was coming to interview you, I contacted Mr. Hazelton in the hope he could provide some legal support if needed."

George gave me a quizzical glance, and I glared back. Yes, I was stretching the truth a bit, but it hardly mattered now.

Before he could reply, a tap sounded at the door, followed by Blakely entering with the tea tray and a decanter of spirits, presumably the requested whiskey. While the butler laid the table, Charles took the decanter and set it aside.

I lifted the teapot and gave him a questioning glance.

He smiled. "Yes, Cousin Frances, I do believe tea would be the better choice after all."

"Back to the matter at hand," George said, accepting a cup from me. "Shall we discuss your interview with Inspector Delaney? Clearly, he didn't arrest you, but I am curious about his line of inquiry. Did he indeed treat you as a suspect in Mrs. Archer's murder?"

"He didn't say the words, but I certainly felt like a suspect." Charles took the cup of tea I offered and placed it on the table to his side. "He asked me a great many questions. How long had I known her? Had I ever visited her home? How close was our relationship and why did I decide to end it?"

He glanced at me. "I didn't read about her death in the *Times* until this afternoon. When I spoke to you I had no idea she had died." He dropped his gaze to his hands. "And the bit about foul play came as a surprise. I was prepared when the inspector came calling. But he did seem to view me with more suspicion than I would have thought circumstances warranted."

"I'm sorry you had to go through that, Evingdon," George said. "This case may prove to be a difficult one for Delaney. It's possible Mrs. Archer was involved in activities that would allow for a great many unknown suspects. When Frances mentioned you, Delaney pounced on the chance of at least one known suspect. Did he provide any information about her death?"

"Far too much for my comfort." He sighed. "After that, he asked the questions, and I answered."

"It would be good to hear what your answers were," George said.

Charles gave him a rueful smile. "I met her through Lady Harleigh about three weeks ago. I escorted her to the theater and dinner, in company with several friends two weeks ago. We visited the British Museum last week and had another outing to the theater." He glanced at me. "I enjoy the theater. As that is the whole of my acquaintance with Mrs. Archer, it should be clear it wasn't a very close relationship, more of coming to know one another. And yes, I visited her home on two occasions to collect her for our theater outings. We met at the museum."

"I see. Were you this clear when you spoke with Delaney?"

"Not even close." He dropped his face back into his hands.

George dipped his head close to mine. "Evingdon tends to blather a bit when under pressure," he said by way of explanation.

I raised a brow.

He gave me a scowl and turned back to his friend. "Was that the extent of it?"

"No. I had to provide my whereabouts for the whole of Tuesday, some of which was spent in company and the rest, here at home. And I had to explain why I chose not to see Mrs. Archer again." He threw me a sidelong glance, knowing he had rather dodged that question with me.

George would not be put off. "And?"

"She was keeping company with another gentleman."

This caught George's attention. He leaned forward in eagerness. "Who?"

Charles gazed down at his hands. "I'm afraid I don't know. We had plans for Tuesday evening and Mary sent round a note to cancel. Since I was left at loose ends, I decided to visit a friend who lived near her home. After dining, I drove down her street."

He examined our expectant faces and scowled. "It was on my way home." He straightened his back and placed his hands on his knees. "The point is I drove down her street and saw a man leave her house and rush to a waiting carriage."

He shrugged. "Looking back at the situation, it may have been perfectly innocent, but it didn't feel that way. His was the only carriage nearby, so she wasn't entertaining a group. She had every right to see whom she pleased, but it was just the two of them alone in her home, and I suppose I felt slighted she put me off for another man."

"What night did you say?" George's voice was thick with tension.

"Tuesday."

"Oh, dear. Her body was discovered on Wednesday according to the paper." I glanced at George. "Might she have been murdered Tuesday?"

George raised his hands in a helpless gesture. "It's possible. A neighbor found her early Wednesday morning. He was walking to his place of business and noticed her door open. When she didn't answer his knock, he stepped inside. I haven't heard a more specific time of death yet."

Charles gave him a quizzical glance. "Why would you? Have you some interest in the matter—aside from your concern about me, which I greatly appreciate of course."

George took a sip of tea, then carefully placed his cup on the table in front of him, clearly considering how much he could reveal. "There's a rather sensitive side to this case and I've been asked to lend a hand, but rest assured if I must choose between working on this case or mounting a defense for you, I would certainly choose in favor of you."

"You can't do both?" Charles's confusion showed in his blank expression.

"Not out in the open I can't." George gave him a reassuring smile. "Behind the scenes I may be able to get away with a great deal. My preference, however, is to eliminate all suspicion of you in this matter, so let's get back to the man you saw leaving her house. Did you tell Delaney about him? Were you able to provide any sort of description?"

"I did, but I couldn't tell him any more than I've already told you. It was drizzling that evening. The man carried an umbrella that hid his face from my view. All I could really say is he was tall, not really lean or stout. His clothes were dark. No markings on the carriage, so it was probably hired. There was really nothing to identify him." His brows drew together in frustration. "My memory is unreliable at best, but I can't think of anything else I might have seen from that distance."

"What of your coachman?" I asked. "Would Delaney not take his word that you simply drove past?"

"I took the chaise and drove myself." Charles shook his head. "Just me and the horse and he's not talking."

"Well, Delaney must have given your story some credence, since he didn't arrest you," I said, hoping to ease his despair.

"They are just beginning their investigation," George said. "The police will canvass the neighborhood, and with any luck, someone else will have seen the man. If not, depending on the coroner's determination of the time of death, Evingdon may well have placed himself on the spot at exactly the wrong time, and with no witness to provide an alibi for him." He shifted his gaze to Charles. "There were no other witnesses, were there? You saw no one else on the street?"

"No. Perhaps a neighbor saw something from a window, but I am aware I'm not off the hook even if neighbors confirm the existence of another man at Mrs. Archer's home. I only hope you will come to my defense if I find myself arrested for murder."

"I hope it won't come to that," George said. "But you should be prepared for the possibility. And of course, I will defend you."

I studied George's face for signs of false bravado, but though he frowned, his jaw was set with determination. I still had trouble seeing Charles as a murderer, but neither did I have George's confidence.

"First," he said, "I need to find how far the police have progressed in the investigation, see if they've left any clues dangling that I can examine. And since that will keep me sufficiently busy, I may have to hand my task over to Lady Harleigh."

I held back a gasp. "You mean . . ." My heavens. Was he going to let me read Mary's notes?

George's eyes glittered with amusement. "If you don't find the task too arduous?"

"I believe I'm up to it," I said, fighting against my urge to jump up and dance a jig. The thought that George would trust me with such a responsibility sent a thrill of exhilaration rushing through my veins.

"Does this task involve those unknown suspects you mentioned earlier?" Charles's normally open expression had tightened into severe lines and angles. "If it helps to uncover the monster who murdered Mrs. Archer, I must take part in this as well."

I glanced at George. His hand rose to stroke his chin as he gazed off to the distance. I could empathize with Charles's need to fight this battle himself, or at least take part in it, but really this wasn't my decision. "We're talking about something that's potentially evidence. If I were your defense counsellor, I would be granted access to that evidence."

"If I am charged, you will certainly be the man I ask to defend me." His expression was hopeful.

George's gaze drifted off. "It's a bit sketchy in a legal sense, but I'm willing to give it a go." He turned to me. "From what I've been told, there's a vast amount of information to review. You may need some assistance."

Having ascertained Charles was under no immediate threat of arrest, the three of us agreed to meet at my home the next morning to begin digging into Mary's poison-pen notes. George and I took our leave and climbed back into the carriage, headed for home.

I stared at George's profile as he gazed out the window at the blur of pedestrians and shops we passed. Pondering the best way to help his friend, I'd imagine. Meanwhile, I pondered Charles's story. Driving past Mary's house after she'd broken an engagement with him felt like an intrusion on her privacy. She had the right to break an engagement, and he had no right to snoop.

Her house was located on Baker Street, however, which would take one from Marylebone to Grosvenor Square, and from there to Piccadilly and Charles's home. So, if the friend he visited lived in Marylebone, it would be a logical route for him to take. If that's where his friend lived. Why hadn't I asked?

Even more curious was that he passed Mary's house at precisely the time a man rushed away from her door. But the vague description he provided of the man could also describe Charles. If he were concocting a story, wouldn't he have described the man as short, or round, or thin? I had to remind myself he did not possess the sharpest of minds, but that point made me want to believe his story. That, and George's faith in his friend. I truly wanted George to be right.

"What is our next step?"

He turned back to me, his lips drawn in a thin line. "I've been wondering about that myself," he said. "I should be able to get an update from"—he paused mysteriously—"my contact. Find out what the police have learned from their canvass and from the coroner. They may have found some useful evidence from her home and spoken to her family."

I felt a sudden surge of excitement. "I could speak to her family. As a friend of Mary's, I must call on her sister when she arrives in town, and it would certainly be reasonable for me to pay a condolence call on her late husband's family as well. After you find out what the police learned, you can tell me if there is something you still need to know. As a social equal, I may be able to wheedle those personal details the family may have held back from the police."

"I don't know if they would consider themselves your social equals, Countess," he said with a grin.

"They are new money, to be sure, but our social lives intersect a great deal." I gave him a careless shrug. "And if they view me as a step above them, it will be only that much easier to gain answers to impertinent questions."

He pursed his lips again, the muscles in his jaw tightening. "What?"

"I don't want you to put yourself in any danger. Right now, we only know Mrs. Archer was murdered; we have no idea why. Just because the police have a theory, doesn't mean it's correct. What if one of the family murdered her? I don't want you asking leading questions of a murderer."

"I think you are rather putting the cart before the horse. Why not wait and see what you find out by tomorrow and what you still need to learn? I promise not to ask any questions of potential suspects before discussing it with you first. Will that make you feel better?"

He gave me a suspicious smile. "It might if I didn't think your promise rather ambitious for you. Don't forget, the last time you investigated on your own someone tried to murder you." He raised a brow. "You will consult me before taking any action?"

I widened my eyes in an expression of innocence. "This is your investigation. Just the fact that you're willing to let me participate will keep me on my best behavior. I promise to abide by all your rules and have a care for my safety."

I caught a glimpse of self-satisfaction on his face. What was he up to? "I hesitate to look a gift horse in the mouth, George, but I must know why you're willing to cede some of your responsibility to me."

He picked up my hand in his. Turning it, he placed a kiss on my wrist, just above the lace of my glove. "I like the idea of you working with me, Frances. I think you'd make an excellent partner. And in this particular matter I truly need your help."

His words and actions confused me beyond all measure. When he said *partner,* did he mean in the investigation, or something more?

"Will you be able to help Charles?" I asked.

He nodded. "This will be a difficult case. Perhaps the only thing worse than no suspect is too many suspects. It would be far too easy to make a case against Charles and forget all about the potential blackmail issue."

"Unless I find a more likely suspect among Mary's notes."

"That's my hope."

So, we were to be partners for this investigation. How silly of me to imagine otherwise. But if it was only my imagination, why was he still caressing my hand?

Chapter 5

~✥~

Stepping into my library the next morning, with the hope of a few quiet moments to review my accounts, I found it occupied by every member of my household, including my seven-year-old daughter, Rose, and her nanny.

I dropped a kiss on the top of Rose's head. Her dark, glossy waves, usually contained with a length of ribbon, were now pulled back in two severe braids. "I missed you at breakfast, dearest." After receiving a soap-scented hug, I cast a glance around the room. "I wondered why I had the dining room to myself this morning. Why are you all hiding in here on this lovely day?"

I turned to Lily and Lottie who were browsing the bookshelf behind the desk. "Didn't the two of you have some outing planned for this morning?" Even I had to admit my tone was a little peevish, but this was my library after all and I'd hoped for a bit of privacy.

Lily's blond curls bounced as she turned around. "We do. Leo's obtained bicycles and we plan to ride through Hyde Park."

Bicycles? I hoped Lottie was more competent on wheels than on her feet. "Do be careful."

"I'm waiting for Uncle Graham." Rose clung to my hand, bouncing up and down on her toes. "He's coming to work with Aunt Hetty, and Nanny and I are going back in the carriage to his house to play with the boys."

The boys were her cousins, Graham's sons. They were a few years older than her but because Graham's family had moved into the old manor with us, while in mourning for my husband, the children had become close. Rose would be eight soon, putting her only two years behind Graham's youngest. She loved following them around and I daresay they enjoyed showing off to her.

For my part, I was thrilled she had playmates. Most families kept their younger children in the country. Even her kitten, a gift from Lily's fiancé, preferred the country life. She went into hiding when Rose and I returned to London from Harleigh Manor a few months ago, and we had to leave without her. From all reports, she was growing and earning her keep as a mouser in the stables. Lovely for her, but Rose missed her little companion. Perhaps I should consider finding another pet for her.

I glanced at Hetty, seated behind my desk. "I'd forgotten you planned to work with Graham today." Graham was not the spendthrift my late husband was, but his genius was in agriculture, not finance. That was Hetty's area of expertise. The last time he asked her for a loan, she offered to help him organize his finances instead. A strategic move on her part.

"I take it you'll be working in here?" Lovely. Now I'd lost access to my own library.

Hetty sank down in her chair. "Sorry, Frances. I hate to be an inconvenience but we really have nowhere else to work. In the future I'll check with you first before scheduling time here with him."

I tamped down my disappointment. "Don't mind me. I can make do elsewhere." I took a seat across the desk from her as

Rose took Nanny's hand and slipped out through the French doors to the back garden.

"You've been working with Graham for a week now. Just how complicated are his investments?"

"I can't be sure until I sort out his records"—she let out a *tsk*—"which are in a terrible state of disarray. Graham didn't want to trouble his steward with the task as the man had his hands full with estate business, and he didn't want to go to the expense of hiring a secretary." Her lips twisted in a grimace. "So, he managed his investments and their records himself."

"I take it keeping records isn't his forte?"

"Far from it, and sorting through all the documents has been quite a task. I'm becoming rather frustrated."

"I could assist you as secretary."

We both turned to find Lottie standing beside my chair, her eyes wide and head bobbing as if in agreement with her own suggestion. "I'm very good at organizing records," she said. "When I volunteered at the Metropolitan Museum of Art back home, I spent most of my time working on Mr. Cesnola's records."

Hetty brightened. "Well, that might be just the thing, my dear. I could certainly use someone with organizational skills."

I stared at my aunt as the image of Lottie spilling ink all over Graham's documents ran through my mind. "You are here to enjoy yourself, dear. We can't put you to work."

"I wouldn't consider it work. I really enjoy organizing things."

"Well, I won't ask you to cancel your engagements, but if you can lend me your spare time, I'd be grateful for the assistance." Hetty locked eyes with me and lowered her brows, daring me to interfere.

I shrugged. "If the two of you are in agreement, I won't stand in your way." Hetty gave me a satisfied smile while Lottie beamed. Odd what some people do to amuse themselves.

"Excellent," Hetty said. "I'll review everything with you when you return from your outing this afternoon." She turned to me. "And speaking of afternoons, wherever did you vanish to yesterday? You left to speak with Hazelton and I didn't see you again until we passed each other in the hall when I went out for the evening. Surely you weren't discussing Mrs. Archer's murder the entire time?" She lifted a brow suggestively.

"Sorry to disappoint, but indeed we were." I leaned over the desk, and keeping my voice down, told Hetty what little I could reveal.

Her expression grew more concerned as I spoke. "I always suspected Hazelton was more than just an idle gentleman, so I won't inquire how he became involved in this case. And I can certainly understand he'd want to defend his friend, but why on earth is he handing this task, as you call it, off to you?"

"The task is a simple parsing of documents, which may produce some evidence." I shrugged. "He thinks I can help."

"Perhaps Lottie would be of better use assisting you than me?"

"Cousin Charles has asked to help."

Hetty's expression grew clouded. "Is that wise? I understand he's your cousin, dear, but a woman was murdered and Delaney has reason to suspect Mr. Evingdon."

I shook my head in a firm negative. "I'm quite convinced he is perfectly innocent and it's my fault he finds himself in this mess. Not only did I introduce the two of them but I'm the reason Delaney suspects Charles of murdering her."

Hetty gave me a warning look and placed a hand over mine. "I'm confident Hazelton will do his best to protect you, but be careful all the same."

As if on cue, Mrs. Thompson knocked on the door and announced George and Charles. Both Lily and Lottie turned to cast admiring gazes on the latter as the gentlemen entered the room. To my eyes, Charles faded into the background when standing next to George but I suppose everyone has her own preference.

Charles made his preferences clear when after greeting the rest of us, he walked straight over to Lottie. "Miss Deaver," he said, giving her a shallow bow. "Delighted to see you looking so well, though I suppose I don't actually know if you are well. What I mean to say is you appear perfectly uninjured." He gave her his boyish grin. "After your misstep yesterday."

Her cheeks pinkened. "I am indeed well and uninjured, thanks to your assistance."

I left them to their conversation and turned to George. "It seems Aunt Hetty and Graham have plans to work here today. Could we conduct our business in your library?"

"Of course," he said. "I was planning to suggest that anyway as the documents I've acquired are more numerous than I'd expected. If you're ready, we can go now."

"But if you rush off, you'll miss Leo," Lily said.

"I'm afraid we must, dear." Mostly because I was itching to dig into Mary's files, and worried that George could change his mind about my involvement at any moment. I had no wish to wait around for Leo. "Please make our apologies."

Lily's lips turned down in a pout. "At least try to remember we are to dine with the Kendricks tomorrow."

Oh, yes. Dinner with the Kendricks. Actually, I was eager to become better acquainted with Lily's future in-laws, but the business at hand had pushed it from my mind. Lily didn't need to know that. "Of course I remember, dear. Saturday evening."

With that, George, Charles, and I stepped into the garden, where I gave Rose a hug, and we took my sneaky back path from my garden to George's, and from there to his library.

"Rather convenient, that private route," Charles said. He choked back a chortle as George turned around and glared. "Not that I'm suggesting anything," he added.

George grunted a reply I didn't quite hear and pulled a

leather satchel from behind his desk, dropping it with a thud on the desk.

"I hope it's the bag that's so heavy and not its contents," I said.

My hopes were dashed as he unbuckled the straps and removed several large files bound in stiff paper and fastened with strings. He gave me a crooked smile. "I'm sorry, but I'm afraid it's the contents."

Charles surveyed the stack of files and let out a whistle. "What is all this?"

I raised my brows as I turned to George. "You haven't told him yet?"

"Told me what?"

"The police suspect Mrs. Archer was involved in a blackmail scheme," George said, watching for a reaction.

Charles's head jerked back as if he'd been struck. "The devil, you say! She was being blackmailed? Whatever for?"

"No, Charles." I placed a hand on his arm. "The police believe she may have been blackmailing someone. Perhaps many people."

He sank into a chair near the desk as if he were deflating. "No, no. That's impossible. She was a kind and caring person."

George gave him a sympathetic look. "These files contain information of a personal nature about nearly every prominent member of society. More investigation will have to be done to determine if she was using it to blackmail anyone, but the fact that she has this rather strange collection of facts about so many people in society, suggests it may be why she was murdered." He shrugged. "Particularly since no other motive has surfaced."

He tapped the top file with his index finger. "Someone found out she had damaging information about him and murdered her to keep it quiet. I daresay his name is in here."

It sounded like a logical conclusion, but something was

missing. "If the police found these files in her house, why didn't the killer take them before he ran? Or at least take the note that pertained to himself?"

"He may have searched for them, but he wasn't as thorough as Delaney. The whole bundle was found under a loose floorboard in a closet, covered by a rug."

"Why'd the police turn them over to you?" Charles asked.

"Let's just say a friend called in a favor. The files are said to be rather scandalous and he'd rather have me reviewing them than the police." He leveled his gaze at Charles, then me. "That said, I expect confidentiality from both of you. None of this can be made public."

Charles waved a hand. "Yes, yes. Mum's the word and all that. After all, I'm hardly likely to discuss this with anyone. Not much for gossip myself."

"Though I have every confidence you'll both act with discretion, you'll be taking in a great deal of information. Take care that none of it slips out."

George waited for an affirmative reply from both of us. "All right then, let's get to work, shall we?"

He handed each of us a bulging file of paper.

I seated myself in the guest chair next to Charles. "What exactly are you hoping to find in here?"

George took the chair behind the desk. "Anything that looks like fodder for blackmail. The more damning, the more likely. You might want to start with the most prominent names you find."

"Are you staying to help us? I thought you intended to check up on the police investigation today."

"That was my plan, but the constables were canvassing Mrs. Archer's neighbors again this morning. I'll need to wait for them to leave before I can nose around without causing suspicion. Only Delaney is aware of my involvement, and my official assignment is these files, not removing a suspect from their list."

He glanced at the clock on the shelves behind his desk. "They should be finishing up about now. I'll just stay long enough to get you two started in this quest."

I wondered if his caution about the constables' presence meant he planned to sneak into Mary's house. George had taught me the art of searching someone's residence without their knowledge a few months ago. Since I wasn't sure Charles knew about his friend's more clandestine activities, I decided the question would have to wait. Following George's instructions, I settled the file on my lap, untied the string, and pulled out the first page.

It made absolutely no sense. Letters followed by dashes, sets of initials, and fragments of words littered the page. "What on earth is this meant to be?" I turned the page around to show George and watched his eyes glaze over in confusion as he took it in.

"It appears she's used a type of short writing, or stenography."

"Stenography?" I turned the page back to scrutinize it again. *A.S.W. dning? at Sav wt E.C? or E, PoW? Nt sn in public rms.*

I stared across the desk at George. "How am I ever to determine what this means?"

He leaned back in his chair, stroking his chin while he stared back at me. "The note Delaney showed you, about yourself. Was it written in this manner?"

"No." I stared over his head at the bookshelves and tried to picture the note. "Well, some of the words were abbreviated but Graham's name, and mine, were written out."

"Like this?" Charles handed me a page from his file. I read it aloud.

"'Lady Elinor Finch held a festive gala at the Royal Opera House last Christmas much to everyone's delight—except the proprietors, who wonder if she'll ever pay them.'"

I let out a snort of laughter before recovering myself. "Good heavens, how did Mary hear of this?" I handed the page to George. "And yes, that's precisely how mine was written."

George placed the coded note on the desk, facing Charles and me, and beckoned us closer. "Let's try to decipher this one, shall we? The content may explain why she chose to record it in this manner."

"The letters followed by periods are likely initials, don't you think?" Charles looked at us for agreement.

"A.S.W.," I read. "Alicia Stoke-Whitney?"

"Possible," George muttered. "A number of E.C.s come to mind."

"Oh, my goodness." My hand rose involuntarily to my chest as I glanced at my companions. "There can be only one interpretation for the next set."

"Edward, Prince of Wales." Charles waved a dismissive hand. "No point blackmailing him. The man's never in funds."

"Then E.C. is likely Ernest Cassel." George's gaze darted between the two of us, seeking confirmation.

"Makes sense," Charles agreed. "The two are close friends."

"And bear a striking resemblance to one another." Now that we'd identified the principals in the note, or at least guessed at them, it made more sense. "Look, she is questioning whether it was the prince or Cassel with Alicia. Since she mentions dining, Sav is probably the Savoy."

"Dining is followed by a question mark and she further notes the couple was not seen in the public rooms of the hotel. Leading one to wonder where they disappeared to once inside."

"Heavens, will Alicia never stop trifling with other women's husbands?" Neither man answered my question. Likely because it was commonly known Alicia and my late husband had spent a great deal of time—trifling.

I pondered the note as I stared across the desk at George.

"Alicia's husband threatened her with divorce," I said. "At least that's what she told me a few months ago. This little story would certainly provide him with grounds."

He pursed his lips. "The question is, does Alicia want to hold on to her husband, and reputation, enough to pay a black-mailer to keep this story quiet?"

"Or does the gentleman?" I asked.

He raised his brows. "I'd say that's a contender."

"I agree. The note about Lady Finch, while embarrassing, is hardly worthy of blackmail. Perhaps that's why she didn't bother disguising the note with this stenography-short writing code. Are all yours like that, Charles?"

He raised a few pages in his hand. "Everything I've read so far has been crystal clear and completely dull."

I thumbed through mine. More abbreviations and seemingly random letters. "Well, unless Charles wants to trade files with me, I don't see how I'll get through this lot without a copy of Debrett's."

George held up his index finger as he stood. "I may have one here."

I'd spoken in sarcasm, but on second thought, a guide to the peerage might come in handy. George found the book and dropped it with a thud on the desk beside the first suspicious letter.

"If you find any further likely suspects," he said, tapping the first note, "stack them here and we'll determine what to do about them when I return. In the meantime, if the two of you feel comfortable with this task, I'll move on and see how the police are proceeding."

Charles slapped another page upside down on the desk. "I haven't found anything other than general gossip so far, but I do comprehend the assignment."

George paused in his departure. Charles had spoken the words coldly enough to make me wonder if he were indeed angry with his friend. I gave George a smile and tipped my head toward the door. If my cousin had something on his mind, perhaps he'd tell me.

As soon as the door closed he glanced up at me, a scowl on his face. "Before you say it, I know I was rude. Hazelton's trying to save my worthless neck, and I snapped at him."

"I'd never call your neck worthless, but I agree with you otherwise. Why did you snap at him?"

He dropped the stack of paper into his lap. "He's taking risks on my behalf while I am stuck here reading gossip."

"He can hardly take you with him while Delaney still suspects you. You shouldn't take offense."

"I'm not taking offense. Hazelton is one of a very small group of people who don't consider me a fool. He's a good friend and I'm grateful for his help. I simply hate being in the position of needing it."

"He's helping because he knows you didn't murder Mary."

"Only because he doesn't think I have the brains for it."

My cheeks grew warm. That sounded closer to my opinion. I placed a hand on his arm. "You just said yourself he doesn't consider you a fool. He simply knows you wouldn't do such a thing. As for being in your present position"—I shrugged—"for that you must blame me. I should have stayed out of your affairs and let you find a lady to court on your own."

"Come now, Cousin Frances, I asked for your help." He gave me a crooked smile. "And I did like Mrs. Archer. She was charming, lovely. I just can't reconcile that woman with someone who'd commit blackmail."

He rubbed a hand across his cheek. "And on that subject, how is your stack progressing? Anything blackmail-worthy?"

"As you are well aware, I haven't progressed past the first page."

He leafed through his pages. "I seem to have nothing more than gossip here. Some of it common knowledge, even to me."

He held up a page to read. " 'Miss Leticia Stuart has chosen a rather unique way of refusing her suitor. While in private consultation with Mr. Frederick Thornton in her family's garden, she pushed him into the fountain. Did the cold bath cool his ardor or will the gentleman return to request the hand of this saucy miss again?' "

I raised my brows. "Frederick Thornton. I'd have given him a dunking myself. Humorous, I suppose, but I doubt anyone would pay good money to keep that quiet. What else do you have?"

"Another damp story." He shuffled through a few pages on top of his stack and pulled one out. " 'In an attempt at gallantry, Clifford Worthington leapt from his carriage to rescue a lady's hat from certain destruction as it blew along the path toward the serpentine. He managed to save the hat but not himself. The hapless gentleman tripped over a rock and dove straight into the water himself.' "

"Goodness, I am familiar with that story." I frowned, trying to bring the details to mind. "Oh, yes. It was very embarrassing. Mr. Worthington is the father of my late sister-in-law. I can't imagine what possessed him to attempt such a silly feat. The man is approaching sixty and quite stout. I wasn't the only one laughing at the image of him running to catch up with the blowing hat."

I couldn't contain a smile at the thought. "Mrs. Worthington was furious. But that story was the buzz of town several months ago. If Mary had hoped to blackmail the man over this little on-dit, she left it too late."

He waved a hand at the file. "So far everything I've read has been of this nature, a bit salacious or embarrassing, but generally well known."

"Strange." I dug a little deeper into my stack and pulled out a page with a story I could easily decipher. "Here is something I'm sure His Grace, the Duke of Manchester, would wish to keep quiet. It links him to M.A. and whoever she is, he would never want Miss Zimmerman to hear about it. Though, for my part, I think somebody should inform her of what a scoundrel he is. He's only chasing after her money."

Charles leaned his head against the back of the chair and stared up at the ceiling. "Yes, he's only ever interested in women with money. This other woman is probably just a flirtation."

"I doubt that would make a difference to Miss Zimmerman if she found out. It would still be an insult to her."

"Why would he do it then? Do you think the story's true?"

I gave him a one-shoulder shrug. "It's believable, I'll say that much. He can't seem to help himself. He must marry money, but he can't resist female attention." I turned my gaze back to the file, but he wasn't finished with the subject of the young duke.

"How do you know he must marry money?" He leaned forward to reach a bowl of fruit on the desk. I waved him off when he offered it to me and watched him choose an apple for himself.

"I suppose because he doesn't hide the fact that he has little, if any, money of his own." A little warning bell sounded in my head. Something was inconsistent here. I frowned at Charles who stared, his eyes wide and innocent. "He has no money," I said. "In fact, he is likely deeply in debt. How could he pay a blackmailer?"

"Well, I don't suppose he could. One does need money to pay a blackmailer. Or for anything else for that matter. One can't pay for anything if one has no money. Terrible situation to be in."

I held up a hand to stop him so I could think. "Manchester couldn't afford to pay blackmail, so why would Mary even bother?"

"Would she know that?" He sunk his teeth into the apple with a loud crunch.

"I rather think so. It's common knowledge." I scanned the note again. "She'd be wasting her time blackmailing him."

"Maybe she didn't. She wasn't one to waste her time."

"Then why keep the note? Why take note of it in the first place?" I waved a hand toward his file. "Why gather any of that useless gossip?"

Charles had a mouthful of apple and held up a finger for me to wait. Since I didn't really believe he had an answer, I posed another rhetorical question. "How did she come by all this information?"

This time he merely raised his shoulders. "No idea," he said from the corner of his mouth.

"Well, at this point I can't see Manchester as a likely suspect but I suppose I should place him in the possible stack."

"Have you found any likely suspects?"

I gave him a scowl. "You've been next to me this whole time, Charles. You know I've read only two notes. The first page, yes. The second, doubtful. Why?"

He unfolded himself and rose to his feet. Stepping over to the fireplace, he tossed his apple core onto the grate. As it was unlikely George would have a fire in that grate for the next month or two, it was probably not the best place for food detritus, but I held my tongue.

He turned to face me. "I just keep wondering if Mrs. Archer was really blackmailing anyone." He gestured to the file he'd left on the chair. "I've seen nothing in that file but gossip, most of it well known. I've even heard it before." He waved a hand in my direction. "You've found one possibility and another that's completely impossible. A blackmailer isn't going to bother with an impoverished peer."

"What other reason would she have for keeping all these notes? And you have only just begun to read your file as have I. We may run into many likely suspects."

He stuffed his hands into his pockets, stared down at the carpet as he outlined the pattern with the toe of his shoe. "I suppose I really didn't know her well enough to make a judgment about what she would or wouldn't do, but Mary Archer a blackmailer? I don't believe it." He raised his gaze to mine. "How would she even go about it?"

A good question. "I suppose she could have contacted her victims through the post."

"Her victims!" He raised his hands and face toward the ceiling. "Her victims. How ridiculous that sounds."

Though not without sympathy, I was beginning to lose patience with the man. "Forgive me, Charles. I'm aware these people are not all innocents, but I don't know what to call them other than *victims*."

He waved a hand in my direction. "Apologies, Frances. I understand how odd it is that she collected all this information, but we all have idiosyncrasies. I can't keep two thoughts in my head at the same time. You, it seems, dabble in solving crimes. The fact she collects gossip and scandal does not make her a blackmailer."

"Perhaps, as we examine these files, we'll find another reason for them. But remember, if she wasn't blackmailing anyone, that makes you an even more likely suspect to the police."

He twisted his lips into a sad half smile. "Point taken. I just wish there were another way to prove my innocence than ruining a dead woman's reputation."

He moved back to his seat, and we both continued with our reading. Over several hours and a few cups of tea, I'd gathered a small stack of possible blackmail victims while Charles continued to find none. While we shared the silence of the room, I pondered his questions. Where did this woman find the audacity to threaten so many prominent people with exposure unless they paid for her silence? This was so different from the woman I thought I knew.

And where did she find her information? Mary didn't move about in society much, at least not as of late. Since her husband died, she lived a subdued life in a quiet part of town. I assumed she had a small income from her own family. Enough to allow her to live alone, but it would hardly provide for attending social events.

I worried my lower lip while I considered Charles's defense of Mary. He'd made his case well. He'd planted a seed of doubt. And that was another thing that bothered me. He had made a good case. With barely a word of the gibberish I'd become used to hearing from him. Perhaps he was not as foolish as I'd thought.

Chapter 6

~~

Several hours later, I left Charles in possession of George's library since I could no longer focus on the words before me. Back home, I found Hetty relaxing on the sofa in the drawing room with a glass of some amber liquid.

When Aunt Hetty first arrived in London, I'd been surprised by her taste for strong spirits. I've since found they have something of a restorative value and from time to time I join her. I eyed her glass. Whisky or brandy? Either would be welcome at this point.

"Has Graham left already?" I moved directly to the drinks cabinet.

Hetty raised her brows. "He left about an hour ago. About the same time the girls returned. You've been gone for most of the day, dear."

My gaze darted to the clock on the mantel. Goodness, nearly time for dinner already, yet we'd accomplished little to nothing. I decided on sherry and poured a small glass.

"You look rather done in," Hetty said. "Come sit down and tell me what you've been doing all day."

"Surprisingly little, considering how exhausted I feel." I took a sip and seated myself next to my aunt.

"You mentioned reviewing some documents this morning." She placed her glass on the tea table and turned her scrutiny on me. "What type of document could provide evidence of a murder? And why does Hazelton have them?"

"I'm afraid I can't tell you what the documents are, but you know Mr. Hazelton occasionally works with the authorities when discretion is required. It is definitely required in this case, so he accepted the responsibility of reviewing the documents." I gave her a helpless smile. "Sorry I don't know what else to call them, but they're of a very confidential nature and may lead us to another suspect."

Hetty dropped her hands to her lap. "Do the police still believe Mr. Evingdon murdered her?"

"I don't know if they actually believe it, but he is a suspect and, at the moment, he's rather an attractive suspect." I took a sip of sherry. "Unfortunately, he was near her home the evening she was murdered. He also saw a man leaving Mrs. Archer's house, and the police are checking into that as well. But until such time as they find the other man, or we find something in the documents that turns the direction of the investigation, Mr. Evingdon will remain under suspicion."

"Then you must find something."

I twisted around to find Lottie in the doorway. Heavens, how long had she been standing there?

"Why haven't the police exonerated Mr. Evingdon by now?" she asked, stepping into the room. I winced as she banged her knee on the tea table but she seemed barely to notice.

"It's not quite that simple, dear. I'm afraid a police investigation can take some time."

"Is there anything I can do to help?" she asked. "Mr. Evingdon could never do something so horrible."

I was surprised by the conviction in her voice as well as her determined expression. Before I could reply, Mrs. Thompson ushered George into the room and I turned my attention to him. His weary step and troubled expression told me the heavy satchel in his hand wasn't the only burden he carried.

"Ah, have you come to dine with us, Hazelton?" Hetty asked.

"Dine?" Lottie glared her outrage. "A man's life may hang in the balance."

George stared. Blinked. Then turned his gaze to Hetty. "Under other circumstances, I'd be delighted, but as it happens, I'm seeking only a moment of Lady Harleigh's time."

Hetty stood and took Lottie by the arm. "Dinner will be another quarter of an hour at least. We'll just retire to the library and allow you use of the room."

Lottie opened her mouth to speak but, with a tug from Hetty, allowed herself to be led from the room. I gestured for George to take a seat beside me and inclined my head toward the satchel. "Has something developed?"

He slumped down beside me. "Not as much as I'd like. I visited the coroner this morning for further details of Mrs. Archer's murder. Since then I've been focused on identifying the man Evingdon saw leaving her house." His lips compressed in a thin line. "If she was spending time with another gentleman, they were both very discreet about it. No one has heard of anyone connected to her."

"Then the man he saw was not another suitor?"

"It seems unlikely. I need to move on to questioning her neighbors and in the event one of them is our unknown man, I'd like Evingdon to go with me. He might recognize him. Will you carry on searching for suspects through these notes?" He indicated the satchel.

"I'd wondered why you brought that with you. Yes, of

course I'll carry on. But now that you mention this man, does that not narrow the scope of suspects?" I considered my own question. "Should I eliminate any notes that only implicate a woman?"

"Given what I learned from the coroner, that's a safe assumption. A woman might possibly have strangled her with a scarf or length of rope, but the coroner has ruled the bruises on her neck were caused by a reasonably large pair of hands, probably a man's."

I shuddered as I considered the method of her death, and he placed a steady hand on my arm. "Are you sure you're up to this?"

I waved away his concern. "Yes, of course. It's a rather gruesome image I keep seeing in my mind, but it only makes me all the more determined to help. If going through those files will lead us to the murderer, I'll do it."

"Tell me you've found some worthy suspects."

I frowned. "Sadly, I've found little anyone would pay to keep quiet. Much of it is embarrassing, but hardly scandalous. And most of the notes Charles read from his file were common knowledge."

"I'd like to see what you have."

I had him lift the satchel to the table, and I reached inside to pull out the file I'd been reviewing. "Well, now that I'm eliminating females, I believe there are only three. I haven't gone through the entire file, of course, but we have no plans for this evening so I can keep reviewing them."

I leafed through the pages and handed him the three most likely suspects. "I wonder if these files were already bundled together when Delaney found them."

George was reading through the notes, but he spared me a quick glance. "Do you suppose that signifies somehow?"

"Only that there was nothing of note in Charles's folder.

Everything we've found came from this one. Perhaps Mary already had them separated and my file has all the juicy bits."

"Then why collect the other information at all?" he asked. "And I should remind you there are two more files to be reviewed."

"Yes, I suppose I can't make any judgments until I've seen everything, but I do wonder if there is some other reason she would keep such a collection. Frankly, if Mary was a blackmailer, she was not a very discerning one. She has notes about people who couldn't possibly pay her."

"Perhaps they could grant her favors though." He turned away from the pages to meet my gaze. "And that reminds me, I need to find a way to check with her bank. See if she'd made any deposits lately."

"Isn't Delaney doing that?"

"I'm sure he will, but as my official assignment is limited to reviewing these files, I can't depend on Delaney to share his findings with me."

"I'd be very curious about her financial situation. I realize we've just begun this investigation, but I can't help thinking we're going about this all wrong. How do we even know she was using this information for blackmail?" I gave him a sharp glance. "By the way, do you plan to slip into Mary's house at some point?"

"Is there something in particular you'd like me to search for?"

"Money." I shrugged. "Perhaps she kept it somewhere at home rather than in her bank."

He gave me a half smile. "You're becoming rather accomplished at this investigating business. That's a very good point. I'll try to do that this evening but this time you cannot accompany me as you have a great deal of work to do."

I let out a groan. "I am learning far more about my acquaintance than I ever wished to know. Once I've ferreted out the likely suspects, how do you wish me to proceed?"

"I suppose you should make a list and I'll attempt to learn if they've had any interaction with Mrs. Archer and where they were when she was murdered."

"Ah, in other words are they in possession of an alibi? Excellent notion. You have your hands full, George. I'm perfectly capable of calling on some of these suspects myself."

His brows shot up. "Did you hear what you just said? I will not have you placing yourself in such a dangerous position. I'll handle it."

I harrumphed my disdain. "The woman has recently died. No one would become suspicious if I, very casually, ask how well acquainted they were. I realize no one will admit to having murdered her, but while you are busy hunting for Charles's mysterious man, checking Mary's house for evidence, and analyzing her bank account, I can narrow down this list for you."

He relaxed against the back of the sofa and graced me with a smile. "I suppose that will help, but I don't want you speaking to anyone on your own."

"If only Fiona were here. She'd be perfect for this task. No one can extract information from people the way she does."

"Unfortunately, my sister is unavailable for this task. Though perhaps that's not such a bad thing. Fiona is also good at sharing information, and since the murderer may be someone prominent in society, we must be careful not to show our hand."

"Speaking of showing our hand, I have three guests in my home who are becoming curious about what we're doing. They already know the police consider Charles a suspect. I've told them you are working to prove his innocence and I'm assisting you. I'm certain they'll keep this confidential and perhaps I could ask Hetty to accompany me. She's the soul of discretion."

George narrowed his eyes as he considered my proposal. "Have you told your aunt Hetty what I do?"

I leaned back and took him in with a glance. "Heavens, George. I don't even know what you do—not exactly. If you recall, it was Bridget who told me you previously worked for the Home Secretary. All you said"—I poked a finger into his arm—"was you were still loosely attached to that office. Regardless of how little I know, I've mentioned nothing to Hetty about it. But since you helped us deal with that murder last spring, she has her suspicions. I'd imagine Lily does, too." I shrugged. "They'd never dare ask you about it."

He smiled. "I do believe you're up to the task and I'm sure I can trust their discretion, but judge carefully. Don't put yourself in any danger."

I was warmed by his trust in me. "I promise to take care. Now I believe you have work to do." My gaze took in the satchel on the table. "And I suppose I do as well. Don't worry about me. I promise to take care."

As it happened, Hetty was not able to spare any time for me the next day as she was closeted in the library with Graham again. Neither was Lily free to join me in my investigation. By process of elimination that left me with Lottie. This did not bode well.

I'd spent several more hours last night poring over the files until my eyes were red and dry. As a result, I'd only found nine notes in which the gentlemen in question might be willing to pay Mary to keep their secrets. Four of them were in the country for the summer so I had no way of contacting them. I could devise no excuse for contacting two of the remaining five and would have to leave them to George.

The remaining three would be difficult but not impossible. I couldn't leave everything in this investigation to him, so I devised a plan to come across them completely by chance. One of them was far afield, so I'd need to borrow George's carriage as waiting for the train would take far too long. With Lottie by my side, I might be able to pull this off. She was, after all, a visitor to London. It would only be reasonable for me to take her about town. And reasonable for her to be highly inquisitive. Timing would be essential though as we had three separate stops to make today.

I tore my attention from my notes as Lottie entered the drawing room and I gestured her over to the card table I'd claimed for my work. Its surface was now scattered with pages from Mary's files, but with Hetty and Graham ensconced in my library, my choices were limited to here or my dining room.

She pulled up a chair beside me and I explained what our activities would be for the day. Her bright eyes revealed her eagerness to begin. Poor dear. Either she was completely smitten with my cousin, or so bored, she considered any activity exciting. Since her arrival in London her days had been rather dull. At least today she'd see something of the town and make some new acquaintance, though one of them might be a murderer. I tucked that concern away. We'd be perfectly safe.

By the time I'd explained our itinerary, Mrs. Thompson came in to announce Mr. Hazelton's carriage had arrived. We gathered our belongings and were on our way. I have to admit, I was every bit as excited to begin as my young companion.

Our first stop was just a short drive away in Knightsbridge. Once I'd narrowed my suspects down to three, it became necessary to devise a way of meeting up with them. Daniel Grayson was easy. Leo had mentioned a few days ago the young man had a horse to sell and would be going to Tattersalls today to oversee the sale. It was already ten o'clock when we left the carriage. I hoped we'd arrived in time.

"Who are we meeting up with here?" Lottie asked as we strolled past the subscription rooms and entered the covered courtyard.

"Daniel Grayson, if he's still here," I said as I took in the scene before me. Grooms led horses through their paces in the open arenalike area, while patrons milled about the perimeter. About two dozen or more. Mostly men, here to either buy or sell their horseflesh.

"You think there's a chance he may have murdered Mrs. Archer. Is that correct?"

Though that was exactly the point, her words startled me. While I didn't for a moment consider us to be in any danger, it was certainly unseemly at best to ask a young lady in my charge to speak to a potential murderer. What was I thinking?

"Lottie, perhaps it would be better if you waited in the carriage."

She turned to me with an expression of disbelief. "You can't mean to send me away, Lady Harleigh. I must have a chance to help prove Mr. Evingdon's innocence."

I was about to insist, but at that moment my gaze landed on Grayson. Almost directly across from where we stood. He smiled when he caught my eye and we nodded at one another.

Lottie took in the exchange and gave me a nudge. "Are we going over to him?"

I released a sigh. "I suppose it's too late now to send you back, but let him come to us." I glanced at my young friend in her walking dress with its fitted waist and drapery at the hip, clearly the latest fashion from Paris. The dress, in that particular shade of blush, showed off not only her curves and creamy complexion, but her wealth. Grayson was a second son with little money of his own. I gave her a smile. "Once he sees you with me, I'm certain he'll be right over."

"He's very handsome."

Indeed. Tall, rather lean, with flaxen blond hair, and dressed in a perfectly tailored morning coat, he was the image of a fashionable London gentleman. "Don't let him turn your head, dear. He would not make a good husband." In fact, he once courted Lily while carrying on with a married woman.

"Just follow my lead," I whispered as Grayson arrived at my side.

"Lady Harleigh, how good to see you."

I turned to give him my most charming smile. "Mr. Grayson. It's been some time since we last met."

"Indeed. Don't tell me you are considering a purchase? And with no one to advise you?"

Well, this was a twist. Was he planning to push his own horse off on me? I waved a hand toward my companion. "Why, in fact, I do have an advisor. Have you met Miss Deaver? She's a friend of my sister and is visiting us from New York."

I made Grayson known to Lottie. He took her outstretched hand, a smirk on his face. "Are you a good judge of horseflesh, Miss Deaver?"

She gave him a confident smile. "Well, I should be. My father breeds racehorses on our ranch."

Grayson tilted his head, narrowing one eye. "Isn't New York a city? Is that not rather crowded for a proper ranch? I would imagine such an operation would take a bit of space."

Lottie released a tinkling laugh. "Of course it does. Our ranch is nearby in Brooklyn."

Grayson threw me a glance as I struggled to turn a bark of laughter into a cough. "That's fascinating, Miss Deaver. Has he bred any champions?"

"I'm surprised the two of you haven't already met." I considered it best to turn this conversation before Lottie began spinning tales of the Kentucky Derby. "Were you not at Lady Fiona's gathering Tuesday evening? I was sure Lily told me she'd seen you there."

Grayson allowed the change in conversation and turned to me. "Your sister must have been mistaken. My mother was in town briefly and I escorted her to a card party at the home of my aunt."

I smiled. His alibi would be easy enough to verify. We spoke of horses for another few moments until I felt it was time to depart. "It was lovely to see you again, Mr. Grayson, but I'm afraid we must be off." I linked my arm with Lottie's.

"But didn't you just arrive?"

"Oh, no. We've been here for some time now," Lottie said. "I haven't seen anything to recommend to Lady Harleigh, but perhaps we'll have better luck next week."

I leaned toward her as we walked out. "Very well done, dear. But a ranch in Brooklyn? What were you thinking?"

She released a merry laugh. "That he'd never trouble himself to discover the truth."

Well, well. "I take it Mr. Grayson failed to charm you."

"I think Mr. Grayson will always hold himself in higher regard than anyone he chooses to court." She gave me a glance from the corner of her eye. "I am not as sheltered as you imagine, Lady Harleigh. Nor am I fooled by a handsome face. I assume you were trying to determine if he had an alibi for the time of the murder?"

Perhaps she wasn't as sheltered as I'd thought. "We must still determine if it's true."

"May I continue as your assistant, or do you intend to have me wait in the carriage?"

I gave her a rueful smile. She had done well. "Just don't let your mother find out."

Her laughter rang out as we reached the street and headed for our carriage. I believe I was going to enjoy this day with her.

Lottie and I did enjoy our day. In fact, we chatted and laughed all the way out to Twickenham, where the rowing club had scheduled a meeting at half past twelve at the reading room of the

Twickenham Literary Society. We arrived just in time to greet my suspect at the door along with seven other finely built young men.

"Heavens, are all of you gentlemen here to discuss Mr. Henry James's latest work?"

My inquiry was met with eight blank stares. I tried again. "Are you not part of the literary society? We are to discuss *The Turn of the Screw* this afternoon." I held up a thin volume of *The Two Magics,* which contained the work.

"We're here to discuss our next race, ma'am."

"It's *my lady,* if you please."

Digby Fairchild, my suspect, stepped forward and gave me a nod. "I'm afraid you must have the wrong day or time, Lady Harleigh. This is the meeting of our rowing club."

After some feigned embarrassment, surprise, and flattery, Lottie and I managed to extract what I supposed was an excellent alibi from Mr. Fairchild. The club met every Tuesday evening when they had a race the following Wednesday morning, and they did indeed meet last Tuesday evening.

Once their meeting began, we were back in the carriage and heading to London for Regent Street, and our next and final suspect for the day. By the time we arrived it was after two o'clock and we were both rather hungry.

"I'm afraid we'll have to wait for luncheon until we return home," I said. "However, this shouldn't take much longer."

She gave me a cheeky smile. "I don't mind. Who is our final target?"

"You are speaking like a spy." I returned her smile. "Or like someone who is enjoying this far too much." She really was such a delightful companion. I can't imagine how I didn't see this sooner. "We are waiting for Mr. Oscar Goulding."

She sobered and seemed to study me. "And how has he managed to become a suspect, Lady Harleigh? Why do you suspect any of the men we spoke to today?"

The simple answer was because Mary had a note about Mr. Goulding's daughter. It seems she was caught in a compromising situation with a married gentleman. And somehow, Mary found out about it. And a girl's father might do anything to save her reputation.

"To be honest, I find it hard to believe any of them could have murdered her, but their names are on a list. The only way to take them off the list is to find out if they have an alibi."

"Why do you expect Mr. Goulding here?"

"I spoke with him at the garden affair the other day. He mentioned he was picking up a gift for his wife today and it would not be ready until two, which was very inconvenient for him and required that he rearrange his schedule."

"Why didn't he have it delivered?"

"It's to be a surprise, and he didn't want Mrs. Goulding to learn of it until he presented it."

"How sweet." Her lips pulled down in a frown. "Is it wrong to hope he is innocent?"

I wasn't so sure he could be called innocent. Mary's note about the young Miss Goulding made some mention about the apple not falling far from the tree. Whether the reference was to Mr. or Mrs. Goulding, I couldn't say.

"Not at all. I would hate to believe it of him myself." A movement on the street caught my eye. "Ah, there he is."

The driver assisted us in climbing out of the carriage and we made our way across the street to the jeweler, arriving at the door precisely as Mr. Goulding entered.

"Why, Lady Harleigh." He was all smiles. "What a wonderful bit of luck to find you here." He held the door and ushered us inside. "I am just picking up that little trinket I mentioned the other day. If you have the time, I'd love to hear your opinion of it."

Lottie was right. It was impossible to imagine this genial

man had committed murder just a few days ago. At a fit fifty years, he had the wind-lined face of an outdoorsman. If I recalled correctly, the family hailed from Cornwall so seafaring was not out of the question either. He was a rather no-nonsense type, so I was surprised to observe a hint of indecision in his expression.

"We'd be delighted to give our opinions, though if you chose it, I'm certain Mrs. Goulding will find it perfect."

As the proprietor vanished behind a curtain to retrieve Mr. Goulding's purchase, I introduced Lottie and launched into my questions. "When I last spoke to you I neglected to ask if you were at the Prince of Wales Theatre for Tuesday's performance. I thought I caught a glimpse of you in the lobby, but by the time I made my way through the crowd, you were gone."

"Had I been in the lobby, I would have been happy to wait for you, but as it happens, I was at my club Tuesday evening, so it was not me." His brow knit together. "*A Tale of Two Cities* is still playing there, is it not? We saw it earlier this year. How did you enjoy the performance?"

As I'd been nowhere near the theater that evening, I would have been hard-pressed to come up with an answer. Fortunately, the jeweler returned at that moment with a small velvet pouch. He placed a length of black velvet on the glass-topped counter and spread a lovely diamond and pearl bracelet on its soft surface.

"Oh, my!" Lottie leaned forward for a better view and turned to Goulding, her face full of wonder. "Your wife will be thrilled, sir."

Both Goulding and the jeweler beamed at her praise. "I can only echo that sentiment," I said. "Is the gift in honor of a special occasion?"

Goulding gestured for the man to wrap it up, clearly pleased by our reactions. "The anniversary of our wedding." His expression grew reflective. "It has not been an easy year for my wife. I'd hoped this would allow her to have some good memories of it."

I dug my teeth into my lip. George would have to check on his alibi, but of the three suspects we'd approached today, I truly hoped this one was innocent of this crime.

Our spirits were subdued by the time we returned home. It had taken nearly the entire day to track down three suspects only to eliminate all of them—well, pending confirmation of their alibis. When I considered I'd barely gone through half my file and there were still three other files to be reviewed, this investigation became a daunting prospect.

Mrs. Thompson waited for us in the foyer. "Mr. Hazelton is in the drawing room, my lady," she said, taking my hat and gloves.

"Excellent. I'm eager to hear his news."

George was rifling through the files I'd left on the card table and stood when we walked in. Just a glimpse of his grim face told me his news would not be good.

"Oh, dear, I'm afraid to ask how your day progressed."

"Not well."

Lottie and I seated ourselves on the sofa. "What happened?"

He took the chair across from us. "Evingdon and I canvassed the neighborhood as planned. We received no real information from any of the neighbors. Nor did he recognize any of them as the man he'd seen leaving Mary's house. Unfortunately, one of them recognized him. A woman who lives across the street from Mrs. Archer told the police she'd also seen a man leaving Mary's house that night."

"I don't understand. That's good news, isn't it?"

He bounced his fist off the arm of the chair. "Not at all. The description she gave of Mrs. Archer's unknown visitor also fits Evingdon. Since he's already admitted to being in the area, I can understand Delaney's suspicion. He had two constables waiting at Evingdon House all afternoon. When he never came home, Delaney thought to check in with me. He arrived just as we returned from our canvass."

I felt a sick sense of unease. "George, what are you saying?"

He raised his eyes to mine. "Evingdon is now in police custody."

Chapter 7

"Arrested!"

Lottie jumped to her feet, her outstretched arm just missing my head.

"In custody," George corrected, holding up his hands as if to halt her panic. "There's a world of difference. Delaney doesn't feel Evingdon was completely forthcoming when he questioned him. This is rather an intimidation tactic to make a suspect either provide more information or confess."

"Do you suppose he was less than forthcoming with Delaney?"

He pressed his lips into a grimace. "It's more likely he was incoherent."

"Wouldn't such intimidation make him even more so?"

"That's my fear, but I've instructed him not to answer any questions until I'm with him. I only stayed home long enough to get word to the viscount, Mr. Evingdon's brother," he added for Lottie's benefit. "Then stopped off here to see if you've learned anything I can pass on to Delaney. Otherwise, I'll leave it to the viscount to intervene and put a stop to this."

I raised my hands helplessly. "Though we still need to check their alibis, everyone we spoke with did indeed have one."

"Then I'll go see Evingdon now." He turned from my stricken expression to Lottie's. "All is not lost, ladies. Witness descriptions are notoriously unreliable and Delaney is well aware of that fact. It will take a good deal more evidence to convince him Charles Evingdon is the culprit. And no matter what happens, they can only detain him for so long. Even if they decide to charge him, the viscount should be able to gain his release. Then we still have about a week before the assize to find the real murderer, or at least provide Delaney with a better suspect."

I swept my gaze over the files waiting on the card table. Only a week to find some clue in that stack of notes.

I walked George to the door and asked if he'd had the opportunity to search Mary's house or check on her bank account.

He ran a hand through his hair. "No, I didn't want Evingdon involved in that sort of search and he was with me all day."

"I know you have to mount a defense for him but promise me you'll check on those issues as soon as possible. Meanwhile, if I must double my efforts to review Mary's notes, I may need help."

He nodded. "Right now, let me see to your cousin. We can discuss that later."

Once he left us, I had little time to prepare for dinner with the Kendricks. Charles's difficulties nearly drove the engagement from my mind. But Lily, of course, reminded me.

With the help of Bridget, my lady's maid, I'd made it. Preparing myself mentally for the ordeal might take significantly longer. Not that I had a problem with the Kendricks. They were lovely people, and I wanted to become better acquainted with them. However, we'd be discussing Lily and

Leo's engagement this evening. Just the fact of Lily marrying so young and leaving the safety of my home made me squeamish.

Well, I suppose the safety of my home was questionable considering a man had been murdered in my garden just a few months ago, but that was not the point. Lily would be surrendering herself to the care of a husband, a man she'd known only a few months. How could I not equate her situation with mine? Or rather, what my situation had been.

I'd only known Reggie, my late husband, for a short time before he and my mother agreed on our marriage. She wanted his title. He wanted my money. The moment he laid hands on it, I disappeared for him. Became part of the furniture. It was not a happy marriage. I had to wonder if given more time to get to know Reggie, would I have married him?

I know there were differences in our situations. For one thing, Leo was not marrying Lily for her money. Yes, she had a large dowry, but Leo's family was well-to-do, so her fortune hardly mattered. Their feelings were clearly engaged, Lily was of an age to know her own mind, and both sets of parents had agreed to the match. Still, I felt the need to push for a long engagement. I was sure I'd be the only one with this opinion.

I'd kept Leo close in the past months, trying to learn as much about him as possible and I found him to be a fine young man. Now I needed to learn if his family would accept and love Lily. As this was almost a fait accompli, there was no point in my agonizing over it. Leo was not Reggie. Lily had made a good choice.

In an effort to distract myself, I asked Bridget what she had planned for her afternoon off tomorrow as she put some finishing touches on my hair.

"Very exciting plans, my lady. A good friend of mine is in service with Miss Zimmerman, a lady from America who's staying at the Savoy. Well, my friend also has the afternoon free, and she's arranged for us to have tea there." She beamed at the prospect. "So, I'll be dressing in my finest and meeting her there."

Excitement shone from Bridget's eyes. How lovely for her. It amazed me how Bridget managed to have such a rich social life considering she had so little time off. I assessed her features in the mirror while she pulled my hair into an intricate mound of twists and curls. She had a pink and cream complexion and a mass of blond hair under her cap. "Would you be overdressed if I gave you my rose silk poplin dress? You're a bit shorter than I, but I know how fast you are with a needle. You could certainly alter it in time."

Bridget blushed furiously. "I might be mistaken for an upper-class lady, ma'am, but I have to say I wouldn't mind a bit. Thank you, my lady. I wondered what I could wear to such a posh place as the Savoy."

"I'm sure it will suit you beautifully, Bridget." The rest of her words sunk in. "Did you say your friend works for Miss Zimmerman? Helena Zimmerman from Cincinnati?"

"Just lately. She really works for the hotel, but Miss Zimmerman's maid took ill so Sadie—that's her name—was asked to fill in."

My brain worked out a plan so furiously, I was surprised steam wasn't billowing from my ears. Perhaps it was as Bridget, watching me in the mirror, chewed nervously on her lip. "If I were to fund the tea for both of you, would you be able to steer the conversation to the Duke of Manchester?"

Bridget frowned. "What is it you want to know?"

What I needed to know was if the duke would murder someone to keep Miss Zimmerman from learning of his peccadillos, but I could hardly tell her that. I quickly improvised.

"Just whether or not her mistress is aware of his exploits with another heiress in town."

Bridget compressed her lips as she gave the matter some thought. "That should be easy enough. Miss Zimmerman may have talked to Sadie about the duke, asked for details and such." She gave me a bright smile. "Consider it done, my lady."

"Excellent. I'll give you a note for the maître d'hôtel to send the accounting to me."

I left for my dinner with a much-improved outlook.

The Kendricks had a lovely home on Green Street, just off Park Lane. A slightly smaller mansion than the Argyles' home where the garden party had been. As George had taken his carriage to the police division, to rescue Charles, the Kendricks had kindly sent theirs for us. So Hetty, Lily, Lottie, and I arrived in style. Lily was in high spirits, her excitement contagious. We were all laughing as a liveried footman assisted us to the pavement. I turned at the sound of a squeal, just in time to see Lottie tripping off the carriage step, almost colliding with Hetty. Apparently, she'd missed the hand the footman held out to steady her as she climbed down and caught her heel in the hem of her gown.

I took her arm. "Don't worry, dear. I'm sure Mrs. Kendrick's maid can see to your hem in a trice."

The gaslight of a massive chandelier cast the foyer in a warm glow. The Kendricks waited there to greet us, and when Mrs. Kendrick placed an arm around Lily's shoulder, the gesture went a long way toward easing my concerns. I knew Patricia Kendrick beyond the general social whirl and was fond of her. The second daughter of a second son of a baron, her venerable family line dated back to the Tudor reign. Her marriage to Henry Kendrick came as quite a shock to society. Mr. Kendrick was of less distinguished stock. His father had gained his fortune in the mining industry, which allowed him to give his sons a proper education among boys of the upper classes.

The Kendricks would have been a worthy family in the States but here they were seen as new money social climbers. Rather like I'd been regarded when my mother and I first came to London. But the Kendricks' marriage took place a good fifteen years before I'd arrived, so I imagine the outrage engendered when he managed to steal an aristocrat's daughter from under their aristocratic noses was far greater than anything I'd experienced.

With Patricia's status, the family had a toehold in society and Henry Kendrick hoped to solidify that with grand connections for his children. In that sense he had a great deal in common with my mother. But I'd try not to prejudge.

"Thank you for having us, Patricia," I said, taking her extended hand. Indeed, she exuded a pink and golden glow that made her appear far too young to have a son of twenty-five. She wore her light brown hair in a twist, Gibson style, with tendrils brushing her neck and shoulders. Her gown was a light shade of amber, trimmed in gold netting.

"Have you met Lily's friend, Miss Charlotte Deaver from New York?"

Patricia smiled. "Indeed, we met last week. Oh, dear," she added as Lottie stepped forward. "Has something happened to your hem?"

"Er, I seem to have torn it." Lottie took a step back onto the loose fabric and would have tripped again had I not caught her arm.

Patricia extended a hand toward the girl. "Let's take care of that right now, shall we? Henry, take everyone into the drawing room." With that, she swept the young lady up to her boudoir for the repairs, leaving Leo to perform the introductions for the rest of his family, which consisted of his father, Henry Kendrick, and two sisters, Anne and Clara. Leo and his sisters were an interesting collection of their parents' traits, with little resemblance between them except their father's warm brown eyes.

"Our eldest, Eliza, and her husband regret they couldn't be here tonight but I sent Arthur to the North Country to take care of some business for me. Naturally, he'd want his wife along. I'm very fortunate in my son-in-law, Lady Harleigh," he added, gesturing for me to precede him down the hall. "That boy is like a second son to me."

I'd turned while he spoke and caught a glimpse of Anne, his second daughter, mouthing his very words. Clearly, he'd made that statement more than once.

We all progressed to a tastefully decorated drawing room for conversation and a glass of wine before dinner. Intriguing land-scapes hung on the walls and one could move about the room without cracking a knee on unnecessary tables covered with tatted doily stuffs and assorted knickknacks. Here I was able to observe the elder Mr. Kendrick as he saw to our refreshments. I'd heard much about his business acumen, but not possessing much of a head for business myself, I found myself more inter-ested in his personal qualities. He came to my side as soon as we each had a drink in our hands.

"I cannot begin to tell you how delighted we are with your sister, Lady Harleigh. Leo has certainly chosen well." He gave me a hearty smile. I believe he barely restrained himself from slapping me on the back.

I gave him a warm smile. "We are equally pleased with Leo. And you should dispense with my title. As we are to be family, I should like it if you called me Frances at such family gather-ings as this."

Contrary to my expectations, a frown clouded his counte-nance. Ah, yes, I remember the man was coveting titles for his children. But one couldn't be a countess to one's relations. If it was so important to him, he could introduce me to his friends as Lady Harleigh and talk about me thus in conversation with others, but here among his family I'd insist he use my given name if I had to glare him into submission.

It worked. "Yes, yes, of course. We will all be related soon after all. I am Henry, as you know."

I nodded. I also knew he had just realized he was on a first-name basis with a member of the aristocracy other than his wife. Why that was so important to some, I will never understand. I decided to draw Hetty into the conversation. "Did you know the Kendricks have a mining interest in the North Country?"

At this, Hetty's brows shot up, and she entered into the conversation with enthusiasm, asking pertinent questions about his business. With Henry thus occupied, I wandered over to make the acquaintance of Leo's sisters. The youngest, Clara, was in conversation with Lily but Anne turned toward me when I approached.

"How are you passing the summer?" I asked. "Society is a little thin in town at this time of year."

The look she turned on me could have curdled milk. And quite frankly, the way she lifted her nose, one would think she was smelling it.

"Anne doesn't think much of society events," Clara inserted with a large dose of sarcasm. "She is only interested in improving her mind." Clara was perhaps seventeen or eighteen years old. A pretty, vivacious young woman with a sparkle in her eyes, which I'm sure drew young men to her wherever she showed her face. And from that sparkle I gained the impression this was not the first time she'd teased her sister about "improving her mind." Since she'd waited until Leo had moved away with Lily, I suspected she'd been reprimanded for doing so in the past.

I gave Clara a sweet smile. "It sounds as though you don't find that a worthy pursuit."

"I think she'd do better to pursue a marriage." She pushed her lower lip out in a pout. "Men don't like women who try to act mannish and her actions reflect on me."

"Goodness, you do have strong opinions. I believe I've heard gentlemen bemoaning that trait in young ladies as well."

Her eyes widened as she let out a small gasp. "Have you indeed?" With my nod, she wandered off to ponder this new bit of insight to the male psyche. I turned to Anne, who was trying very hard not to smile.

"I don't need you to defend me," she said finally.

"Actually, I don't think I was defending you so much as women in general."

She gave me a sharp look. "Really?"

"Men will always find something to complain about as far as women are concerned." I shrugged. "And I suppose women do the same. But I can't abide it when society tries to keep women ignorant simply so men can feel superior."

Her face was a study in amazement. "You can't?"

"Of course not. Women have brains; we should use them. Where does the rest of your family stand on this issue? Are they in Clara's camp or yours?"

She thought a moment. "I'm not sure they are firmly embedded in either camp now that you ask. Father encourages my studies, but he'd never let me involve myself in his business." She shrugged. "Leo certainly respects a woman's intelligence, if you're concerned for your sister's sake."

"I would worry if Lily had to pretend to be a fool to please her husband, but she's not very good at pretense, so I'm sure Leo knows she has a brain."

Patricia Kendrick and Lottie joined us just then, as the butler stepped in to catch the lady's eye. Ah, dinner was ready. When Henry offered me his arm to lead me into the dining room, I saw his wife lift her eyes upward and heave a sigh. Goodness, I hoped Mr. Kendrick wasn't observing such formality on my account, but as I had no choice, I took his arm. Patricia and Leo entered next, leaving Hetty and the girls to follow. I was seated next to Henry, with Hetty on his other side. The silver gleamed and the crystal sparkled under the glow of the chandelier overhead. Amid all this formality, I gave thanks Leo seemed so levelheaded.

Once the soup course was served, everyone seemed to relax, and the scene began to feel more like a family dinner. Hetty picked up her conversation with Mr. Kendrick where they had left off in the drawing room. "You were saying you aren't familiar with the South Sea Equity Consortium, Henry? Lord Harleigh told me his banker recommended it highly." She frowned. "I wish I could remember the man's name, but Lord Harleigh's investments are so scattered among different institutions."

"Not a bad idea to diversify," Henry said. "I would be curious to learn who has the management of the fund. It sounds as though it would be a lucrative investment."

Hetty made some murmur of agreement. "I would have thought so, too. And it was initially, but recently it's suffered a loss and I've been unable to discover if there's any chance of a recovery. I understand storms are to blame."

"Henry, do leave off discussing business if you please. You're not in the office now." Mrs. Kendrick couched her rebuke with an indulgent smile.

"Has anyone heard anything more about the poor woman who was murdered last week?"

Mrs. Kendrick shot Anne a glare of exasperation upon the introduction of such a subject at dinner. She seemed ready to chastise her, but Lottie picked up the conversational ball.

"Mrs. Archer was a friend of Lady Harleigh."

All those Kendrick brown eyes turned to me.

"I'm so sorry for your loss," Patricia murmured.

"Archer, you say." Henry lowered his brows as he studied me. "Any relation to Gordon Archer, at Bates Merchant Bank?"

"Gordon Archer is her late husband's brother," I said. "I do believe he is a partner at that bank. Are you acquainted with him?"

"Indeed. Mostly in a business sense, but we meet socially from time to time." He frowned down at his soup and dipped his spoon into the bowl before turning back to me. "I saw him just yesterday. Odd he didn't mention a death in the family."

The conversation had picked up around us, but Henry's comment caught my attention. Was it odd? "Is it common for men to discuss family matters over business?" I asked.

He pulled himself from his musing and gave me a smile. "Not common, no. But I do know the family socially. Been to their home. Met their children. Seems I should have met the sister-in-law at some point, don't you think? Or at least it seems I should have been aware he had one."

I gave the matter some thought as he sipped his soup. Was Mary at odds with her late husband's family? "I suppose that depends on how long you've been acquainted with Mr. Archer. After all, Mary went into mourning for her husband"—I paused while I did the calculations—"well over a year ago now. She hasn't had much of a social life since."

"Ah, that explains it. That's about the time I met Archer." He sat back and allowed the footman to remove his bowl. "At any rate I'll have to attend the funeral."

"Henry." Patricia's voice held exaggerated patience. "First business, then funerals. Surely you can find another topic for conversation."

"Yes, of course, my dear. We should be discussing plans for the engagement party, shouldn't we?"

Lily blushed and smiled across the table at Leo. I struggled to restrain a sigh. Well, I'd known this was coming.

Mrs. Kendrick turned to me with a warm smile. "Do you have any objections to holding it next week? Perhaps a week from today?"

I blanched. I hadn't realized it was coming this soon. I glanced at Lily, who had developed a rapt interest in her napkin.

"Is it necessary to move so quickly? Few people are in town this time of year. Would it not be better to wait until the fall?"

Both the elder Kendricks observed me with surprise. Patricia recovered first. "I think we can gather enough of society to fill a ballroom."

"But isn't Margaret Henderson having some sort of gathering that evening?"

Henry pinned me with a hard look. "One might almost think you had some objection to the match, Lady Harleigh, as you seem intent on putting off the announcement."

I opened my mouth to deny anything of the sort, but Patricia spoke first. "Nonsense, Henry. Frances is right. Margaret Henderson has already sent out her invitations for Saturday next. Aside from that, it's awfully short notice. Perhaps two weeks from today will work with your schedule, Frances?"

Trapped, I cursed Lily for not warning me. Across the table, Hetty pushed the corner of her mouth upward with her pinky finger, giving herself a crooked smile and reminding me this was a happy occasion. As everyone else at the table watched me, I was the only one to notice. I forced a smile.

"I must insist I have no objection at all to the match. My only concern, if it can be called such, is the short length of time Lily and Leo have known each other. Announcing the engagement will give rise to the expectation the wedding will take place within a few months."

Again, the occupants of the table stared at me. "I believe Lily and Leo have expressed their intention of marrying before the Christmas holiday." Patricia spoke in a tentative voice, realizing for the first time I was unaware of the couple's wishes.

"Have they?" This time I stared at Lily until she was forced to raise her eyes. She gave me a nervous smile.

"We are very certain of our affection for one another, Frances, and hope you'll indulge us in our haste."

What could I say? I had absolutely no objection to the match. Even my parents approved it. My father had already finalized the marriage settlement. Just because haste had been a mistake in my marriage, who was I to say Lily didn't know her own heart? She certainly knew how to get her own way. "Then I won't stand in your way. If you wish to be married before Christmas I'm sure we can arrange it."

The gratitude shining from Lily's eyes told me she was certain of her decision. That was all I could ask for. "Well, if we are to have an engagement party in two weeks, we had better get to work on the guest list."

Chapter 8

Sunday morning found me managing multiple assignments. In addition to finding a blackmail victim, and possible murderer, I was charged with the task of preparing a guest list for the engagement party as invitations must go out today. Bridget would be doing some snooping for me this afternoon as to just how familiar Miss Zimmerman was with the duke's romantic liaisons. Sadly, I wouldn't hear if she'd learned anything until tomorrow. George had sent round a note with a footman, saying he would call on me at noon, both to give and receive an update on our progress. Rather a busy day.

After breakfast with Rose, I set to work. With Hetty, Graham, and Lottie using my library, Lily and I set ourselves up in the drawing room. I'd given her a guest list I'd helped Fiona prepare for a soiree she'd held two months ago. Many on the list had gone to the country, but at least it was a place to start. Lily sat at the card table writing invitations to those she knew to be in town. When she was unsure of someone, she called out their name to me, as if I knew the whereabouts of everyone in society.

Meanwhile, with the use of a lap desk, I sat on the sofa, making notes of my progress from yesterday and reading through still more of Mary's files. I'd chosen the file with the uncoded notes as they were easier to read, then sifted through all the pages for Charles's name. I was ashamed at myself for doing so. I suppose it was disloyal, but I couldn't help but wonder if Mary had learned something about him and confronted him with it. In the end, I'd found nothing with his name, which gave me great relief, though the process had made my head throb.

"The Fontaines, Frances. Are they in town?"

"No, but they are only in Oxford. I'd send them an invitation anyway as they're close enough to come. And we will certainly invite them to the wedding."

Back to reading the notes one by one. Hmm, what's this about Lord Herford? I read further. Good heavens, was she implying he'd drugged a racehorse? I placed that sheet in the stack of possible blackmail victims. He'd do anything to keep that from getting out. The next was a breach of promise suit brought by Harriet Farmer against a Mr. Richardson. I didn't know Mr. Richardson, but I was familiar with Miss Farmer, and frankly, the gentleman should consider himself lucky to escape with only a lawsuit.

"What about Sir Robert and Lady Nash? They are in the country, are they not?"

"Yes, and they are too far away to attend the party, but you must send an invitation to Fiona and tell her of your engagement, as I have no time at the moment to write. Indicate that you don't expect her attendance, but only wish to give her the news."

Back to the file. The next was about the Duke of Manchester. Again? Miss Zimmerman was the only one likely to care about his exploits, and Bridget was already checking into that. Lily's voice broke into my thoughts.

"Do you want me to tell her you don't have time to write?"

"Who?"

"Lady Fiona."

"Heavens, no!" I whipped my head around to glare at her. "You can't tell Fiona I have no time for her. Just indicate you are including her in your happy news. I will write her later."

"Then should I tell her you'll write her later?"

Her questions made me want to beat the sofa cushion with the file in my hand, but I took a calming breath instead. "No. You should leave me out of it altogether."

Back to the file. I scanned the next sheet with a jaded eye. As titillating as this information had been at the outset, I could barely take it in now. I had absolutely no interest in who was doing what with whom—or to whom. I put the current page in the minor gossip pile.

As I reached for the next page, Lottie slipped through the door. I watched in fascination as she caught her sleeve on the door handle, tugging until the embroidered trim wrapped around the handle several times. Lily came to her rescue, deftly twisting the trim away from the metal handle and voilà, Lottie was freed. With trim dangling from her wrist and a newspaper in her hand, she made her way toward my working area, stopping midstep as she took in my harried expression.

"They're discussing something rather confidential," she said, tossing her head back toward the hall. "I thought I'd give them some privacy. Is it all right if I wait in here?" She inched closer toward the sofa.

"Of course," I said. "But not—"

She seated herself on the other side of the sofa from me and my stacks of paper, jostling the cushions, and sending the pages into a heap on the floor.

"—there."

"I'm so sorry, Frances. Let me get those." I didn't bother to stop her. I knew she'd simply bundle all the carefully sorted pages, but if I'd tried to intervene, we'd likely clunk heads, or tear the pages, or cause some other disturbance.

My nerves grew taut and I longed for the return of my library.

As expected, Lottie returned all the pages to me in one lump. I smiled as she reseated herself and opened the paper, flicking it out before her to straighten the folds. I returned to sorting the papers into two stacks.

"What about Mr. Hazelton's brother?" Lily asked.

"If you mean the earl, I believe Mr. Hazelton mentioned he's in town. You should send him an invitation."

"Why, there's no gossip column again today," Lottie said, her voice bordering on a whine. "I so enjoyed reading it, and this is the third day without one."

Having enough gossip in the pages on my lap, I chose to make no comment.

"Have they given any explanation?" Lily asked.

"No, and I truly miss it. I've been reading it every day since I've been here and the last column hinted at a breach of promise suit between a Miss Farmer and a Mr. Richardson. I was curious to see if anything had come of it."

I was ready to throttle the two of them for disturbing my concentration when Lottie's words registered with me. I glanced up sharply. "You read about that in a gossip column?"

She jumped as if not expecting me to speak, her movement tearing the paper. "I'm sorry, Frances." She bit her lip and glanced at me from the corner of her eye. "Have you read this already?"

I waved a hand. "It's of no matter, dear. Tell me about this gossip column."

She brightened. "It's fascinating. It usually refers to people only by initials, but Jenny and Mrs. Thompson have helped me identify whom she's speaking of. The columnist has definitely created a stir as she seems always to be on the mark."

"She?" That was an interesting twist. "The columnist is a woman?"

Lottie nodded. "A Miss Information. Isn't that clever?"

Actually, I thought it a ridiculous name, but that was beside the point. My brain was telling me this was important, and I needed to learn more about this column. "You say there hasn't been a column for three days? And you read about the breach of promise suit—when?"

"Sometime last week. If it's important, I can fetch it for you. I keep clippings of her columns."

"Do you? Yes, please fetch them. I think I need to read this column."

She folded the paper and set off like a shot, leaving me to wonder what these notes actually represented. Were they fodder for a blackmailer, or simple gossip? I needed more information. Was there some connection between Mary's files and the gossip column? After all, much of what I found in her files was common knowledge. Was it common because everyone had already read about it in the newspaper?

A steady tapping sounded behind me. I turned to see Lily resting her chin on her fist and drumming her fingers on the table. At my raised brows, she stopped. "Frances, why are you so concerned about the gossip column? I've never known you to indulge in gossip, other than listening to Lady Fiona, that is."

I reacted with a snort. "You give me far too much credit. While I do my best not to spread it, I am human after all and just as curious as anyone else."

"But why is this so important?"

"I'm not sure it is, but I'd like to find out. Now don't you have invitations to attend to?"

She scowled but went back to her work just as Lottie returned, her hands full of clippings.

Heavens. "How did you acquire so many of these? You've only been here three weeks."

I carefully removed my stacks of notes to the tea table so she could sit on the sofa and spread the clippings out between us. "It's a daily column and I began clipping them after I read the first one." She shrugged. "I thought it would help me to learn who was who around town."

I glanced through the clippings, reading a sentence here and there. "Well, I doubt it's providing you with everyone's best qualities, and I must warn you much of the gossip in the papers is simply made up. Though if even a portion of this is true, you might take it as a warning about whom you should avoid. Now, where is the one that mentions the breach of promise?"

She sifted through the papers and, settling on one, handed it to me. I scanned the column, then found the page in Mary's notes that corresponded. They were identical, word for word. Unfortunately, this proved nothing unless I knew which came first. It would be odd for Mary to copy the contents of a column when she might simply have clipped the item from the paper as Lottie had done. But I couldn't rule that out.

All right, what could rule it out? I leaned my back against the sofa and gazed up at the ceiling, tapping my fingertips against my lips. There were no dates on the notes. But they'd arrived in separate bundles. I focused on the stack of folders I'd left on the tea table. The one I held was the thinnest and I'm sure it was the one Charles had been leafing through. What if . . .

I gathered the clippings and thrust them into Lottie's hands. "Let's go through those one by one. You can give me the salient points of the column and I'll try to find a corresponding note in here."

It took the better part of two hours to match them up. Hetty had stepped in after the first hour, hoping to take Lottie back to the library, but the intensity of our search had her backing away without her assistant. One by one, we matched the notes to the clippings Lottie had collected. There were at least three notes to each clipping. In the end, about twenty pages of notes remained unmatched.

I gazed across the stacks of paper to find Lottie staring back at me, her brows lowered in concentration. "Does this have something to do with Mrs. Archer?"

"I'm not sure yet." I stared past her into the distance. "If all the notes in this file match a column in the newspaper, then should we assume these other files are columns yet to be written?"

The girl's eyes widened. "Are you saying Mrs. Archer was Miss Information?" She caught her lip between her teeth. "Does this help Mr. Evingdon's cause?"

Oh, dear. "It certainly seems like more than a coincidence, but I don't believe it helps him at all." Heavens, this might actually remove the motive of blackmail.

"You should inspect the other files." I turned to see Lily had given up all pretense of writing invitations and was watching us intently. "They can't all be gossip columns. It hasn't been running for that long. What are the other files for?"

Good question. I turned my gaze to the three other bundles tied up in heavy paper covers. "We've reviewed two of them. This one is filled with rather inflammatory information."

I pushed it to the side, remembering it also contained the note about me. Though I certainly didn't want anyone else to see it, I could hardly remove it as it was evidence. "I have yet to examine the other two files."

As I picked up one and opened it, I wondered if I should take them to my bedchamber or send Lottie back to Hetty. Delaney hadn't wanted to admit they existed, and George wanted to keep them confidential. But that was when we all thought the files were for the purpose of blackmail. If Mary was only writing a gossip column . . .

"There's a note on this folder that says *Do not use*."

I glanced over at Lottie to see she had untied the strings binding the fourth file and was examining the inside of the paper cover. Setting aside the pages I'd been reading, I turned back to the inside cover of my folder and saw the words *December 1898 through May 1899* written in pencil. Could this relate to the columns for that time period? I reached for the file that contained the current columns and turned back the cover. *June 1899 through—*.

Lottie craned her neck to see the note. From her expression, I saw we'd arrived at the same conclusion. Our gazes moved to the file I'd pushed aside, still sitting on the table. I moved the two from my lap to the sofa and pulled open the file I'd been reading yesterday. The note on the inside cover also read *Do not use*.

"Perhaps these notes weren't interesting enough for her column."

"I've read some of them. I suspect just the opposite is true."

She turned to the first note.

"I'd rather you didn't read those, dear." I reached out to close the folder just as she spoke.

"She uses Pitman shorthand."

I stopped my hand in midreach. "You're familiar with this style of writing?"

"Oh, yes." She waved a hand over the file. "I found it very useful when I took minutes at the board of directors' meetings." She raised her brows at my blank stare. "My volunteer work at the Metropolitan Museum. Recording minutes became much easier when I learned this type of stenography. Perhaps I might help you go through these files?"

Before I could answer, Mrs. Thompson escorted George into the drawing room. I leaned closer to Lottie. "I'll have to speak to Mr. Hazelton about that. Can you give us a moment?"

"Of course." She greeted George and excused herself to return to the library with Hetty and Graham. Lily pretended to be working intently on her invitations. I motioned for George to take a seat next to me.

"It seems we've made a discovery," I said.

His gaze took in the files on my lap and strewn across the tea table. "We? Never say the young ladies have been working with you?"

"Not in the manner you think." I handed him the newspaper clippings. "Lottie has been collecting these clippings from the newspaper and they match Mary's notes perfectly. We strongly suspect she was writing the Miss Information column."

He gave me an empty stare. "Misinformation?"

"No. *Miss* Information." I tapped the heading on the clipping he held. "It's a play on the word and a column in the *Daily Observer.*"

"Interesting. Tell me more."

I gave him a summary of our morning's business. "Though I can't say for certain she isn't blackmailing anyone, the files filled with the scandalous tales are marked as *Do not use.* What do you make of all this? And have you discovered anything yourself?"

"What I discovered is making a little more sense now that I've heard your information." He flicked a glance across the room at Lily, now paying more attention to us than to her own work.

I huffed. "Lily, those invitations are not going to write themselves. And they must be delivered today."

George waited until Lily returned to her work before speaking. "In checking with Mrs. Archer's bank, I found regular deposits of a fairly small amount. Either she was utterly inept as a blackmailer, or she had some other source of income. Until now, I assumed it was some type of allowance from her family or the Archers; now I wonder if it was from her employment."

"I'm beginning to wonder if she was not on the best of terms with her late husband's family. The Archers are quite well-to-do. If they were giving her an allowance, she would at least have been able to keep a maid-of-all-work, and that was not the

case. Last evening, Mr. Kendrick told me he's been a social acquaintance of the Gordon Archers for a year now and yet he
knew nothing of Mary's existence. I suppose that doesn't mean
they were at odds, but it does make me wonder about her relationship with that family."

"What of her own family?"

I let my fingers roll the edges of the papers in my lap as I
tried to remember something about Mary's family. "Her parents are deceased, I think, and her only sister is married to the
third son of Viscount Spencer. A prominent family, but not
much money. He's a solicitor with offices in Oxford." I chewed
at my lip, wondering what sort of income a solicitor might
earn. "I doubt they could provide an allowance for her."

"Well, I suppose it should be easy enough to verify if she was
employed with this newspaper."

"If she was, that is not good news for Charles." As I spoke
the words, it occurred to me I had no idea what was happening
with my cousin. "Good heavens, how could I forget to ask
about him? Is he still in police custody?"

He chuckled. "I wondered if you had forgotten about him in
the excitement of your new discovery. The viscount is seeing to
his release as we speak. I expect him to arrive at my house this
evening. I've invited him to stay for a few days."

"Why should he stay with you?"

"Rather ironically, I'm concerned about gossip. Reporters
haunt the police divisions for just such a story as this. So far,
they've been discreet in this matter and the viscount has threatened the career of any constable who breathes a word of
Charles's questioning." He shrugged. "Still, word could get
out. I thought it best if he stayed out of sight and out of society
until the police make it clear he is no longer a suspect."

"I hope that will be soon, but if we confirm Mary was Miss Information, that eliminates blackmail and makes the case against

him even stronger. Though I will be happy to stop searching for potential victims."

George rested his palms on his thighs and leaned toward me. "I'm sorry to contradict you, Frances, but simply because the file says *Do not use* we cannot make any assumptions. She might still have been blackmailing."

"But you said she had no large deposits to her account."

"Yes, but I haven't obtained access to her house yet. She might have money hidden there. We can't rule it out yet."

I frowned. "So, we still don't know anything."

"I'm afraid not. But you have uncovered a helpful clue in this gossip column. We should make Delaney aware of it."

"We?"

"Yes." He gave me a sheepish grin. "I bumped into him at the Chelsea division this morning and he inquired, with some asperity, why I wasn't inspecting Mrs. Archer's files."

I raised my brows. "You told him?"

"Merely confirmed his suspicions. Delaney knows Evingdon is my friend and that I'd been investigating on his behalf." He raised his hands in a gesture of helplessness. "He had to know someone was poring through the files. He's a clever fellow. I'm sure he suspected that someone was you."

"And he didn't object?"

"He might have done if it were known among his superiors, but as long as we're discreet, I'd say he's just happy he doesn't have to do it himself."

My hand fluttered up to my chest and I struggled to suppress a smile. That Delaney hadn't objected to my participation was very much like a vote of confidence. My pleasure faded a bit when I considered the prospect of digging through these files again. I wondered how far I could push his goodwill.

"How do you suppose he'd feel if I enlisted some help?"

He raised a brow. "Your aunt Hetty?"

I took a glance over my shoulder, surprised to see Lily hard at work. Apparently, she'd given up trying to eavesdrop. I turned back to George and lowered my voice. "Lottie."

He twisted the corner of his mouth downward. An objection was clearly imminent, so I pressed on.

"I would not normally ask a young lady to read material of this nature, but she has just the skills for this and, having met her mother, I doubt any of it will shock her."

He leaned away and stared through narrowed eyes. "You have just shocked me. Her mother?"

"Is carrying on with a French count—a married French count." I raised my hand to forestall his response. "Don't misunderstand me. Lottie is a lady in every sense of the word. I suspect her volunteer work is a way to escape her household. The most important part is she can read stenography."

His expression cleared. "I see. That would be helpful."

"Indeed, it would. If you agree to let her assist me, I'll be certain to stress the confidential nature of these notes."

His expression told me he was beginning to see my point. "We'll move through these files much more quickly with her help," I added.

George looked up to the ceiling and scrubbed a hand down his face. "All right," he said finally. "She would certainly be an asset to the investigation, but she must not breathe a word of what she is doing."

"I will vouch for her. And since you mention keeping things to ourselves, could we wait to tell Delaney about the gossip column? I don't want to give him any more reason to suspect Charles."

A smile crept across his face. "May I assume once he's a free man you'll have no further reason to withhold information from the police?"

"Goodness, I suppose that is what I'm doing, isn't it? Well, it's only until Charles is released. And as you said, just because she was writing a column doesn't mean she wasn't blackmailing someone as well." I shuddered. "I hate saying something like that about a friend, especially a deceased friend."

"That reminds me. When is the funeral?"

"Tomorrow morning."

"Damn." He raised his gaze to mine. "Apologies. I'd hoped to attend, but I don't see how I can make it. Are you going?"

"Yes, I'd planned to. Why?"

He moved closer and lowered his voice. "Try to pay attention to everyone there—family, friends—even minor acquaintances. Take note of anyone who seems out of place. Anyone who didn't know her well, whom you wouldn't expect to see there. Or anyone just acting out of character."

"Goodness, that's a great deal of attention to pay. I shall have my hands full." I studied him through narrowed eyes, searching for whatever he wasn't telling me. "Are you asking me to watch out for the killer? Do you think he might go to her funeral?"

"It happens quite frequently." He placed a hand over mine. "Mind you, I don't want you to take any action yourself. Just make note of anyone who seems suspicious to you. If it's at all possible, I'll meet you there. I daresay Delaney will attend. If you have a concern about any of the guests, tell him."

"I can do that." A thrill of excitement coursed through my veins. If I weren't so worried about Charles, I might actually enjoy this investigative work.

Chapter 9

Once George departed, I organized my troops. Lily had finally finished her invitations, and we sent them with Jenny to the Kendricks for delivery. I appropriated Lottie from her work with Graham and Hetty and brought her back to the drawing room.

Since the three of us were already seated around the tea table, and since it was nearly four o'clock, we made our battle plans over tea. There was no longer any point in secrecy as I needed Lottie's help. I had no authorization to involve Lily, but quite honestly, I felt rather guilty leaving her out. I'd simply restrict her to the common gossip files. Once we each enjoyed a bracing cup of tea, I explained Delaney's blackmail theory.

"But didn't we decide she was using this material for her gossip column?" Lottie waved a hand over the files on the sofa between us.

"We haven't yet verified that she was writing the column," I corrected. "But even if she was, we must still consider the files marked *Do not use*. Though she may have chosen not to use them for her column, that doesn't eliminate the possibility she was using them for blackmail."

"Just how much does a blackmailer earn, do you suppose?" Lily wondered aloud. "How do they determine what to charge?"

"We still haven't verified that either, Lily—whether she was blackmailing anyone or if she received any payments," I said as I reconsidered Lily's involvement in this task. "Perhaps this was her first attempt."

"Oh, dear," Lottie said. "It seems she chose the wrong person to threaten."

Lily tipped her head to the side. "If someone she blackmailed murdered her, wouldn't he take the notes about himself?"

I gave the girls a summary of everything we'd learned so far about the case, including the fact that the notes had been hidden.

Lottie's mouth fell open as she drew in a gasp. "Are you saying this is all of society's dirty laundry?"

"Heavens, no. I'm certain it's just a small sample. And I think we should refer to it as salacious gossip. Just because we're reading it, doesn't mean we should lower ourselves by speaking in such a common manner."

Lily almost choked on a biscuit, recovering after a quick sip of tea. "We get to read this?" She waved her hand over the files on the table.

"All of your invitations are done?"

She slid forward to the edge of her chair and eyed the files. "So many people are away from town right now, it didn't take nearly so long as I expected."

"I'm allowing Lottie to read the rather nasty files only because she understands this code they're written in." Biting my lip, I turned to her. "Do you mind, dear? I'd rather not involve you, but I truly need the assistance."

She waved away my concern. "If this will help Mr. Evingdon, I'm happy to do it."

I reached for the first *Do not use* file and froze as my fingers closed around it. Sitting back in my seat, I stared openmouthed at Lily.

"What?" she muttered, leaning away to distance herself from me.

"So many people are out of town." The information was slowly processing through my brain. I clamped my mouth shut and stared at her. "Lily, do you have a list of those people? The ones who were out of town?"

"Well, they were on the original list and their names are now crossed off."

"Where is it?"

Setting down her tea, she stepped over to the card table where she'd been working. I should have known she wouldn't have picked up after herself. Sorting through the mess on the table, she returned with the list.

"All right. As we go through these notes, check the names of the parties involved against this list. If they've been gone longer than a week, they should go in a stack on the table."

"If one intended to commit murder, I hardly think they'd balk at traveling back to London to do so." Lily raised her brows with the challenge.

"I agree, so we won't completely exonerate them. We'll simply set them aside for the moment. But if someone had already removed to the country then returned for a short time, people would notice. It's almost impossible for someone of prominence to sneak back into town. Their servants would need to provision the house and word would get out. Even if they stayed at a hotel, they'd draw attention to themselves. And a murderer wouldn't want to do that."

"That means our most likely suspect is someone who is still in town," Lottie said.

"But someone who left just Wednesday is even better."

"How will we know when they left?"

"If we aren't sure, we'll just consider them out of town. We can review that group later."

With our assignment established, the girls eagerly pulled pages from the files. I scooted toward Lottie. She might be able to read the notes, but she'd need help with the initials.

"Before we begin, you must understand you are not to breathe a word about anything you read today. All of this information stays in this room."

I obtained a promise from both of them and we continued in silence, Lottie transcribing the notes, while I inserted the appropriate names. We then placed the pages in the various stacks. By the end of two hours we had a stack about three inches high for those who had been out of town for some time. Another stack held about ten pages. These were the people who had left within the past week, though we didn't know the exact day. A third stack held about fifteen pages. These were the people who were still in town.

I'd cringed at some of the things I'd read, but still found it hard to believe anyone would kill to save their reputation. I also wondered how Mary managed to collect this information on her friends and acquaintance. Although it was marked *Do not use*, she'd gone to the trouble of making note of it. Would she have used it as blackmail if necessary? And what would make it necessary?

It wasn't that difficult to put myself in Mary's position. Alone in the world and without funds. It wasn't so long ago I'd have been in the same position if not for Lily and Aunt Hetty. As soon as I'd left the Wynn family home, Graham had filed a suit to claim the funds in my bank account and the bank denied me access to them until the suit was settled. If my mother hadn't sent Lily and Aunt Hetty to me, along with a large bank draft to cover their expenses, I'd have been penniless in a matter of weeks.

But what if they hadn't come along? Would I have made some attempt to support myself, or crawled back to the safety of my late husband's family? If there was a rift between Mary and her in-laws, it must have been something important since she chose to support herself selling gossip rather than turning to them for assistance.

Or was I simply projecting my distaste for this manner of earning a living onto her? I didn't know Mary very well. Yet she had notes about me. How had she obtained that information? I considered who knew about the financial dispute Graham and I had a few months ago. Obviously, he and I. Mr. Stone, my solicitor, Lily, Hetty and George. Oh, yes, Fiona and her husband. Fiona was an incurable gossip, but she was also my best friend. She would never carry that tale to anyone.

Lily and Lottie were reviewing the "still in town" stack. I must have been very deep in my thoughts, for when I looked up they both stared at me with concern.

"I was just wondering," I said, "how Mary came by all this information." I lifted a page and gave it a cursory read. "One does not overhear details about Lord Frobisher's financial situation in a crowded ballroom."

"That's true." Lily sat back and threaded her finger through a stray curl at her neck. "You might hear someone hint about someone else's financial distress, but you would never hear details about such a thing."

"Do you remember the difference of opinion I had with Graham earlier this year?" I raised my brows, hoping Lily would remember the bank account story without requiring me to spell it out in front of Lottie.

Lily nodded while Lottie discreetly tried not to pay attention.

"Mary knew about that."

"How?"

"I can't imagine. None of you would ever speak of it."

"Servants?" Lily suggested.

"Did you say anything to the servants?"

"Of course not."

"Neither did I, though I expect they were well aware of it. I can't imagine Mrs. Thompson, Bridget, or Jenny carrying gossip outside the house." I shook my head firmly. "They have far too much integrity."

"What about Graham and Delia's servants?"

Now that was possible. Graham and his late wife wouldn't have said anything directly to one of their servants, but they might have been overheard in the battered old manor house they'd lived in. I certainly did my share of eavesdropping on them. I pondered the matter.

"All right, let's assume Mary received her intelligence through servants. In my case, that means she either had a correspondence with a servant at Harleigh Manor, which I find unlikely, or she obtained this bit of gossip from Graham's valet. When the earl came to town, he only ever brought his valet."

"Well, that rather narrows it down, don't you think? We need to have a talk with Graham's valet."

I held up my hand. "Not we, dear. Why on earth would he admit anything to us? The gossip was about me, for heaven's sake. I think we'd have a better chance with Jenny."

Jenny, while not a maid-of-all-work, was certainly a maid of much work. Pretty enough for the parlor, she was also strong, capable, and efficient. Though only seventeen, she'd been in service with the Wynn family from the age of twelve and knew well how a house should be run. I brought her with me from Harleigh Manor after she'd caught me eavesdropping on a conversation between Graham and his late wife. Not a breath of my indiscretion escaped her lips.

"Jenny used to work with Graham's valet," I said. "After the funeral tomorrow, I'll pay a call on Harleigh House and take her with me. While I'm visiting with Graham, perhaps she can wheedle something out of the valet."

Lily and Lottie exchanged a look. "It's as good a plan as any," Lily said.

Chapter 10

Why must it always rain at a funeral? I peered through the misty drizzle at perhaps two dozen of my fellow mourners, huddled under their own umbrellas. If George was correct, one of them might have taken Mary's life. The thought further chilled me.

He'd been correct about Delaney. I noticed him as soon as we arrived at the cemetery and moved to his side at the back of the group. All the better to observe everyone, I suppose.

Closest to the casket was Mary's sister, Louise, and her husband, whose given name escaped me. They were dressed appropriately in black, but Louise's outdated dress was all the more notable as she stood next to Caroline Archer, Mary's sister-in-law. Her gown, which had probably been designed and made within the last few days, hugged her figure like a glove. Likewise, the hat with its peekaboo veil flattered her high cheekbones. Jet earrings replaced the more precious stones that usually dripped from her ears.

Moving along the line, Mary's brother-in-law, Gordon Archer, came next. Tall, fair, and well, businesslike. In fact, he looked every inch the banker he was. Two more Archer siblings and their spouses stood to his left, but it was Gordon Archer and his wife, Lady Caroline, who interested me most. As wealthy as they were reported to be, they had left Mary to live in what would have to be considered reduced circumstances. Yet they stepped up to organize her funeral. Curious.

I leaned closer to Delaney. "Are you aware of any rift between the Gordon Archers and Mary Archer?"

He kept his gaze on the crowd. "What have you heard, my lady?"

I glanced at him through the tail of my eye. "Nothing, but it strikes me as suspicious. Archer is quite well off. Why leave his brother's widow to fend for herself?"

"It would be suspicious if you were making a case for Mrs. Archer to murder Gordon Archer, but not the reverse." This time he turned his gaze to me, a half smile on his lips. "The case is still under investigation and there are plenty of suspects. You don't have to throw more of them under my feet."

"Is anyone here worthy of your particular attention?"

He shrugged. "So far, no one more than your cousin. I assume you'll be happy to hear he's been released."

"Indeed, I am, though it doesn't sound as though you've changed your mind about Mr. Evingdon."

"We haven't charged him, but you should understand he is still a suspect. At this point, our best suspect." He lowered his shaggy brows. "And you can tell him he needn't hide. No one should know he was brought in for questioning."

I raised my brows. "Where exactly is he hiding?"

Delaney tipped his head to the left. I took a peek beyond him to see a man holding an enormous black umbrella. More accurately, I saw only the torso of a man. The umbrella completely hid his head and shoulders. I chuckled behind my hand, though I had to admit it was a rather effective disguise.

The movement of the crowd distracted me. The service had ended, and the group dispersed to their carriages, either to go about their business or return to the Archer home. I bid Delaney good day and walked over to my cousin.

He tipped the umbrella to reveal his face as I approached and greeted me with a smile.

"I'm surprised to see you here, Charles. Mr. Hazelton said you'd be staying out of society for the next few days."

"Probably should be, but I wanted to come to the funeral." He shrugged. "Seemed the right thing to do."

"Delaney thinks no one has found out you were ever in police custody so hiding may not be necessary. I'm pleased you managed to survive the ordeal with no ill effects."

We fell into step as we walked back to the carriages lining the street. "Ordeal? Oh, yes. The inspector chap had a great many questions but no beatings, no rack. Though I don't think they torture prisoners anymore, I was only there the one day, so I couldn't say for sure. My brother came and vouched for me, you know. So here I am. Fit as a fiddle."

"I'm happy you have your freedom once again. Are you going back to the Archer home?"

By this time, we had reached the carriage. Once again, I'd borrowed George's. His driver opened the door and took my umbrella while Charles assisted me inside where Jenny had been waiting for me.

"Truth is," he said, "I hired a hack to bring me here as I was hoping to tag along with you back to the house. I want to pay my respects, especially to Mary's sister, but I'm not sure the Archers are aware Mary and I were keeping company, and I'd feel rather uncomfortable wading in there alone."

At my invitation, he joined me in the carriage. Why had I never thought to ask him about Mary's relationship with her in-laws? Heedless of Jenny's presence, I put the question to him.

"She spoke of her sister quite frequently but not the Archers. We spotted them at the theater once, but she wanted to avoid them. She said they did not get on and she'd rather not spoil the evening by conversing with them." He cocked his head to the side. "It struck me as odd, but I decided she knew best and didn't push her for an explanation."

Interesting. Jenny pretended to ignore us, her gaze glued to the window as we traveled through the streets. "Do you have any idea why they didn't get on? Was there a disagreement?"

"Afraid I never asked. She spoke from time to time about her late husband. Well, not time to time actually, more like once, and it was more of a mention. But she never spoke at all about his family."

The carriage came to a stop as we reached the Archers' home in Belgrave Square. I gave Jenny leave to do as she pleased for the next half hour. As the rain had stopped, she might like to stretch her legs.

Charles assisted me from the carriage and we took ourselves inside. "I took note of everyone who attended the funeral today," I whispered. "It might be wise to do the same here."

As we entered, I could see a large group had gathered in the drawing room, far more than had attended the funeral, everyone speaking in hushed voices. Even if it were not a mournful occasion, the drawing room itself was magnificent enough to engender whispered tones. Dwarfed by the expansive space and soaring ceilings, we mere mortals gathered in small groups so as not to be overcome by the overt display of wealth. It truly resembled something an Astor would build, and, in fact, would be much more at home on Fifth Avenue.

As we planned to stay only long enough to pay our respects to the family, we'd have to note our observations quickly. We hung back near the entrance to the room so as to have a good view as everyone arrived. When I spied Mary's sister entering the drawing room, I stepped up to speak to her.

"Louise, dear."

Louise, Mary's older sister, was a short, solid woman in her mid-thirties with a matronly air about her. Premature, given her age, but likely a result of giving birth to five children and the concern of how to feed them all. Her face registered confusion before she recalled who I was. A sad smile played about her lips as she reached for my hand. "Frances, how good of you to come. We haven't met for an age."

"Not since Jasper's funeral. How sad it is that these are the events that bring us together." I squeezed her hand. "I am so sorry for your loss."

"Thank you, my dear." She sighed and gave me a brave smile.

"Mary and I had lost touch once we both became widows, but in recent weeks we've revived our friendship. She was such a lovely person. Her death must have come as a shock to you."

Her gray eyes misted. "Indeed. She lived a rather quiet life this past year or so. We corresponded regularly but I have absolutely no idea why someone would wish her harm." She dabbed at a stray tear with a black-edged handkerchief.

"Has the police inspector in charge of her case spoken to you yet?"

She tucked the handkerchief into the cuff of her sleeve. "We just arrived from Oxford yesterday. We are to meet with Inspector Delaney tomorrow."

"I had some experience with Inspector Delaney when someone broke into my house last spring. He's quite competent, and I'm sure he will find out what happened in this case."

I'd hoped my comment would reassure her, but her face registered her distress. "Someone broke into your house?" She tutted. "I knew Mary should have come to live with us. This city is far too dangerous for a woman alone."

"Did you ask her to move to Oxford?"

"Of course. As soon as Jasper's funeral was over, and several times since then. She and Jasper moved out of the family home not long before his death so I wasn't sure the Archers would help her." Her chin trembled and she took a breath. "Mary was adamant about supporting herself, though I can't fathom how she did it. I suppose the Archers must have provided some small pension as she did manage living alone." She retrieved the hand-kerchief and dabbed at her eyes again. "She never asked anything of us."

"I'm sure she could have moved back to the Archers' home if she found it difficult to manage her own household."

Louise shook her head. "I'm not sure that was possible. She never spoke against them, but she gave me the impression their relationship had cooled. I don't know why, but she did have an independent streak."

"I can attest that living with another's family is uncomfortable at best." Clearly Louise was not the source of Mary's income. If she didn't know how Mary supported herself, who else would?

Louise cast a glance over my shoulder and I saw Charles had come up behind me. I took my cue and introduced them. She brightened when I mentioned his name.

"My heavens," she said. "Mary wrote to me about you, told me what a good man you are." Her eyes watered once more.

Heat rose to his face and I felt his anguish. He'd cut Mary's acquaintance due to a misunderstanding, though of course, Louise didn't know that. As far as she was concerned, they'd been a courting couple. Now that I considered the matter, I daresay it's what Mary had thought as well.

"Lovely woman," he murmured. "I do hope we find the villain who took her life."

We? Heavens, perhaps he should be in hiding. "I'm sure you mean the police, Cousin Charles. You hope the police find him."

"What?" His brow furrowed. "Oh, yes. Them, too."

Louise's face softened as she gazed at him. "You poor dear. And when you cared so much about her, too."

Either Charles had given Mary a much stronger impression of his affection or Mary had done so to her sister. As Louise was now fawning over him, I felt secure in leaving them alone, and crossed the room to speak with Mary's in-laws.

Like their home, the Archers were impeccably, and fabulously, turned out. Both of the Archer brothers had married into the upper class. Lady Caroline was the third daughter of a viscount who was more than happy to marry her off to any man who didn't require a dowry. The Archer family had been principals in Bates Merchant Bank for two generations, long enough to have amassed a fortune, but not quite long enough to become accepted in the highest circles of society. Lady Caroline and Mary, whose family was landed gentry, provided that acceptance.

Now Mr. Archer belonged to any club of his choosing, had a wife who visited duchesses, and children who attended the best schools.

Caroline gave me a sad smile in exchange for my condolences. Mr. Archer merely quirked his lips then directed his attention to a gentleman behind him. I turned back to his wife.

"I was surprised to see you at the funeral service, Frances. It's so kind of you to call on us at this sad time."

"But of course I would call. Mary and I were friends after all. I suppose our shared widowhood gave us some common ground on which to come together."

Caroline arched a brow. "She kept so much to herself but I'm pleased to hear she maintained some of her more refined friendships." She leaned in and lowered her voice. "It appears she associated with some unsavory types as well."

Unsavory? "What leads you to believe such a thing?"

She gaped at me as if I were dim. "She was murdered in her own home, Frances. That would not have happened if she'd been under our roof, keeping the right company, and living a blameless life."

I tried not to stare, but for heaven's sake, was she truly blaming Mary for being murdered?

Caroline took a step back. "That may sound harsh, but you know I'm correct."

Apparently, I had been staring. "I'm sure she would have

been safer under your roof, Caroline," I said. "Has there been any progress in finding her killer?"

"None that I am aware of."

Her chilly tone told me she was eager to distance herself from such a distasteful topic. I lifted my brows. "Haven't the police consulted with you? I would think as her family they would expect you to have some knowledge of her acquaintance, or who might want to harm her."

"Yes, well, of course they asked a great many questions when they came to inform us of her death." Her tone softened along with her expression. "It's painful to admit we were unable to enlighten them as she kept herself so apart from the family."

Caroline's demeanor confused me. In one breath she condemned Mary's style of living and in the next she was hurt by her distance. I supposed a murder of so close a relation must bring on a storm of emotions. Many of them at odds with each other. Perhaps Caroline herself didn't know how she felt.

"You should not take it to heart," I said. "Mary always gave me the impression that she truly cherished her independence."

"Her death makes me feel so sad about the distance between us," she said with a sigh. "We were not overly close when Jasper was alive, but since his death, she separated herself from us completely."

"I'm so sorry to hear that. Usually one turns toward family for comfort in times of grief."

She pressed her lips into a thin line. "Not Mary. She'd never accept an invitation to our home." She lowered her voice. "We tried to assist her, but she wanted nothing from us."

I could not ask, of course, but assumed Caroline meant financial assistance. Mary's situation was becoming more and more interesting. If her sister and sister-in-law were to be believed, she refused support from both families. The Archers hadn't cut her off; it was the reverse. I could understand her need for independence if it hadn't meant turning to such a distasteful way of earning a living. I doubted Louise and her husband had much to spare, but why had Mary refused help from the Archers? If she would not visit them, it would suggest something more than just a need for independence.

Caroline shook her head. "I often wonder if we've done something to offend her."

"Perhaps your company just reminded her of her husband, something she might not have been ready to face."

"The cold truth is the woman thought herself above us, but ultimately involved herself with people of low character. It's just as well she separated herself from our family."

Mr. Archer had turned to join our conversation, but his words, spoken in a harsh tone, made it clear he'd been listening all along. Strange and rather unnerving. Why had he been eavesdropping? The set of his expression was strained, contradicting his rather cold words. Archer was approaching his fifties but until now, I'd always thought he appeared younger. The gray at his temples blended well with his blond hair, still quite plentiful, and he maintained a fit physique. Perhaps it was simply the strain of the past few days that put the shadows under his eyes and the lines of worry between them.

Caroline placed a restraining hand on his arm as if she'd only just realized they'd been airing private family matters. And a rather strange family they were, in my opinion. Heavens, I thought my in-laws were difficult to live with.

"You must excuse us, Frances. In our grief, we keep searching for reasons why this tragedy happened, and wondering if we could have prevented it."

I made some comforting response and after extending my sympathy, excused myself from the two of them. I glanced around the room for my cousin, taking note of the faces in the thinning crowd. It was time for us to leave as well. One did not want to impose on the grieving family, however much one might wonder about their grief. And I still must pay a call on

Graham. I caught a glimpse of Charles across the room, but before I could reach him, I was stopped by Hugo Ridley.

"Lady Harleigh, we meet again." He stepped into my path and took my hand in greeting.

"Indeed, Ridley, you keep popping up everywhere." I frowned. "This time it's such a somber occasion."

"Somber?" His brows drew together. "Why, I would call it tragic myself. And you should take note of it. A woman living alone in this city is completely vulnerable to such an attack. I'm surprised Mrs. Archer's fate has not sent you back to Harleigh House."

I repressed a sarcastic snort. To some degree, he was speaking the truth, however much it might irk me. That said, neither marriage nor living with my in-laws had provided me with any security in the past, and as it came with so many other problems, I'd rather risk living alone.

"Do you believe her death was due to some random attack then?"

He shrugged. "What else could it be? Mrs. Archer was a middle-aged widow. I hardly think she had connections with anyone of a criminal bent."

Middle-aged? I ground my teeth behind a closed-lipped smile. She was only a few years older than I. A man would consider himself in his prime. At forty-something, Hugo likely still did so. Men. At least he wasn't blaming Mary for her own murder.

I bit back my annoyance and pressed on. "Were you well acquainted with Mrs. Archer?"

"A bit. More so with her husband. And of course, the elder Archer, her brother-in-law." His face split with a grin. "One must always be on good terms with one's banker, you know. I wouldn't want to miss out on any good investment advice, and Archer is always on to the latest scheme."

Hmm, was he indeed? Perhaps Graham should talk to the man. Perhaps I should.

I made a show of perusing the room. "Does it seem to you

the guests are divided into two camps?" He followed my gaze. Once I noticed, the division was obvious. Mary's sister and her husband held court on one side of the room, with the Archers on the other. How had that come about? Perhaps there was something to Archer's theory that Mary, and in this case her family, looked down on him.

Ridley's gaze returned to mine. "It's the age-old prejudice, old family versus new money. I would place a bet on the new money to win."

"In this case it appears Mr. Archer does a great deal of winning. I should speak to him about investing my funds."

"You might. But remember, the greater the reward, the higher the risk."

Chapter 11

As Charles was without a carriage of his own, we arranged for him to take George's carriage back home—that is, to George's home. Jenny and I could easily walk from the Archers' to Harleigh House, only a few doors down, where I would call on Graham and collect my daughter. The carriage would return for us in half an hour.

I'd already consulted with Jenny on her assignment. In some manner, she must find out if the valet had ever provided information to Mary Archer. Specifically, information about the battle Graham and I fought for possession of my bank account. Failing that, perhaps she might at least learn if he had ever had any dealings with anyone in Mary's former household.

I counted myself fortunate in having trustworthy servants like Jenny. Not only could I depend on her discretion, she was also a willing participant in intrigues such as this. In fact, she might just enjoy them as much as I did.

We separated outside Graham's door where Jenny skipped down the steps to the service area and I rang the bell on the front door. Crabbe, the butler, led me to the drawing room where I was delighted to see Rose waiting for me. Well, she wasn't exactly waiting for me, but she was in the room with Graham and his boys, enjoying tea.

"It appears I've come just in time for elevenses."

Proper young men that they were, the boys, Eldon and Martin, twelve and ten years old respectively, came to their feet and gave me a polite bow. The boys looked almost exactly as Graham and my late husband might have looked as boys. Eldon was the image of his father with dark blond hair, fair skin, and gray eyes, while Martin could have been Reggie in miniature with his flaxen hair, rosy cheeks, and vibrant blue eyes.

Rose drew my attention away from the boys as she ran up to take my hand, twisting it at she danced around. "We took our ponies to the park today, Mummy. And I got to ride Pierre on Rotten Row."

Graham had closed up Harleigh Manor several weeks ago in anticipation of selling the portion of the estate not entailed with the title. He and the boys were now living in town and in a rare moment of kindness, he brought Rose's pony along with the boys' mounts. Fortunately, he was stabling them near Hyde Park so I didn't have to worry about Rose riding through the busy streets.

"You went riding in the rain?"

She giggled. "No, it stopped by then. We just got back."

I squeezed her hand and gave my nephews a smile. "It's very kind of you boys to invite Rose on your outings."

Martin shrugged and stuffed a small triangle of sandwich into his mouth while Eldon returned my smile. "Rose is a good horsewoman, Aunt Frances. She doesn't slow us down at all."

Rose basked in her cousin's praise. "I want to teach Pierre to jump so I can take the fences with the boys."

My stomach knotted. I wasn't much of a rider myself and the thought of my daughter sailing over fences on a horse was almost enough to make me forbid riding altogether. "Dearest, Pierre isn't a jumper. Besides, the rider needs to learn a thing or two about jumping as well. I'm afraid that will have to wait until you have a new mount." I gave her a stern frown. "And some instruction."

"I'd wager Pierre would jump," Eldon said, sweeping his arm in an arc. "He's a real goer, Aunt Frances. I could teach Rose how to take a hedge."

Young Eldon was not my idea of either a horse trainer or riding instructor. Rose, on the other hand, sent a beaming smile over her shoulder to her cousin, clearly delighted with the idea.

"I believe you should stick to the flat for now, Rose, and don't try to make little Pierre jump."

Rose pushed out her lower lip and wiggled onto the divan beside her cousins.

Graham had been standing patiently during this exchange. I finally realized his tea was cooling, so I took the chair beside him. "How was the service?" he asked, reseating himself.

I pulled my reticule from my wrist and set it on the tea table, accepting a cup from Rose. "Sad," I said. "But very interesting. Are you well acquainted with the Archers?"

Graham crossed an ankle over his knee. "Well acquainted? I shouldn't say that. Archer's a fellow member at Brooks, though I can't imagine who put him up for it, so I see him from time to time. Not socially though. Don't travel in the same circles, you know."

I should have realized Graham would be too high a stickler to socialize with someone like Archer, conveniently forgetting that his own brother had married new money. This house and Harleigh Manor had both reaped the benefits of my family's funds. I shook off the annoying thoughts. "What about business? Have you any dealings with him or his bank?"

"Of course. The man rather has a nose for a good investment. I've been urging Hetty to talk to him, but she wants to investigate all the dealings we've had to-date, make sure they've been profitable before diving in again. She's wonderful with all the little details like that."

Yes, little details like determining if your investment is actually making money. What a novel idea. Graham had no concept of how one earned money, only how one spent it. "Do you recall what type of investments you have with him?" I racked my brain for terms I'd heard Hetty use in the past. "Bonds? Securities?"

From the expression on his face, Graham had to stretch his concentration even further than I. "Not sure exactly what you'd call them. Stocks, I suppose. Last scheme he told me about was a company building a railroad somewhere."

"I see. You and other investors provide the capital for a company to do business and as a result, you receive a percentage of the profit. Is that more or less it?"

"Yes, you've got it." Graham rewarded me with a beaming smile. "Financial minds must run in your family, I'd say."

"Well, thank you, Graham. Perhaps I'll urge Hetty to pay a call on Archer on my behalf as well."

Graham agreed that I should and as the children had finished their tea, I called for Jenny, and she, Rose, and I took our leave. In a way, Archer reminded me of my father, and Hetty for that matter. Everything they touched seemed to turn to gold. I wondered what it took to make Mary turn away from such a family. Not that wealth was of such great importance, but the Archers could have made her comfortable. With their help she wouldn't have had to spread gossip to earn a living.

But she would have had to live with them. Archer's words at the funeral had been cruel, but before I judged him, it would be helpful to know which came first. Had she turned away from him because he was cruel? Or was he cruel in response to the insult of her turning away?

As Rose was in the carriage with us, I restrained myself from questioning Jenny about any conversation she may have had with Graham's valet. But the moment we arrived at home, I signaled for her to come up to my bedchamber, as Hetty was likely using my library again.

"Well?" I said as soon as the door closed behind us. I found it difficult to keep the excitement out of my voice.

Jenny smiled back at me. "I reckon you were right, my lady."

Barely containing a squeal, I took her hand and led her over to the bench at the end of my bed, where we put our heads together like young girls sharing secrets.

"Cook and the housekeeper were about to take tea when I arrived. They invited me to join them, but I said I'd stay out in the main area with Mr. Fletcher and keep him company." She twisted her lips into a grimace. "I'm sure they thought I wanted to stay and flirt with him, but at least they can't accuse me of being rude."

I repressed my impatience. This all seemed like useless information, but I trusted Jenny would eventually get to the point if I let her tell the story in her own way.

"He was polishing the earl's shoes, so I took my tea over to the table where he was working and just started talking, casual like."

"That sounds like a good beginning,"

"Well, Mr. Fletcher was never very happy in his position and once we got to talking, I could tell nothing had changed. He likes being a valet, but the earl's not so very good to work for." She worried her lower lip between her teeth, studying my expression.

"I'm not going to judge anyone, Jenny, and I'll tell no tales."

Her expression cleared. "You see, we didn't always get our proper wages from the earl, and not always on time either. For Mr. Fletcher, it could be worse. He scorched one of the earl's shirts not long ago and later he found out the cost was deducted from his wages. When he mentioned it to His Lordship, the earl told him it would teach him to be more careful."

While this practice was not unusual, I tsked in distaste. Graham was such a pinch-penny. Servants were human, for heaven's sake.

"Well, of late it's become a regular practice for the earl to be nipping here and there at everyone's wage packet. I told Mr. Fletcher that I thought it was wrong, and he just smiled and gave me a wink. Tells me he managed to find a way to make a few shillings off the earl. I asked him what he meant by that, but he wouldn't say right out."

This was promising. "But he must have given you some indication." I struggled to keep my tone calm.

"Just that the earl always had a lot to say when they were together, and Mr. Fletcher reckoned more people might want to hear it. I kind of scolded him, saying he shouldn't be telling people outside the household things he heard the master say. He shrugged and said he only told one person, and if the master paid him proper he wouldn't have done that."

Her gaze was cautious. "I feel bad he did that, my lady, repeating gossip outside the house, that is." She tucked her lower lip between her teeth. "But I understand why. A few shillings here and there, deducted from our wages, makes a big difference to the likes of us, and if a body doesn't like it, well, it's not easy to find another situation. And even if you did, who's to say it would pay any more?"

"I understand, too, Jenny. I'll find some way to point out to the earl how unfair he's being. And I'll make sure not to implicate either you or Mr. Fletcher." I squeezed her hand. "Thank you for taking this on for me today."

"Anytime you need me, my lady. I'm happy to help." She stood as she spoke, bobbed a quick curtsy, and let herself out the door.

As soon as the door closed, I remembered I was without Bridget this afternoon. Rather than call Jenny back to assist me I decided to remain in my funeral wear. It was a dull, serviceable dress but as I wasn't expecting company, it would do.

I made my way to the drawing room to piece together what I'd learned today, feeling a little resentful that I never seemed to have the use of my library anymore. The door was open and upon my approach I saw Charles and Lottie ensconced at the card table. Goodness, had they been alone together since he'd come home? I straightened my spine. Cousin or not, he had better not be imposing on that young lady. No matter how much she might welcome it.

Lottie's eyes lit as I entered. "Was your mission successful?"

Charles rose from his seat. "Miss Deaver has been apprising me of your progress with the files and that you hoped to discover the source of Mrs. Archer's information while visiting Graham today." His gaze dropped to his shoes. "Frances, I can't tell you how grateful I am for your help on my behalf."

I blushed. Now it seemed rather churlish to take them to task for their behavior. I'd just have to be careful to chaperone them in the future. At least they'd left the door open.

He pulled out a chair for me at the table and I passed on the details I'd just learned from Jenny. "Mr. Fletcher didn't reveal who bought his information, but considering the story ended up in Mrs. Archer's possession, I think we can conclude she was the buyer."

"I must admit, I'm a little confused," Lottie said. "You told us yesterday the valet would never speak about Lord Harleigh to us. Why would he speak to Mrs. Archer?"

"I assume because he knew she'd pay him."

She leaned forward in her seat. "But she wrote the column anonymously. How did he know to go to her?"

Oh, dear. Perhaps I'd been too hasty in my presumptions, but Mary did have the information and Mr. Fletcher had admitted to telling someone. "You make a very good point. How would he have known?"

"The market, I'd say."

We both turned to Charles. "The market?"

"The market," he repeated, lifting his hand and slapping it

back down on the table as if that settled the matter. "Where one purchases food and household goods."

"I know what a market is, Charles," I said. "What I don't understand is how it comes into play in this circumstance."

"Well, I can't say for certain. Never done my own marketing, you see. But I'd think if servants are gathered there, out of the watchful eyes of their employers, they'd pass the time of day with one another. Maybe share a few stories."

I still wasn't following, and my blank stare must have said as much. He leaned forward as he elaborated. "Mrs. Archer had no servants, only a woman who took in the laundry and did some heavy cleaning. She would have done her marketing herself. As would the servants from all the larger houses in town." He shrugged. "She's at the market. They're at the market. She wants gossip. They have gossip."

"But they'd be housekeepers or cooks, not a valet."

He made a circular motion with his finger. "Word gets around. Once she became friendly with a few of them, maybe paid for a bit of gossip here and there, they'd spread the word." He lifted one eyebrow. "Maybe to someone they felt sorry for—someone who'd just been docked for ruining a gentleman's shirt."

Understanding dawned on Lottie's face just as I caught on myself. I couldn't believe it. "Charles, I think you've sorted it out."

He reddened and gave me a beaming grin, dimples and all. "Did I? Well, it just seemed to make sense."

It made perfect sense. In fact, it was the perfect plan, so simple yet so ingenious. Working with their servants, Mary could obtain a boundless supply of gossip about every member of society. And no servant would ever admit to selling her the information for fear of losing his position. Therefore, they could never betray her. But it brought me no closer to understanding why she'd done it.

"So now we have a theory for how and where she obtained the information for her columns," Lottie said. "But how did she obtain this employment in the first place, and why was she doing it?"

"I'm not entirely sure, but both her sister and sister-in-law told me today she'd refused any support from them." I turned to Charles. "Was she simply determined to be independent?"

He stared in confusion. "Independent? I'm not sure we came to know each other quite that well." He drummed his fingers on the table, screwing up his face in concentration. "That is to say she was always quite agreeable to any outings I suggested. Agreeable to everything, in fact. She never expressed strong opinions or insisted on having things her way."

I released a long breath. Why on earth had I asked him?

"I'm trying to make sense of everything I heard about Mary today. You said she didn't want to meet up with the Archers at the theater because she didn't get on with them."

"That's what she told me," he said.

"Caroline Archer made quite a point of that today," I said. "It bothered her that Mary had become so distant with the family since her husband's death. On the other hand, Gordon Archer sounded angry rather than hurt."

"You must be very good at this, Lady Harleigh, to get them to confide in you that way," Lottie said.

In truth, I'd done nothing to deserve such a confidence from them. I closed my eyes, trying to bring the Archers' words to mind as well as the emotion behind them.

"At first, Caroline Archer might have been trying to distance her family from the shame of Mary's murder." I glanced at Lottie. "I gather this holds true among the old families in New York as well. If a woman's name appears in the paper for any reason other than her birth, marriage, or *natural* death, she has made herself notorious, and the family would prefer simply to disown her."

She grimaced. "I suppose that's true, though hardly fair in this case. Mrs. Archer was murdered."

"Caroline implied she'd brought it on herself by living alone and associating with a lower class of people."

Charles released a grunt of disgust. "Her life was perfectly circumspect. Clearly her relations didn't care much about her. Why would she want to live with them?"

This left us no further ahead. Either Mary was so fiercely independent she would refuse all support, or the rift between herself and the Archers was a sore enough point with her that she'd prefer employment to taking assistance from them. Or even more odd, did she simply enjoy airing her friends' and neighbors' indiscretions?

And did it really matter? Must we know why she wrote the gossip column in order to determine why she was murdered? I scribbled a note on a page of Lily's leftover stationery and decided to speak to George about it.

As if thinking of the man conjured his presence, Mrs. Thompson escorted George to my drawing room within fifteen minutes. Charles had just taken his leave of us through the garden pathway. A good thing, too, as George was accompanied by Delaney. I doubted my cousin would be eager for a meeting with the inspector after their recent encounters.

Lottie clearly wished to linger but good manners forced her to excuse herself once the introductions were performed. Upon her departure, Delaney and I made ourselves comfortable, each of us taking a chair, while George chose to pace back and forth behind the sofa.

"I apologize for intruding on you in this manner, Frances," he began. "But I happened to meet up with the inspector and thought it time we brought one another up to date on our findings."

Delaney, who had just opened his notebook, raised a brow at

this. "I'm happy to hear any information you have for me, but you understand I'm not at liberty to divulge evidence we've discovered through our investigation."

George reached the end of the carpet and turned back. "Of course, Inspector, though perhaps you'd be willing to confirm one or two items we've found. For example, through my investigation I've learned something of Mrs. Archer's financial situation. She had a small income, source unknown. Have you arrived at the same conclusion?"

Delaney dropped his notebook in his lap and leveled a glare at him. "She made regular, small deposits herself. And no, we don't know where the money came from."

George inclined his head in my direction. "Lady Harleigh has made some progress with the notes, which may shed some light on that income."

"Is that so?" Delaney turned his gaze to me. "Anything indicating blackmail, Lady Harleigh?"

"Obviously I haven't been able to examine every note in Mrs. Archer's files, and after the first day's sorting, I found only a handful that appeared to have potential for blackmail. But after speaking to three of the people in question, all had alibis for Tuesday evening, which I assume was the time of the murder."

"You spoke to them?" The vehemence in Delaney's voice even stopped George in his tracks.

"Of course. How else was I to learn anything?"

His brows drew together. "Reviewing these files is one thing, but confronting potential suspects is far from your area of expertise, Lady Harleigh. You should have given a list to me, or to Hazelton, so one of us could question them."

"And waste precious time?" I waved away the suggestion. "You were both too busy with your own assignments. This was nothing I couldn't deal with and I'll be happy to give you that list now as someone still needs to confirm those alibis."

Delaney ran a hand through his already-disheveled hair and

turned to George as if for support. George just smiled and raised his hands. "She managed it well enough."

"You knew about this?"

I let out a huff of impatience. "Enough. Mr. Hazelton told me to use my judgment, and I did. Allow me to know when I am putting myself in a dangerous position. Every meeting took place in public and the gentlemen in question had no idea I was interviewing them." I thought it best not to mention I'd taken Lottie along for those meetings.

"Now," I said, addressing Delaney, "aside from the interviews, I have learned more about these notes and I believe it relates to the income you discovered."

Delaney made a growling sound in his throat but gave me his attention. I explained about the columns, their relation to the files from Mary's house, and that the columns stopped running shortly after Mary's death. I concluded my report with our theory that she was working for the *Daily Observer.*

Delaney had been taking notes while I spoke; now his head shot up. "The *Daily Observer,* you say? Are you certain of this?"

The question took me by surprise. "Of course we're certain. I read clippings of the column myself just yesterday. It was definitely the *Observer.* Why?"

Delaney pursed his lips and let out a long breath. "Because a man who works as an editor for that newspaper has also been murdered."

Chapter 12

⟨⟩

George's head snapped around at Delaney's words. "An editor at the newspaper? You say he was murdered? How?"

The older man scrubbed a hand across his jaw as he leafed through the pages of his notebook, released a heavy breath, and dropped the book on the table. "Only heard a bit here and there. Not my case or even my jurisdiction. If I remember correctly, his name was Milton, or Morton. No, Norton. That's it. He was murdered at his offices after hours."

He rubbed the pencil against the stubble along his jaw as he stared upward as if a police report were written on my ceiling. "Quite sure he was shot. That's about all I heard. I'm not even certain what day, but it was recently." He opened his notebook to slip the stubby pencil inside. "I'll have to pay a visit to Bow Street to get the details. It's their case."

"Shot, you say?" George's brows inched upward.

Delaney twisted his lips into a wry smile. "Hardly sounds like a coincidence, does it?"

"Coincidence?" My gaze traveled between the two men. "What coincidence? Mary was strangled, not shot."

"She was," George agreed. "But the police believe she attempted to defend herself—with a revolver. A bullet was found lodged in the wall of her sitting room. They discovered a case for a revolver in her desk drawer, but the weapon was missing."

He turned to Delaney, who nodded in confirmation. "The firearm may have been missing for years, of course, but the bullet in the wall leads us to believe she fired at her attacker. Chances are, he now has the weapon."

"And perhaps used it on this editor," I said.

"That would be pure speculation, my lady." Delaney jotted a few more notes in his book. "I should get this information to Bow Street. With any luck the inspector in charge has made some headway in his case. He may have a suspect, or at least some idea of the motive for the editor's murder."

"Do you suppose they were both involved in blackmail?" I asked.

George resumed his pacing then stopped abruptly, turning to face us. His expression was of someone who wasn't certain if he'd just discovered a new planet or merely a speck on his telescope lens.

"What if this had nothing to do with blackmail? This Norton was a newspaperman after all. What if they were going to expose someone?" He placed his hands on the back of the sofa and leaned forward as if he were interviewing a witness in the box. "If there was no question of withholding the story in exchange for payment, and their intent was to expose some wrongdoing, perhaps that person felt it necessary to stop them."

"Or maybe they already had exposed someone," Delaney added, "and were murdered out of anger. Revenge."

"I've read her last fifteen or so columns. She wrote nothing that would push someone to murder. And a threat of exposure, or exposure itself might explain the murder of the editor, but why murder Mary? How would the killer have known she was writing the columns?"

"Do women really keep secrets that well?" Delaney spoke as if he were wondering aloud. "She must have confided in some- one, and that person let it slip to someone else, and so on, and so on. Wouldn't all of society know by now?"

My spine stiffened at this. "Women most certainly do keep secrets, and this is something Mary would never have confided in anyone. She had a reputation to maintain as a gently bred lady. She could never reveal she was employed. To think she'd tell anyone she was paid to spread gossip is beyond belief." I shook my head, giving Delaney a firm negative. "And if all of society were aware of it, Mary would have been considered be- yond the pale. Her friends, even her family, would disown her."

Delaney stared in amazement, then turned away, muttering under his breath.

"Someone had to know," George said. "Otherwise this is amazingly coincidental."

I raised my hands in surrender. "I'm not saying no one knew about her employment. Just that Mary wouldn't have told them." A thought struck me. "If you two are correct about this, then Mr. Evingdon ought not to be a suspect. I specifically searched for his name in her files and found nothing."

Delaney came to his feet. "I'm not quite ready to see it that way. If they were a courting couple, she might have confronted him, face to face, with something that so outraged her she threatened to have it published if he didn't stop. He was at her home that night, with a chaise. He could have murdered her, then gone off to murder the editor."

I rose to my feet. "If he wanted to stop her from publishing something, all he had to do was threaten to reveal to the world what she was doing."

"You toffs are amazing." Delaney's voice was a low growl. "There's no shame in trying to make an honest living."

"Not everyone would agree with you that spreading gossip about one's acquaintance for profit is an honest living."

George raised a hand before our argument could become more heated. "There's also the chance the editor was murdered first and the killer found a connection to Mary in his office. One of her handwritten columns or a payment voucher made out to her. It could be any number of things."

"Well, if I'm to find out, I'd best get myself to Bow Street."

"Will you keep us apprised of the other case?"

He shot me a glare. "My lady, this is police business. If we find those notes are no longer important to the case, I'm sure someone will inform Mr. Hazelton and come by to collect them. Otherwise it would be in your best interests for both of you to stay out of it."

With a grumble about private citizens allowing the police to do their work he bid us good day and was off.

I huffed in frustration and turned to George. "Well, that's gratitude. He's happy enough to take information from me, but not inclined to reciprocate."

He gave me a quelling look. "He thinks you're exceeding your bounds. Remember, you took on my assignment, which was limited to reviewing the files." His lips quirked up in a smile. "Good thing you didn't tell him about Miss Deaver helping you. By the way, did you really go through the files looking for Evingdon's name?"

I bit my lip and retreated a step. "I feel rather disloyal about doing so. He's your friend and my cousin, but—"

He held up a hand to stop me. "I understand. In fact, though he's my friend and your cousin, he might also have become my client, so I took the precaution of verifying his whereabouts on Tuesday evening."

We exchanged looks of chagrin. "I knew Delaney would be questioning both the friend he'd been dining with and Charles's butler. I had to know what they'd report."

"Don't leave me wondering. What did they say?"

"Based on the time he left his friend's house, and the time he returned home, he appears to have driven straight there."

"Then why won't Delaney exonerate him?"

"It's Delaney's job to be suspicious. Either man could be lying after all."

"I still feel rather guilty about my suspicions."

He took my hand. "It doesn't make you disloyal, Frances, just a good investigator. Suspicion is part of the job."

He narrowed his eyes. "I am curious about one thing you mentioned. Would you have cut Mrs. Archer if you learned she was writing a gossip column?"

I frowned as I considered the question. "I don't approve of publishing other people's personal affairs, but I am impressed that she found a way to support herself independently. No, I wouldn't have cut her, but as we weren't close friends, I doubt my support would have made her life any easier. She would definitely have lost friends, and come to think of it, she might have lost her job as well. The very nature of her column demanded she work in secret."

"What if someone just guessed?"

I gave him an incredulous stare. "How?"

Still holding my hand, he led me to the sofa. "What if someone confided in her, told her something only they would know, then saw that very on-dit in the gossip column?"

"Mary was too clever for that." I rubbed my head with the heel of my hand. "It would be easier if we had more information. How long has she been doing this? Who was that editor? Could he have let anything slip, or did anyone else at the newspaper know about Mary? Was he even the man who employed her? We are perhaps jumping to conclusions about their connection."

I eyed him suspiciously. "Do you really intend to wait for information to trickle in from Delaney?"

"Not when you're asking such good questions." A smile slid across his lips. "Care to come with me?"

"To the newspaper office? You'd take me with you?"

"Experience tells me if I don't take you with me, you'll simply go on your own." His face suddenly lit with wonder. "In fact, I've just devised a frighteningly good scheme." He drew me to my feet, his gaze taking in my funeral garb. "You're even dressed appropriately. Come, I'll explain in the carriage."

George's idea was pure genius, but as we descended from the carriage and approached the offices of the *Daily Observer*, I felt the first twinge of nerves. I wasn't altogether confident in my ability to play this role. At that moment George opened the door and placed a hand against my back. Too late to back out now, I supposed. And I had to admit it: I wanted to justify his confidence in me. I could do this.

It was already late afternoon when we walked into the reception area where a young gangly man sat behind a desk. Painfully thin and barely an adult, his long fingers clacked away at a typewriting machine, a pencil clenched in his teeth. He jerked around at our approach, dropping the pencil as if he'd forgotten it was even there. I goggled at the machine while George asked to see Mr. Norton. The boy paled.

"Mr. Norton doesn't work here any longer," he said. That was an understatement.

"Did he have an assistant? Someone who is now overseeing his work?"

"Um, well. Mr. Mosley is the assistant editor. He might be able to help you. May I ask what this is about, sir?"

George gave him a hard stare, then raised a brow. "No," he replied. "We'll speak with Mr. Mosley if you please."

The young man shrank back in his chair, eliciting my motherly concern. "There's no need to be rude, George." I leaned toward the boy and lowered my voice. "What's your name, young man?"

He blinked his large brown eyes once as he gazed up at me. "Travis Ryan, ma'am."

"Well, Mr. Ryan, we're here regarding the Miss Information column. So, I'm sure you understand our need for confidentiality."

He eyed us suspiciously as he rose to his feet. "Yes, ma'am. If you'll just take a seat," he said, indicating a row of three straight-backed chairs stuffed between an empty coatrack and the door. "I'll see if he's in." He backed away and turned into a hallway behind his desk.

"I think you rather intimidated the poor boy," I whispered.

George's lips moved, but his response was overpowered by shouting from the hallway. "Some reporter you'll make if you can't even learn someone's name! You'd be better on the street hawking papers."

We barely had time to exchange a glance before Mr. Ryan returned and made a beckoning gesture. "Please follow me. I'll show you to Mr. Mosley's office."

We followed him down a short hall and made a left turn at the first door. Hardly worth the escort. Mr. Mosley, a portly man perhaps in his late thirties, with side whiskers and a beard, rose from behind a cluttered desk as we walked in. George stepped forward, shook the man's hand, gave his name, and introduced me as Mrs. Smith.

"How can I be of help to you?" he asked, indicating with a sweep of his hand that we should take the two chairs opposite his desk and sat back down. "And what are you hanging around for?"

Mr. Ryan jumped and dashed down the hall.

"Useless git." Mosley dragged his bulk from behind the desk and shut the door.

"We're here about my sister, Mrs. Archer." I settled into the chair while George remained on his feet. "She was working with your colleague, Mr. Norton."

"Yes?" His expectant gaze darted between the two of us as he lumbered back to his chair.

"Are your familiar with the Miss Information column?" George asked.

The man pulled at his collar. "Familiar, yes, but we aren't running that column any longer."

A hint of suspicion lit his eyes as a grin spread across his face. "Wait! Your sister, you say? Come now, are you her?" He grasped my hand and pumped it with enthusiasm.

George leaned over the desk between us. "This is not Miss Information."

Mr. Mosley released my hand.

"My sister, Mary Archer, held that position."

Mosley hooked his thumbs in the pockets of his waistcoat, his grin fading. "Well, if she's willing to work with me, I'll be happy to keep the column going."

"That won't be possible," George said. "I'm afraid she's deceased."

"The writer? She's dead, too?"

"Not just dead," I replied. "Murdered."

"The police didn't say anything about that." Mosley sank back into his chair. "Did you say 'Archer'? We ran a story about her murder. I didn't know she was Miss Information."

"They hadn't tied the crimes together yet. My sister was writing her column in secret after all."

"That's true enough. Norton kept everything on the quiet about her. I had no idea how to find her to collect her columns, and she never showed up here. So now what? The police think whoever done him in killed her, too?"

"It would seem so," George put in smoothly. "What day was Norton murdered?"

Mosley leaned back and crossed his arms over his girth.

"Tuesday, though I'm not sure why that's any of your business."

"I'm investigating on behalf of my client." He tipped his head in my direction. "I'd like to hear anything and everything you can tell me about the arrangement between Mr. Norton and Mrs. Archer."

"Why should I tell you? The police already came around. I answered their questions."

George placed his hands on the desk and loomed over it. "Are you daft, man? They weren't aware of the connection. It took Mrs. Smith to uncover that information. The police will likely be back with more questions, but this is her sister. She deserves to know if Mrs. Archer lost her life because of her employment with this newspaper."

Two beads of moisture popped up on Mosley's forehead. He raised his hands, palms out. "All right, all right. Like I said, Mr. Norton kept everything about that column to himself. He was the editor and he did things his way. I only worked for him and he didn't bother explaining himself, just made decisions. Like that poor excuse for a clerk up front. A thief is what he is. Tried to pick Norton's pocket, and instead of having him arrested, Norton gives him a job. Takes him off the streets and puts him on a desk. Now I'm stuck with him, the useless git."

This sounded like a favorite refrain of Mr. Mosley's.

George took a seat and crossed his arms. "About the column?"

"It was just gossip, right? About posh folk. Most of them liked being talked about." He shrugged. "Never had any trouble. No one coming in screaming for a retraction. No one threatening to sue. Can't imagine someone wanting to kill the two of them for what they wrote."

"How long was she writing it?"

Now that George was seated, Mosley seemed more relaxed. He scratched his head as he did some mental calculations. "Close to a year by my reckoning."

"Goodness, how did they manage to keep her identity quiet for so long?" I asked.

"Well, seems like they didn't, don't it? I mean, someone found out, didn't they?"

"It would seem so," George said. "How did Mrs. Archer deliver the columns?"

"Norton picked them up from her twice a week. Paid her the same way—in cash, mind you. Like I said, he was real secretive about her. I don't think she ever came around here, but since I didn't know who she was, I can't really say."

"Did he leave anything lying about his office? Did the police search it?"

"They did. Took whatever they needed, I suppose. Want to have a gander?"

We certainly did. Mr. Mosley led us to Mr. Norton's office, which was immediately across the hallway. It appeared after the police did their search someone had come in and cleaned up. The desk was pristine. Books on the shelves. Copies of the newspaper stacked neatly on a table. Nothing to indicate someone had recently worked in this office.

George stepped around the desk and opened drawers. Except for a few pens and pencils, and an unused stack of paper, they were all empty.

Mosley shrugged. "The owners came in after the police. Guess they wanted the place cleaned up. Still have a paper to put out, you know."

"Was Mr. Norton married?"

"Naw, career man, he was. Always chasing a story."

"Where did he live?"

Using the pencil and paper from the drawer, Mosley wrote down the editor's address. George glanced around the room with an air of disappointment until his gaze landed on a closet door. He opened the door, peeked inside, released a tsk, and returned to the desk to take the address from Mosley.

"Like I said, they cleaned the place." Mosley shrugged. "If you two are done here, I've work to do." He started out of the office, then stopped and turned back, fingers stroking his beard. "That column was real popular, you know? Sold a lot of papers." He lifted a brow and leveled a gaze at me. "Don't suppose you know anyone who'd like to take it on?"

I bristled at the suggestion. Indeed, I did not. Before I could express my indignation, George touched my arm.

"That's not such a bad idea," he said.

"You can't be serious. In what way is my writing a gossip column not a bad idea?"

"Whoever murdered Mrs. Archer and Mr. Norton probably wanted to keep something from being printed. If the column continues, the murderer may believe the secrets he worked so hard to keep may still see the light of day." He raised his brows. "It might be enough to flush him out."

My jaw slackened as I stared. "Out where? I have no wish to draw a murderer to my home."

Mr. Mosley held up a hand to calm my indignation. "Only the three of us will ever know who's writing the columns, and I'll never give you away. Under threat of death I'll never give you away."

George waved the man's words aside. "Yes, yes, we have complete faith in your integrity, Mosley."

I gaped. Did we now?

"Hear me out. I don't know what the owners are going to do about Norton's job, but I'll admit I wouldn't mind stepping into it. That column sold papers, and it'd be a feather in my cap if I could bring it back. I can promise you no one will ever learn your name."

"That's very admirable, Mr. Mosley," I said. "But the threat of death is a definite possibility. Someone murdered the last editor, and my sister, over this column. Surely a promotion isn't worth your life."

"I worked my way up to this job." Mosley puffed out his chest, a fond smile in place. "The things I used to do to get a story." He chuckled. "Let's just say I know how to take care of myself."

"Regardless, Mrs. Smith is right. Have you done anything to secure the building since Mr. Norton was murdered?"

"My old firearm's in my desk drawer," he said.

"I'd prefer to have a constable stationed here," George said. "I'll talk to Delaney."

Mr. Mosley had an eager glint in his eyes. "So, you'll do it? I could come by every Tuesday and Friday to pick 'em up, same as Norton did."

"That won't be necessary," I said, still not certain I wanted any part of this. "I'll have someone drop them off."

"What's your deadline for tomorrow's paper?" George asked.

"Usually six o'clock, but if you're certain you can bring it by, I'll hold a spot open until ten. Then it has to go to print."

George nodded. "I'll bring it."

As our business was concluded, George rose to his feet. I placed a hand on his arm and turned to Mosley. "You said Mr. Norton picked up the columns from Mrs. Archer on Tuesdays and Fridays? Did he pick up the columns this past Tuesday?"

"Of course. Just like usual. Went to her house, then brought 'em back here to work 'em up. There were only two on his desk though, so we could only run the column through Thursday."

George and I exchanged a glance. Was Norton the man Charles had seen leaving Mary's house that night? I turned back to Mr. Mosley.

"Could you describe Mr. Norton for me?"

Chapter 13

Mosley provided a very detailed description of Mr. Norton. We also learned that he'd been carrying an umbrella when he left the office Tuesday evening to retrieve Mary's columns, as was the man Charles had seen. Though since it had been raining, off and on, that evening, anyone out of doors would likely have had one on hand.

George used the telephone on the editor's desk to place a call to Inspector Delaney, leaving a message about the possible identity of the man seen leaving Mary's house on Tuesday.

"If Evingdon is still under suspicion, the fact that Norton was also at Mrs. Archer's home should help his case," he said as we returned to his carriage. "The police really have no other evidence with which to accuse him."

He assisted me into the carriage and settled in beside me. "I'm not so sure about your theory," I said, the carriage rocking as we moved into the street. "If the man Charles saw at Mary's house was only her editor, picking up her columns, then no one saw the murderer. Wouldn't that make Delaney even more suspicious of Charles?"

"But if he did pick up the columns, then Mrs. Archer was alive at the time your cousin drove past. And I now have a connected crime to investigate, which I hope will provide more evidence. I can't believe the police allowed Norton's office to be cleaned and cleared." He sighed. "But I have a contact at Bow Street who may be able to tell me what they know about that murder—any evidence found, who they interviewed. We'll see where that leads us. And I have yet to search Mrs. Archer's home." His eyes fairly sparkled with the thrill of the chase. "So, all is not lost. Though I do wish we'd known about her connection to that column before the newspaper stopped printing them."

"I could probably make some comment in the column I write, explaining the omission of the four issues. Although unless I can write a column by this evening, I'll be explaining the absence of five."

"Let's think about this a moment." His brow furrowed. "We're assuming since both Mary and her editor were murdered, the killer knows she wrote the column, and the column had something to do with the murder."

"You suggested he was trying to stop something from coming to light."

"Yet you didn't find anything inflammatory in her files."

"I beg your pardon. We found a great deal of inflammatory information, but it was marked *Do not use*. Additionally, I have yet to review everything in those files. As Lottie transcribes them into plain English, I try to provide the names from the initials Mary wrote. From there I work off Lily's invitation list of who is and isn't in town in order to eliminate suspects." I shrugged. "It's a slow process. I'd say we're only about halfway through the notes. But if you believe one of those notes is tied to the killer, then we have a great deal of work to do as there are still many notes to review."

I shook my head. This task seemed endless. "And now I must write a gossip column." I paused as a thought struck me.

"Oh, dear, I neglected to ask Mr. Mosley what I'm to be paid for my work."

George gave me a look of incredulity.

I drew back and squared my jaw. "Well, I'd like to know what I'm worth. Though I suppose it's of no matter as it's only temporary."

He smiled as he reached for my hand, entwining his fingers with mine and placing a soft kiss on my gloved fingertips. "You are worth everything to me," he said.

I gazed into his eyes, certain mine were filled with longing. I didn't want to move, or breathe, or do anything to break the spell of this moment. I'd never been worth everything to anyone before.

He leaned forward, his brows drawn close. "Frances, are you well?"

"Well?" Good heavens, how long had I been staring at him? Mooning over him, really. Flustered, I glanced out the window. We'd already stopped in front of my house.

I turned back to George. "Are you coming in?"

He flashed me a charming smile. "No, I'm afraid you've far too much work to do."

"You're not going to assist me?"

"Me? No, I'll be busy as well, investigating the second crime."

He reached across me and opened the carriage door, eager to leave me and get on with his work. "I can't thank you enough, Frances. Your assistance in this case has been invaluable."

My *assistance* was invaluable? I threw him a glare before climbing down to the street and saw his expression of confusion as I slammed the door. Guilt assailed me. I suppose it wasn't his fault I let my imagination carry me away.

I let myself into the house. Pulling the pins from my hat, I left it on a table in the entryway. When I turned to the open doors of the drawing room, it was to see all of my houseguests, plus Charles, gathered there.

"Goodness, is it time for dinner already?" I hadn't thought it was quite that late, but a glance at the clock on the mantel told me it was half past seven and I was still in my funeral clothes from the morning. Well, Bridget would be back by now, so I had just enough time to change.

Before I could excuse myself, Lily's voice rang out. "Where have you been?"

She'd risen to her feet, planted her hands on her hips, and with the scowl she wore, resembled nothing so much as our mother. Quite frankly, the image stirred rather unpleasant sensations.

"I've been to the offices of the *Daily Observer*," I said. "Though I'm not aware I was required to apprise you of my whereabouts."

She had the sense to look abashed, but only for a moment. "When I came home you were nowhere to be found. Lottie told me she last saw you a full two hours earlier, locked up in the drawing room with Mr. Hazelton and Inspector Delaney. No one had any idea where you'd gone."

The three other occupants of the room inched away from us. Charles tugged at his collar. All were uncomfortably aware of the tension between us. I forced a smile. "Mr. Hazelton and I had an errand to run. If you'll allow me to freshen up, I'll come back and explain."

"You've been working on this investigation again, is that it?" Lily had seated herself and appeared somewhat mollified, but her voice still scolded. "This work is taking more and more of your time."

I frowned. "Is there something I've neglected to do?"

"Well, I had hoped you'd join me for dinner with Mrs. Kendrick this evening. We are to go over some of the plans for the engagement party."

A moment's panic rushed through me. How had I forgotten a dinner engagement? "Lily, I'm so sorry, I must have neglected to post it to my schedule. When did you tell me of this?"

"She didn't tell you," Hetty said, with a sharp glance at Lily. "Mrs. Kendrick sent over a note this morning asking the two of you to come for dinner. I told her she could hardly expect you to be available at the drop of a hat, so I am going in your stead."

I stared at my sister in amazement. "You are angry with me about missing an engagement you never told me about?"

Lily shrugged. "I would have told you but you were out pursuing criminals all day."

"I was at a funeral." It was absurd to argue with her. "Thank you, Hetty, for standing in for me this evening." I turned to Charles and Lottie. "I am hoping to enlist your aid on our investigation this evening." Lily huffed in exasperation. I ignored her.

After obtaining Lottie's and Charles's agreement, I left the room to go upstairs and change my gown. And to quiz Bridget, who waited for me at my dressing room door.

"I already picked out a dress for you, my lady." She swept an arm toward the gown laid out on the bed. "I hope it's all right as you barely have time to change."

"It will do perfectly, Bridget." We both set about removing the serviceable gown I'd been wearing all day, which as it turned out, had been a good choice for visiting the newspaper office as Mary's sister.

"How was your luncheon?"

Her face took on a dreamy expression. "Oh, my lady, it was everything wonderful."

"How lovely." I placed a hand on her shoulder as I stepped out of the black dress.

"The dining room was so elegant, filled with small tables covered with snow white cloths." She paused, assessing my waistline. "We'll have to tighten your corset a bit, I think." She turned me around and got to work. "Well, when they rolled the tea cart over to our table, I just wanted to order one of every-thing. Scones, seedy cake, and the tarts—all so luscious."

"Ooof" was the best response I could manage as she pulled my laces tighter. I drew a tentative breath. Yes, I could breathe—barely. "Bridget, you do realize I'm going down to dinner, don't you?"

She slipped the gown over my head. "I'd advise you not to eat overmuch, my lady."

"I doubt I'll be able to." I worked my arms into the tissue sleeves and gave her a glare over my shoulder.

She smiled. "I have some information on the matter you asked me to check into as well." She settled the dress on my shoulders and began working the buttons.

"Ah, do tell."

"Well, my friend Sadie says Miss Zimmerman is one of the nicest people she's ever worked for, so she was real eager to talk about her. On and on she raved." Tugging the fabric together at my back, she peeked over my shoulder, a scowl marring her features. "As for the duke, it seems people are always telling Miss Zimmerman about his antics."

"Really? People in general, or her friends?"

"Sounds like these people are no friends, ma'am. And I don't think there's anything about him that would surprise her. She's well aware he's only after her money."

"Well, at least her eyes are open." I turned to inspect myself in the mirror. Yes, I'd do. Bridget was bundling up my dis-carded gown. "Thank you for your assistance today, Bridget. And I'm glad you enjoyed yourself." I sighed. Another suspect off the list. Another ninety or so to go.

Fortunately, dinner included only Lottie, Charles, and my-self so we were at liberty to discuss all the new developments of the day, from who had attended the funeral, to my new job as a columnist, to the possibility that it had been the editor Charles saw at Mary's house the night she was murdered.

"And since he's also been murdered, I am once again the most likely suspect." He lifted his wineglass in a mock toast before draining its contents.

I frowned. It wasn't his first glass. "But if it was the editor you saw then, as Mr. Hazelton pointed out, Mary was alive at the time you drove past." I hadn't noticed a thing I'd eaten at dinner, but since only cheese and fruit were left on the table, it appeared we'd finished. I wasn't sure if it was the turn of events or drink that made him increasingly maudlin, but it seemed a good idea to move him away from the source of wine. I suggested we retire to the drawing room.

Lottie seated herself at the card table covered with Mary's files, while I drew the drapes across the street-facing window, and Charles turned up the gas on the overhead lamp. "What do we do now?" she asked when we joined her at the table. "Do you and Mr. Hazelton still believe Mrs. Archer threatened to publish someone's secrets unless they paid up? And since the editor was also murdered, does that mean he was also involved in the blackmail scheme?"

"The only thing I'm sure it means is that someone knew they were working together." I picked up Lily's forgotten pen and tapped it on the table. "But we haven't determined how they found out."

"She would never have told anyone," Charles said. "And you're certain no one at the *Observer* knew Mrs. Archer's identity?"

My gaze drifted upward while I considered the question. "We didn't specifically ask, but no one from the *Observer* tried to contact Mary when Mr. Norton died. And Mr. Mosley indicated Norton kept her identity to himself. I feel fairly comfortable that she worked with Norton alone."

"Perhaps a servant had a case of conscience and told his master."

"That servant would not only lose his employment, he'd never work again. Facing such an end, I think he'd choose to live with the guilt. But you make a good point, Charles. What if the servant hadn't passed any gossip on to Mary, but knew of her and her system of obtaining it? Might that servant have mentioned it to his master?"

He pursed his lips as he considered the suggestion. "If I'd been Mary, I'm not sure I would have used my true name while collecting gossip. But I suppose the servant might have known her by sight."

"Just to play devil's advocate," Lottie said, "even if someone recognized her from a servant's description, why not just expose her? That would put an end to the gossip columns and shame her in society."

Blast, she was right. "I fear we're going in circles. We keep coming back to her threatening someone."

Charles slumped back in his chair.

"It isn't necessarily blackmail," I said, and explained George's theory that Mary was about to expose someone's wrongdoing. "Frankly, that sounds more like the woman I knew," I added. "But it must be one or the other. If blackmail, the leverage of holding a scandal over someone's head is the only thing that would protect her from exposure. If she was acting as a vigilante, then the issue was so egregious, she'd risk exposure."

"Either way, we are still looking for something scandalous in these files, aren't we?" Lottie asked. "Is that how you want us to proceed?"

"Perhaps you two could make a list of anyone who was at the funeral and has a note in the scandal files." I picked up the two *Do not use* folders and handed one to each of them. "Meanwhile I'll try to write a column or two from the gossip files. Mr. Hazelton said he'd have a footman deliver them to the *Observer*, and Mr. Mosley is holding a space for it, so I'd best get busy."

"I still don't understand why you're writing the column."

Before I could attempt an explanation, Lottie spoke up. "If someone murdered Mrs. Archer and Mr. Norton to stop them from printing something, seeing the column in the paper again might make him fear that his story may be published after all." She rose from her seat and began leafing through pages before her. "And I have another idea."

Goodness, she fairly buzzed with excitement. I simply must provide alternative entertainment for the girl.

"Along, with the regular gossip stories," she said. "I suggest we publish one or two of the more scandalous notes. Or perhaps just a portion of the note."

She glanced from Charles to me and bit her lip as she realized we were not following her. She pulled a page from her file. "Here's a good example. We determined this one was about Lord Larkin and Mrs. Frazier spending two days together at a hotel in Paris when Mrs. Frazier was supposed to be buying a new wardrobe. Why don't we publish just a suggestion of it? *Was Lord L. acting as a modiste while in Paris? If this writer learns there is more to this rumor, dear reader, I will report.*"

Yes, I definitely needed to find a more suitable form of amusement for her. This was not the type of experience Mrs. Deaver had planned when she'd left her daughter with me. Still, I had to commend her ingenuity. "So, we tease the readers with a glimpse of a story to follow. I like it."

Charles blew out a breath. "I don't understand it."

"Mr. Hazelton thinks the return of the column will draw the murderer out. But we all agree no one would kill to put an end to the minor gossip. But if we reveal just a hint of the more salacious stories we have, he's bound to become nervous and make some attempt to find out who is writing the column again."

"What about something like this one?" Lottie pulled another page from her file and placed it in the center of the table. "It's one we weren't able to decipher."

SSE, CTS, W-H & S, CACC. 6 March, 1898. LH, SH, LM, LR at least J.

"I still have no idea what it means or to whom it relates," I said.

She frowned as she stared at the note. "The date is clear, but everything else is just letters or initials."

Charles leaned forward to peruse the note. "Gad, my eyes are crossing trying to make sense of it. Must be old news though, judging by the date."

I hadn't noticed, but he was right. "Mr. Mosley told us Mary had been writing the columns for close to a year. This is several months earlier."

"If she kept it, it must still have some significance, don't you think?" Lottie moved around the table to get a better look. She ran a pencil along the handwritten lines. "Though I'm not sure how we'd use it."

"Why don't we print the first set of initials, then a dash, followed by the second set? Then ask, *Is someone up to no good? This writer will find out.*"

Lottie smiled. "I like it." She foraged through the notes on the table for Lily's leftover stationery and began composing the column.

I turned to Charles who sat back and raised his hands. "I'll leave this to you ladies and make my list of the funeral guests. Should I include the Archers? Did you find any scandalous notes about them in here?"

"Only if it was even more cryptic than that last note." He and I moved our conversation across the room so as not to disturb Lottie's writing. I felt a slight twinge of guilt that she was doing my work, but it passed quickly.

"Besides, if she was getting her information from servants, then the Archer servants would know her. She wouldn't dare approach them for gossip."

"No, I suppose that would be very reckless, wouldn't it? But even if she didn't approach one of them that doesn't mean an Archer servant didn't get wind of the system."

Charles leaned casually against the sofa back, arms crossed in front of him. "As far as the family members themselves, can you be sure no one in the family knew Mary was writing the column?"

I chewed on my lip, pondering the thought. "Louise definitely thought the Archers were providing Mary's support. I'm quite sure she had no knowledge of the column."

He observed my hesitation. "But Lady Caroline?"

"She was harder to read. She mentioned Mary was involved with a lower class of people." I closed my eyes and struggled to bring her exact words to mind. "At the time I assumed she was just throwing barbs at her sister-in-law, but perhaps she knew Mary was working with servants and journalists."

"Is there a way to find out?"

I gave my cousin a smile. Sometimes the man was quite clever indeed. "There may be a way, but I'll need your assistance."

Chapter 14

The next day Charles and I set out to call on Lady Caroline. It was somewhat improper to call on a grieving family so soon after the funeral, but my cousin was known for his rather eccentric behavior, and as long as he was his usual self, we'd likely get away with this.

Nevertheless, my mother had drummed these social rules so deeply into my head, my legs shook as we stepped up to the door. To my surprise, the bell knob was bare. No draping of black crepe. None on the knocker either.

I turned to Charles and lifted a brow. If the Archers were not designating the house as one in mourning, perhaps my hesitation in calling was baseless. Interesting.

After seating us in a small sitting room, the butler took my card to his mistress to determine if she was at home. Within ten minutes, the lady herself walked into the room, wearing black, and a smile that crinkled her hazel eyes. Hmm. Observing mourning but not necessarily feeling it.

"Frances, how kind of you to call."

We both stood on her entering the room. "I'm relieved to

hear that, Caroline. I was concerned about intruding on you too soon."

"Heavens. We are old friends, are we not? Surely a quiet visit would offend no one's sensibilities."

Actually, it would likely offend many sensibilities, but I allowed her to be the judge. I presented Charles, and Caroline sat down with us. We discussed the weather, the visitors from the prior day, and other generalities. Finally, I brought up my ruse for calling.

"My cousin believes he lost his watch fob here yesterday, and it's rather dear to him. Would it be too much trouble to inquire if anyone found it in your drawing room?"

"Of course not. In fact, let us go there now and I'll ring for refreshments."

Once in the drawing room, Charles nudged me away from the sofa and over to one of the chairs while Lady Caroline walked away from us toward the bellpull. "What?" I whispered, giving him a glare.

As an answer, he made some strange contortions with his face and bobbed his head at the chair. Once I glanced in that direction, I realized a newspaper was lying on the table. The *Daily Observer*—perfect. Goodness, we were far enough away from Caroline that he could have just whispered to me.

I took the chair and picked up the paper, quickly leafing to the gossip column, while he made a show of searching under the furniture for his lost fob. By the time Caroline joined us, I'd returned the paper to the table, folded with the column prominently displayed.

"Mr. Evingdon, it's not necessary for you to check the room yourself. A maid will be here momentarily. I'll simply ask if they've found anything." She made as if to sit on the sofa until Charles, with a shooing motion, herded her over to the chair next to mine. I ignored the look of confusion she threw my way, pretending I'd just discovered the paper.

"I was seated here for a time yesterday," he said, indicating the sofa. "I should check the cushions." He began dropping the loose pillows to the floor.

"Must be a rather valuable piece," Caroline muttered under her breath.

I leaned across the table and smiled at her. "He's a little eccentric," I whispered. "But very nice."

Caroline returned my smile then addressed the maid who had just entered the room. "We'd like tea, Bertha. And can you ask if a watch fob was found when this room was cleaned?"

"This is good news," I said, once the maid had left. "The Miss Information column has returned today. Do you read it?" I lifted my gaze to keep a close watch on her expression while Charles pulled cushions from the sofa.

She glanced down at the column as I tapped it with my index finger then took it from the table. "Yes. I've read it from time to time, but not with any regularity." She turned back to me with some surprise on her face. "I wouldn't have thought this to be the sort of thing to interest you."

I released a tinkling laugh that sounded fake even to me. Perhaps I should quell my enthusiasm. "You forget I have two young ladies in my household. They've been bemoaning its absence for days now, so I'm delighted for its return."

A frown furrowed her brow. "Do you really think this is appropriate material for young ladies?"

I gave her a one-shoulder shrug. "I've found that forbidding something often makes a girl try all the harder to obtain it. If you've read the column, you know it's relatively harmless. I wonder where she gets her information."

Charles had finally given up his search and piled the cushions haphazardly back on the sofa. Caroline threw him a glance as he plopped himself down. "Do you really think the writer is a woman?" she asked.

My spirits sank with that question. "I assumed simply from

the title—Miss Information—that she was, but I hadn't given it much thought."

Caroline wrinkled her nose. "I don't believe a woman could work as a journalist. It is such a man's world, don't you agree?"

"One could make the case that every line of business is a man's world. Wouldn't you agree, Charles?"

He squirmed a bit under the weight of our gazes. "I would never underestimate the skills of the female gender, but if the columnist is a woman, she would find herself dealing mostly with men."

I struggled to repress a chuckle as he grinned back at us. He'd struck the perfect balance with his answer, neither insulting nor condescending.

"But as you say, where would she get her information?" Caroline folded the paper and placed it on the table between us, staring off to the distance as if contemplating the matter. A smile blossomed across her lips. "Unless she bribed the servants."

The remark was followed by a light ripple of laughter, which I attempted to join with little success. It was difficult enough not to stare at the woman with my jaw hanging open. Remarkably, Charles came to my rescue.

"If that's true, Miss Information has spies everywhere." He waggled his brows. "You should watch what you say around your servants, my lady."

Caroline waved a dismissive hand. "No good servant would tell tales outside their household."

The maid returned with our tea and the assurance that no watch fob was found in the entirety of the house. Her presence effectively cut off our conversation.

By this point I couldn't be certain if Lady Caroline had unwittingly stumbled on to the truth, or if she'd known all along her sister-in-law had been Miss Information and was simply baiting me. We stayed for another uncomfortable fifteen minutes, sipping tea and speaking of social engagements. As I could devise no way to broach the subject again without making her suspicious, we took our leave.

We argued all the way home.

"I'm sure she knows about the column. Why else would she say such a thing?"

"Though I'm inclined to agree, a passing comment cannot be deemed proof."

He crossed his arms and sank back into the leather upholstery of the carriage. "It would explain why the Archers were so angry with Mary. Rather than return to the family home, she chose to work for a living."

Indeed, it would. "But even if Caroline knew Mary wrote the column, she certainly couldn't be the murderer."

He raised a brow. "But what of her husband? Perhaps she left the dirty work to him."

"Now you're jumping to conclusions. I suspect you'd be prepared to see anyone as the murderer so you aren't required to examine those files again."

"Those files." He groaned. "It's like looking for a needle in a stack of needles."

"Under those circumstances, Charles, I'd say one is quite likely to find a needle."

"Yes, but would it be the right one?"

The fact I found logic in his statement rather unsettled me. Perhaps I was spending too much time with Cousin Charles. Fortunately, we'd arrived home. He helped me from the carriage and saw me to the door which, surprisingly, was opened by George Hazelton.

"Where have you two been?" The question came out in a growl.

Was I always to be questioned as to my whereabouts when I returned home? One glance at his rather thunderous face halted my glib response. Good heavens, what was wrong?

After handing my hat to Jenny, I led the gentlemen into the drawing room where Lottie awaited us, looking nervous. I gave her a smile and turned to the large man hovering over me. "What brings you here today? Has something happened?"

"Happened? Heavens, no, Frances."

I hadn't thought it possible, but his countenance grew even darker. "Only that when I arrived here half an hour ago, I fully expected to find you safely ensconced in your home. Then upon speaking to Miss Deaver, I learned you were out questioning suspects. And Evingdon may or may not have been with you; she wasn't sure."

Oh, dear. Now I understood. "Your information isn't entirely accurate. And as you can see, he was indeed with me."

"I had no idea where you were," he continued as if I hadn't spoken. "Or how much danger you might be in. I only knew it had something to do with Archer."

I glanced at Lottie, who raised her hands in defense. "I was working on the columns last night and only half listened as you and Mr. Evingdon made your plans for today."

"Completely understandable, dear. I'm sure you weren't expecting Mr. Hazelton to arrive and quiz you." I turned back to George who stood with his hands clasped behind him, rocking from heel to toe and back. Heavens, what was the man so angry about?

I returned his scowl in kind. "You act as though I've done something wrong. We were simply trying to gain some information from Lady Caroline, whom I don't believe is a suspect in this case."

He drew in a long breath. "At least Evingdon was with you."

"Yes, I believe I mentioned that." I took his elbow and guided him to a chair. "You told me to use my judgment. I wouldn't do anything foolish. Now, perhaps we can all sit down and discuss how we're all progressing on this case."

Lottie moved from the table and seated herself next to Charles on the sofa while I gave George an update of our findings and how we planned to proceed with the columns. He seemed to grow calmer as I spoke. Perhaps I'd regained his confidence. "We've included just enough information that if we happen on the murderer's story, he should recognize it. I daresay we should tell Mr. Mosley about this so he'll be on his guard in case the killer goes after him."

He nodded his approval of our proceedings. "I take it nothing you've read has caused you to focus on a particular note or person."

I glanced at Lottie and Charles. Both shook their heads. "We actually have many stories that are so scandalous, I have to wonder who wouldn't kill to keep their information from publication. I've seen nothing that could narrow down the suspects, but we've started with those who attended the funeral."

"Have you seen anything that pertains to the Archers?"

"No, and we specifically checked." I raised a brow. "Why do you ask? Do you suspect Mr. Archer?"

"Not necessarily of the murder, but Archer has something to hide, which is why I was so concerned when I thought you were questioning him. He attempted to break into Mary's house last night."

"Aha!" We all turned to Charles as he jumped to his feet. "I knew there was something dodgy about the man. Did you have him arrested? Did Delaney get him to admit his guilt?"

George regarded his friend with some curiosity. "Not precisely."

I shooed Charles back to his seat and turned to George. "What exactly happened and how do you know of it?"

"I've been waiting for a chance to get into Mrs. Archer's house and I was there again last night, hoping the constable would step away long enough for me to gain entrance. I saw Archer myself, trying to break in through the back door. Unfortunately for him, a constable also saw him and took him to the Chelsea police division, where I followed. Delaney wasn't on duty so I couldn't obtain any information, but Archer was released within the hour so he must have come up with some excuse."

"Did you return to Mrs. Archer's house?" Lottie asked.

"I did, but by then a new constable was on duty, fresh and well rested, so it seems I'd lost my chance."

"What do you suppose Archer was after?"

He raised his hands in a helpless gesture. "No idea. But I wish that constable hadn't been so good at his job. I'd have preferred to catch Archer in the house with some damning evidence in his hands."

I gave the matter some thought. "Do we know who Mary's executor is? Archer is a banker and so a likely choice. Could he simply have been trying to settle her estate?"

"In the middle of the night?" Lottie crossed her arms and leaned back in her seat.

"And he isn't her executor," George added. "Louise's husband has that responsibility. From what I understand he has the keys to her house, so Archer had no legitimate reason for being there." He gave Lottie a nod. "Especially in the middle of the night."

"This only makes me more convinced Lady Caroline knew about the Miss Information column," Charles said.

I gave George the details of our visit to Caroline earlier.

"It doesn't necessarily mean she knew Mary wrote this column, but her comment about the servants, combined with Archer's behavior, makes them very suspicious in my view." I glanced over at the files. "Perhaps Mary did have a note pertaining to some scandal about them and we've missed it."

Charles released a grunt. "Needle in a stack of needles."

Lottie turned to him with an inquiring glance, but I pressed on.

"That might be what Archer was after when he tried to break into her house. Perhaps I should pay him a call."

George lurched to his feet. "Evingdon, Miss Deaver, if you'll excuse us, Frances and I need to speak privately."

"Privately?" In this house privacy was at a premium. Before I had a chance to consider where to take him, he clamped a hand on my wrist and led me from the room.

"We'll return momentarily," he said, tossing the comment to Charles and Lottie over his shoulder.

"Hetty and Graham are in the library," I said, scurrying to keep up as he strode down the hallway.

He took a detour to the right and into the dining room. He stopped at the table and, releasing my wrist, turned to face me.

I took a step back. "What's wrong?"

He took hold of my shoulders and gazed into my face with a strained expression. "We need to set some rules before we delve any further into this investigation."

"George—"

"Frances. Everyone you speak to in this case is potentially dangerous." He released my shoulders and circled away, running a hand through his hair. "Perhaps we should forget rules and simply reconsider your involvement."

"But I wasn't doing anything dangerous. We were simply talking to Lady Caroline."

He twisted around and threw me a glare. "If I'd known that, I might not have been so concerned."

"Never say you're going to shut me out of this investigation because I worried you. Is that my punishment?"

"Punishment? Frances, we are working on this investigation together but you must allow I'm the more experienced partner, while you are a novice."

"A novice?"

"Yes, with an ample supply of natural skill, I'll grant you, but still a novice. Your instincts have yet to be tested."

I stared in confusion. "My instincts."

"We don't yet know if they'll lead you into danger or keep you safe." He gave me a penetrating look. "Need I remind you that two people have been murdered?"

I placed my hands on my hips and glared. "No, you needn't. Heavens, George, do you subject all your partners to this lecture?"

He pulled back in surprise, then smiled. "No. I've always worked alone."

I was about to offer a scathing comment about his partnering skills, but held my tongue when he squeezed my shoulders once more.

"Until you. You are my first partner and I couldn't bear it if something should happen to you."

Oh, dear. Why did I always suffer waves of delight when he said things like this? "I do understand and promise to be more careful." I gave him a hopeful smile.

"Yet after what I just told you about Archer, you're willing to go and talk to him alone."

"You said you didn't suspect him of Mary's murder."

"But he is hiding something."

"I'd be completely safe if you came with me."

He shook his head. "Archer's approached me before about investing with him and I told him I had no interest. He wouldn't believe I've had a change of heart so quickly."

"Charles?"

He gave me an incredulous stare. "You're resolved to do this, aren't you?"

I held his gaze, determined not to back down, until he huffed in exasperation. "He might do. He'll keep Archer confused and intimidated at the same time." His expression sobered as he gazed at me. "While I want your help, I don't want you taking risks. Make sure Evingdon goes with you, and from now on someone must always know where you are, preferably me. If you won't agree to that point, then yes, I will shut you out of this case."

My answer was immediate and instinctive. "Agreed, but I

want the same promise from you." I blinked away some foolish moisture from my eyes. "I wouldn't want to lose you either."

His hand moved to the back of my neck and his lips came down on mine. Heavens, this was a proper kiss. Or rather very improper. Deep, delicious, and full of the promise of . . . of something. I didn't know or care what. At last we were getting somewhere. I pressed closer, fairly sinking into him.

He pushed me away. He was gentle, but firm, with a tug at his waistcoat and a brush of his sleeves.

I stared, my jaw drooping. What? Why?

"I know this is not the time or the place," he said. "But someday soon you must decide what you want of me, Frances. You're already aware of what I want."

I blinked. What had just happened? If not for the flush on his face, I'd have thought I imagined that kiss. I straightened the folds of my skirt.

"I'm afraid you give me too much credit," I replied. "I'm not at all sure what you want. When you asked me to marry you it was such a businesslike proposition—beneficial to both parties. You worry about my safety, but is that just your protective nature?"

My words grew more heated as I spoke, my gestures more animated. "You tease me with an occasional show of affection, then call me your partner. Now we have this moment of passion that leads to nothing. No, George, I must confess I am completely in the dark about what you want from me—a friend? A partner? A lover?"

One corner of his lips quirked up in a crooked smile. "Yes. All of it. Isn't that what you want?"

Words failed me. Of course that's what I wanted, but was that even obtainable?

The confusion must have shown in my expression, as he sighed and gave me a weary smile. "I know you're not ready to make this decision yet, Frances. But if you're ever to make it, you must at least open your mind to it."

He took my hand and brought it to his lips. "I'll leave you to make your plans with Evingdon. Now that I think about it, Archer would wonder at the two of us visiting his office together. At least Evingdon is a relation of yours while you and I have no official connection." He smiled. "I'm just the man you sneak through your back garden to visit."

I sighed. If only that's all he was.

Chapter 15

※

I'd waited until the following morning to send a note to Gordon Archer at his office, asking if he had time to see me to discuss some investments. Jenny returned with his reply while I was enjoying breakfast with Rose in the schoolroom. As luck would have it, he would be at leisure to meet with me anytime this morning. I gave Rose a kiss and headed off to dress, hoping Bridget could find something businesslike in my wardrobe. We settled on a pale gray voile with long sleeves extending over my hands. The straight lines of the skirt were edged in a darker gray, making it rather severe. Perfect.

Charles arrived with a hired cab just as I stepped into the hall.

"Mr. Hazelton must be using his carriage today," I remarked as he assisted me into the cab. Riding in private carriages had spoiled me. This one was clean, I noticed as I settled in, but something loose behind the rough upholstery poked me in the back.

Charles slipped in beside me. "Yes, occasionally Hazelton needs his own carriage. I'd considered having mine sent over, but I'm not certain I need to stay with him much longer. I've seen nothing in the papers about my arrest. Have you heard anything of it?"

"You weren't arrested. Delaney simply brought you in to intimidate you. But no, it seems that news hasn't leaked out."

I watched him from under my lashes. "Now that you mention your stay with Mr. Hazelton, may I ask about your feelings toward Miss Deaver? Since you've been living next door you've been spending more time at my home, and I feel I must speak plainly. If you have no intentions of a courtship, I must insist you avoid being alone with her."

He turned away, glancing out the window. "I find Miss Deaver absolutely delightful, but I've no right to any such intentions, Frances. I'm a suspect in a murder investigation."

His voice held a note of dejection I hadn't heard before. It's not that I'd forgotten Charles was a suspect, but I never realized he worried about it. I was ashamed to admit I hadn't believed he worried about anything. I placed my hand over his.

"That impediment will be removed, Charles, and soon, if Mr. Hazelton has anything to do with it. But until you're certain of your intentions, please have a care for her reputation and her feelings."

He turned half toward me, a grin spreading across his lips. "Do you think her feelings are involved?"

Was he serious? Could he not see for himself? The hope in his expression cut off any sarcasm I might have uttered. "I can't speak for Miss Deaver, but my own observations tell me she'd be favorably disposed to your attentions."

He plopped back against the seat, leaning his head on the wall behind him, his hat pushed over his eyes. "Well, I'll be damned," he said under his breath.

The cab slowed to a crawl as we drew closer to the city and the bank on Princes Street. We gave up about half a block away, climbed down to the street, wove our way through the congested traffic, and joined the crowds of business people on the pavement. Goodness, this was nothing like Mayfair, where everything moved at a more leisurely pace.

Eventually we stepped into the lobby and were escorted to Gordon Archer's luxurious office. He rose from behind an enormous desk to greet us and guided us to comfortable chairs facing his desk. The dark paneled walls, thick carpets, and leather upholstered chairs were as fine as any I'd seen in the most elegant of homes.

If Archer was surprised by Charles's presence, he gave no indication of it.

"I'm honored you considered me when you thought of investing, Lady Harleigh," he said. He'd reseated himself behind the desk after we refused his offer of refreshments. "I wonder that your father was not your first choice."

Bother. I'd forgotten my father's reputation would have preceded me. It was no secret our family fortune had been built on his financial acumen. I smiled. "I'd like to strike out on my own just this once. My brother-in-law told me if I wanted a good, solid investment, I should speak to you."

"And of course, your sister-in-law recommended you," Charles added. "Lady Harleigh was great friends with her." He leaned in toward the desk. "Mrs. Archer couldn't praise your talents enough. In fact, she once told me if I had anything to invest I must see you for advice—ouch!"

That last was the result of some rather heavy pressure of my heel on his toe. Had he forgotten the two didn't get on? I maintained a placid smile as I gazed steadily into Archer's eyes. "She did speak highly of you," I said.

"Indeed?"

Archer clearly had the makings of a good card player. His expression remained neutral as he folded his hands on his desk blotter and leaned toward me, clearly ready to get down to business.

"Tell me, Lady Harleigh, when you say you are seeking a solid investment, do you mean safe, or profitable?"

"Safe, by all means," Charles replied. "Risky investments make me nervous."

Archer turned his gaze to Charles and raised his brows. "Are you advising Lady Harleigh?"

"He is not," I said. "I've come to you for that, and I'd like to know why one can't have both a safe and profitable investment?"

"As Mr. Evingdon implied, a profitable investment often comes with a significant amount of risk. For example, you could lose some of your principle." He leaned back to pull a file from his desk drawer. Spreading the pages on the desk in front of me, he proceeded to explain the benefits of an account earning three to five percent per annum. Within five minutes, I stopped listening and nearly dozed off. This conversation was leading us nowhere.

"What about real estate?"

That woke me up. Archer stopped speaking midsentence and turned to Charles.

"The bank's transactions in real estate are on a rather grand scale and not meant for personal investment," Archer said with a chuckle. "Unless, of course, Lady Harleigh is seeking another state for America, which would require significantly more capital."

Charles shook his head. "No, nothing so big. What about Mrs. Archer's house?"

"Mary's house?" Archer's brow furrowed. "What about it?"

I was as confused as Archer, but something told me not to stop Charles this time.

"Well, I rather like the place, and the houses in that neighborhood are not leasehold, are they? She owned it outright, did she not?"

"She did." Archer dropped his hands to his lap and leaned back. "Am I to understand you're interested in purchasing it? Surely you're not thinking of living there yourself?"

Charles bristled at his tone. "It's hardly a poor neighborhood, and quite a nice little place it was, too. Mrs. Archer was happy there."

As his stroke of brilliance waned, I thought it best if I gave him some support before Archer saw through his ruse. "But you were not thinking of living there yourself." I turned to Archer. "Because he has such fond memories of Mary, and her home, he intended to buy it and lease it to a young couple he knows and wishes to assist." I placed a hand on Charles's arm. "It's a lovely idea, Cousin Charles. So much nicer than if an investor bought it and chopped it up into flats."

I addressed Archer before he could speak. "Do you happen to be the executor of Mary's estate by chance?"

He sputtered a bit before replying. "No, I do not have that honor. Mr. Carr, her sister's husband, is her executor. But I advise you to think twice about buying that house. There has been a murder there. You might have some difficulty selling the place in the future."

Charles waved off the concern. "I'd like to take another look at the place in any event." He turned to me. "Perhaps you might contact Mrs. Carr."

"Certainly. There's no damage that you are aware of, is there, Mr. Archer? Have you been to her house recently?"

"Of course not. What business would I have there?" His eyes had widened in surprise at the question, but he made a quick recovery of his poker face. He stood, indicating this meeting was at an end. "If you decide you wish to open an account, Lady Harleigh, I'll be happy to assist you."

Charles and I came to our feet as well. I extended a hand to Archer, which he shook, sparing only a nod and a glare for Charles.

We remained silent until we were tucked inside another cab and on our way back to my house. "Shame we couldn't get him to tell us why he tried to break into Mary's house."

"I hardly think he would have confessed what he was after. But the fact that he denied going there at all tells us he had no legitimate reason for attempting to break in."

He raised his brows. "Ah, I suppose it does at that."

"And since he now expects you to visit the house yourself, he might just attempt it again. We should warn Mr. Hazelton."

"Excellent notion," he said. "All things considered then, I'd say this was a good morning's work."

I considered Gordon Archer. The fact that he had tried to break into Mary's house, and his disdain for his sister-in-law, told me he was up to something. Or at least he had been. It wasn't necessarily murder, but George was right—Archer had something to hide.

Charles saw me to my door, then went off to take care of some business of his own. I slipped inside and peeked into the drawing room. Delightfully empty. Hetty, Lottie, and Graham were undoubtedly in the library but they were unlikely to need anything from me. I fairly skipped up the stairs, removing my hat in the process. Once I'd dropped it off in my room, I could return to the drawing room and spend a little leisure time with the post, or perhaps a book. Yes, I did need to write another column or two but surely, I could take some time for myself.

"There you are."

I jumped at the words and turned to see Lily peeking out her bedchamber door. The vision of a quiet hour on my own quickly dissolved.

"Heavens, Lily, you startled me. Have you been waiting for me?"

I opened the door, and she followed me into my bedchamber. *Stalked* might actually have been a better word. I definitely felt hunted. I dropped my hat on the bed and turned to face her, surprised to see her leaning against the door frame with her arms crossed over her chest.

"Frances, you have barely participated in planning this engagement party at all. I'm beginning to wonder if you even plan to attend."

My spirits sagged at the prospect of the argument about to take place. In all honesty, with Mary's murder, Delaney's suspicions of Charles, and the subsequent investigation, I had all but forgotten about the engagement party.

I walked around her to my dressing table and seated myself. "In my defense, Lily, I have been rather busy lately."

"But this is my *engagement party.*" Lily strode toward me, hands on her hips and a scowl on her face. "This is very important to me."

I raised a brow. "Need I remind you this is also the party that was not supposed to take place for at least a few months? Now I have to be ready for it in less than two weeks. It's hardly my fault I'm in the midst of a murder investigation."

She plopped onto the bed and threw me a glare. "Why are you investigating this murder anyway? You're a countess, for goodness' sake. Society is your milieu, not the seedy underworld of criminals."

"A friend of mine has been murdered. She was neither seedy nor involved in this underworld you speak of. Whatever that is. Mr. Hazelton asked for my help. How could I say no?"

"Mr. Hazelton is just trying to indulge you. You cannot possibly be helping him, so you ought to get back to doing what you're good at."

Well, that stung. "Do you not think it possible I may have more than one talent? Perhaps I don't find planning society events all that fulfilling anymore. Besides, it seems to me that you have everything well in hand."

Lily's scowl collapsed into a quivering lip. "Maybe I do, but that doesn't mean I don't want your approval, or your advice. Maybe I just want my sister to support me."

Oh, dear. I stepped over to the bed and sank down next to

her, pulling her into my arms. "Poor dear," I murmured. "Of course you want support. Marriage is an enormous step. I don't think it's the party you are worried about at all."

"Well, as Leo's wife I'll have to entertain and I want him to see that I know what I'm doing. If the party is a disaster, his mother will assume I'm a disaster and so will he."

"Lily, you're just starting out in your new life and there's something you should know." I backed away to make sure she paid attention. "There are bound to be disasters."

She sniffed. "Not if I plan properly."

I shushed her. "No matter how well you plan. Disasters are a fact of life. Just accept it. Yes, you can and should plan carefully, but you are dealing with humans and they all have their own lives, plans, and needs. There's no telling what can happen when you gather a group of them together. The important thing to remember is when disaster strikes you must face it with aplomb. You cannot fall apart."

"That is not very reassuring, Frances. In fact, I'm even more nervous."

"Don't be. I'll be with you and so will Leo's mother. Leo will be at your side, too, and together you can face down any disaster. Before long they won't seem like disasters to you but rather minor irritations."

"Really?"

"I promise you. Now, I admit I have been neglecting you but I have some free time at the moment. Why don't you get your diary and we'll go over your preparations?"

She glanced up at me through watery eyes. I'd forgotten how important it was to do everything right at her age. And how certain I was I'd do everything wrong. "Thank you, Frances. I truly do want your help."

She gave me a hug and made as if to leave; stopping at the door, she turned back. "And I don't think Mr. Hazelton is just indulging you. I'm sure you're helping him."

I gave her a smile as she left, then went to the mirror to smooth my hair. Lily had put an end to both my private time and my peace of mind. I did believe I was helping to move this case along, but there was definitely a possibility George was pandering to my sense of adventure, my sense of curiosity. I knew he was trying to win my affection. No, he must know he already had that, but he was trying to coax me into marriage. And he was going about it in the best of ways—by including me in his life and his work. But was that the only reason he included me? And more importantly—did it matter?

Lily and I worked on her plans for the engagement party until Mrs. Thompson scratched lightly on the door and informed me Mr. Evingdon and Mr. Hazelton awaited us downstairs. I knew they were coming to dinner. Was it that late already?

We put away Lily's notes and met the gentlemen in the drawing room, where I dug into Hetty's supply of spirits. I'd have to alert Mrs. Thompson that the brandy was running low. Instead, I poured each of us a small tot of whiskey—a fine single malt, Hetty had called it. She and Lottie joined us shortly, and not long after, we were informed dinner was ready.

We didn't stand on ceremony so George took a seat next to me at the table. "Evingdon told me things went reasonably well with Archer today," he said once the fish course was served. "What is your opinion?"

"It was not as productive as I would have liked," I said, swirling a bite of sole into the cream sauce with my fork. "We never had the opportunity to bring up Mary's column. But Archer did lie when we asked if he had visited her house lately. That seemed promising. And he was decidedly nervous when Charles questioned him about the disposition of the house."

He gave Charles a nod of approval. "Well, now. That's very interesting."

"It leads me to wonder if Mary had some scandalous story about him and he was hoping to retrieve it."

"But we have all Mrs. Archer's documents," Lottie said.

"Do we?" I cast George a sidelong glance. "Perhaps you should go through her house."

"I'd consider doing so if that constable would ever move on. The man is nothing if not conscientious."

"Must be angling for a promotion," Charles suggested.

"What about Charles's idea? I could contact Louise and tell her he is interested in buying or leasing the house. Perhaps her husband could arrange for him to have a look at it." I lifted my shoulder in a casual shrug. "She wouldn't consider it strange if you and I were to accompany him."

Lily leaned around George to send a beaming smile at me. "Good work, Franny. That is a decidedly devious idea."

"Indeed," George said. "It may be our only way inside."

"Thank you both for your confidence. It's only an idea, but I'll be happy to contact her if you like."

I'd dropped my hands to my lap. George slipped his hand over them and squeezed. "Please do. Once inside, I'm sure we can manage some type of search."

Our conversation shifted to the weather as Jenny swept in to remove the remains of the fish course and bring in our entrée. Once she left the room, we returned to the business at hand.

"So, you learned nothing else from Archer?"

"He wants to put Frances into a five percent annuity," Charles said with a chuckle.

Hetty's brows rose at that. "From my understanding, that's a far more conservative investment than he normally recommends."

"I was rather disappointed his suggestion for me was so dull. What were Graham's dealings with him, Aunt Hetty?"

She glanced around the table. "I suppose I needn't worry about any of you discussing it outside this room. Archer convinced Graham to invest in a fledgling company involved in shipping between Britain and South America."

George cocked his head to the side. "Convinced him?"

"That may be stating the case too strongly, but he indicated the earl could triple his investment in a year." Hetty released her breath in a huff.

It didn't sound as though this story would end well. "Did Graham lose money?"

"He lost everything. What's worse, he doesn't even have a prospectus on the company. I asked Leo's father if he'd heard of them." She shook her head. "He hadn't, but he promised to see what he could find out about them. To be honest, I think Archer knew the company was questionable at best and wanted to share the risk."

"Hugo Ridley told me Gordon Archer was on top of all the latest investments. After speaking to Archer today, I learned if you want a large profit you must take some risks. It sounds as though this risk did not pay off."

Hetty released a sharp, bitter laugh. "No, this was an absolute failure, but I still want some information on the company. If they were insured, their investors should be able to recover something. But Graham is unwilling to contact Archer."

"It's that aristocratic pride," Charles commented. "Like when a gentleman loses a fortune at the card table he must act as though it's nothing more than a minor nuisance. No matter if he has to lease out his family home and go live in a hut in the woods. Pride must come first."

"Gentlemen can be so ridiculous about such things," I said. "But at least when playing cards, one is aware one is gambling. Did Graham not question the risks of this investment?"

Hetty tipped her head in my direction, her brows raised. "Come now, Frances, you must know yourself Graham has no business sense. If a man with Archer's success tells him he'll make a fortune on an investment, he won't concern himself with something as minor as risk."

Sadly, it had been my experience Hetty's pronouncement was all too true. Graham knew agriculture and very little else, which was why he was relying on Hetty to put his affairs in order.

Lottie turned the conversation to Lily's engagement party, allowing me to ponder what I'd learned about Gordon Archer. He'd tried to break into Mary's house. What had he been after? Was it possible Mary had some gossip about his more dubious investments? I wondered if it would be wise to see if anyone else had lost a great deal of money with Archer.

My musings were interrupted by another touch of George's hand on mine. I turned to find him smiling down on me.

"I delivered your columns yesterday," he said quietly as the group talked around us. "And was told you are not abiding by your contracted schedule."

I blinked. "Odd. I wasn't aware I had either a contract or a schedule."

"Apparently on Tuesdays Mrs. Archer delivered columns for Wednesday through Friday. As you provided only a column for today and Thursday, Mr. Mosley maintains you owe him one more column."

"Heavens, that sounds a great deal like nit-picking to me. I was already dreading working on the next set of columns for him, but now I must produce one tonight?"

He gave me a one-shoulder shrug. "They have a schedule to adhere to, and from what Mosley told me, you are sending the printers into a tizzy. If you think you can write one this evening, I promised to deliver it tomorrow."

I frowned, resigned to my fate. "Very well. I'm sure I can write something suitable for you to take, but only if you tell me why you're whispering."

"I like whispering to you. It allows me to believe we are sharing intimate secrets."

I felt the heat rise to my face.

He leaned closer. "I also like making you blush."

I huffed. "You are rather an expert at it."

"Why, thank you, Frances. I do my best."

I felt the urge to giggle and determined I must put a stop to his teasing before my brain was completely befuddled. "You're getting carried away, George. After all, we aren't sharing secrets now. Everyone at this table knows Lottie and I are writing this column. Your imagination has run away with you."

His smile widened as he squeezed my hand. "Ah, but it's my imagination, and if it wants to run, why should you stop it?" He heaved a dramatic sigh. "And after I was kind enough to bring you a gift from Mr. Mosley."

That came as a surprise. "After demanding more columns, he sends me a gift?"

He reached into his coat pocket and pulled out a thick envelope, laying it next to my plate. I nudged it with my fork, suspicious of this "gift."

"It won't bite you," he said. "You are perfectly safe in opening it."

By now the main courses had been removed and the fruit and cheese served. Several pairs of attentive eyes turned in my direction.

"I know what it is," Lottie stated. "Letters from admirers of your column."

I glanced at George. He shrugged. "They are letters from readers."

"Heavens, from one column? Well, then they are as much yours as mine, Lottie." I smiled at the girl and passed them across the table to her. "After all, you came up with the notion of teasers."

She giggled and opened the envelope. Three letters were enclosed. "We are correct," she said, grinning widely and holding the pages up for all to see. "They are all addressed to Miss Information."

"How intriguing to have a pseudonym," George said.

Lottie read the first letter. "This reader takes exception to the characterization of Lord W in last Thursday's column."

"Ah, not one of ours," I said.

"Wasn't he the man who had drunkenly waded into the Serpentine?" Charles asked. "How else would one characterize him?"

Amid our laughter Lottie opened the next missive. Her frown dampened our merriment. "What is it, dear?"

Raising her gaze from the page, she handed it across to me. It was unsigned and held just a few words, scratched into the paper. The nib of the pen had actually broken through the stiff parchment in a few places. The words read *I know who you are!*

Chapter 16

❦

Louise hesitated on the front porch of Mary's home after turning the key and pushing the door open. I stepped to one side of the door with her, motioning for George and Charles to enter without us. Mr. Carr had been unable to join us so Louise had stepped up to the task. I hoped this wasn't too difficult for her.

"I can wait in the carriage with you, if you'd rather not go in," I said, placing what I hoped was a comforting hand on her arm.

She hesitated. Then, with a sad smile, raised her eyes to mine. "No, if Mr. Evingdon has the courage to go inside, and possibly even live here, how can I do less?"

I gave her arm a squeeze. Charles was endearing, but had Mary really become so attached to him in so short a time? Or was Louise just wishfully thinking? I followed her over the threshold and into a small foyer that led in three possible directions—left and upstairs, forward to the back of the house, or right into a comfortable drawing room. Louise and I turned right. The gentlemen had already moved on through the house so we were alone. I surveyed the room, trying to get a sense of Mary from her furnishings and belongings.

It was an in-between room, neither large nor small, clean nor cluttered. The furnishings were worn but not shabby. I took a seat in a wingback chair and continued my survey. The décor—art, lamps, and the few knickknacks—was interesting, but not expensive. If not for my father's foresight in setting up an account for me when I married, I would consider myself lucky to live in such a house.

I think I understood Mary's choices a little better for having been here. This was her home, not the family home of her late husband, and not the home of her sister's husband. Hers. I knew that feeling. My house was mine. I wasn't required to please other people in order to remain there. I didn't have to worry I was imposing on someone's good nature or their privacy. Or worse, worry the invitation to stay would someday be withdrawn. A woman would give a great deal for that sense of independence and self-sufficiency.

Mary chose a way to support herself by making use of her skills. She could write a clever line and had access to gossip. I might not approve, but I certainly understood. And I was in no position to condemn.

A parlor-sized piano stood against the far wall. Louise seated herself at the bench and rested her fingers on the keys. The piano emitted a pleasant tinkle.

"I wasn't aware Mary played," I said.

"The piano was part of the house when she and Jasper bought it." She stretched her fingers and played a few chords. "I never thought about it before, but it seems the two of them cherished their independence. They were living very comfortably in the family home, had their own set of rooms, but they decided to move out on their own."

She turned back to me and smiled. "Mary told me she wanted to find someone to give her lessons, but in the meantime, she was attempting to teach herself. I have no idea how far she progressed."

I remembered the daily lessons when I was young. Learning

an instrument as an adult must be difficult, which made me admire her even more. She wasn't frightened by a challenge.

Which brought my thoughts to the note Lottie had opened at dinner.

I know who you are!

What did that mean? Was it written when Mary had been the author of the columns? Was it from her killer? Or was it someone we'd mentioned briefly in the current columns? If the former, we'd need to pass it on to Delaney, though I had no idea what he'd do with it. If the latter, we should tell Mr. Mosley. If this was a threat, it might be followed up by the writer visiting the newspaper offices.

Whoever wrote it might be Mary's murderer. And poor Mr. Norton's, too. I kept forgetting about the editor. I wondered how Inspector Delaney was getting on with that investigation. Perhaps any progress in his case would shed some light on Mary's.

We certainly needed something to come to light. Some clue or lead.

Restless, I stood. "I'm going to see how the gentlemen are finding the house."

Louise waved her hand absently, and I stepped back out to the entry, wondering where George and Charles had got to. Moving down the hallway to the back of the house, the next room in my path was a small library. I heard the murmur of their voices before entering the room. Peeking through the doorway, I could only feel relief that Louise hadn't decided to join me.

Mary's desk drawers were empty, the entire contents tossed onto the writing surface in a heap of paper, string, pens, and pencils. "You are supposed to be searching the house, not ransacking it," I said in a low voice.

Charles stepped forward, slipping on a fallen sheet of paper. He clutched the desk to steady himself while George watched with a rather weary aspect on his face. "We did not create this mess," he stated, his voice low. "I don't know if the police left it in this state, or if Archer, or someone else, managed to get inside under the constable's nose."

"Weren't you watching the house last night for just such a possibility?"

"I couldn't watch it all night, Frances. For part of the evening I was at your home, and though I was here for several hours, I am human, you know. I do need to sleep from time to time. Besides, it seemed the constable had everything under control. And as I said, for all we know, the police may have left the room in this state after their search."

"I suppose we can check with Delaney about that. Have you been in here this whole time? Have you found anything of interest?"

George started sorting the papers on the desk into stacks. "No, we entered just a few minutes ahead of you. Evingdon has already checked the upstairs rooms, and I searched the kitchen area downstairs."

"What did you hope to find there?"

"Mary was no fool. If she wanted to hide something, what better place than inside bags of flour or among the onions?"

"Well, her previous cache was under a loose floorboard, not among the vegetables."

"We found no other loose flooring."

"Did you find anything in the kitchen?"

He looked abashed. "No."

"Nothing upstairs either," Charles added. "This, however"—he swept a hand over the desk—"appears to be a good possibility."

George shook his head. "Hate to disappoint, but if it was a good possibility, it wouldn't still be here in plain sight. The police picked it over and decided to leave it. Archer may have done so as well." He tapped the edges of a stack of paper against the desk and stuffed them into a briefcase.

I stepped forward to hold the case open. "If they are insignificant, why are you taking them?"

"Because I'm not going to let the police do my work for me. It's unlikely that they missed anything, but one never knows. Unfortunately, I can't read all this while we're here so we must take them with us. If Mrs. Carr even notices them missing, she'll assume the police took them."

"And you just happened to bring an empty document case along with you today?"

He smiled across the desk at me. "I don't just happen to do anything, Frances. You know that." With that he stuffed the last of the papers into his case and closed it. "We should get back to Mrs. Carr. To her mind, I'm sure Charles has had enough time to view the house."

We headed back down the hallway to the drawing room where Louise still tinkered with the piano. George and I hovered in the doorway but Charles stepped up to her and leaned against the instrument.

"She was coming along in her lessons," he said, smiling down at Louise. "She was determined to improve and practiced every day."

When she turned toward Charles, I could see her eyes were welling up. "Thank you," she said. "If I could not be with her, I'm happy she had someone like you in her life."

He reddened and held out a hand to assist Louise to her feet.

I was filled with emotion. Louise should not have had to suffer this loss. She should not have to cling to this man, who had only courted Mary for a few weeks, in order to feel closer to the sister she'd lost. In fact, Mary should be with us now. She'd simply been trying to earn a living. What could she possibly have written that was so wrong she must pay for it with her life? I felt such anger on behalf of the sisters, I didn't just want to bring the killer to justice, I wanted to hurt him just as he'd hurt these two women.

* * *

We left Louise at her hotel, dropped Charles at George's home, and headed on to Fleet Street, to the *Daily Observer* to deliver my next two columns.

"You are showing a great capacity for writing these columns, Lady Harleigh," George said in a teasing tone.

We sat next to each other in his carriage and I was tempted to give his arm a pinch. "Scoff if you will, but they've proven to be much more difficult to write than I'd anticipated, and I must say, without Lottie's help they would hardly be worth reading." I pursed my lips as I thought about her assistance. "In truth, she wrote most of the columns with a little help from me. Very little. Not much at all."

He gave me a smile that threatened laughter.

"Truly, George. You cannot imagine how difficult it is to have all the facts in your hands while allowing only a hint of those facts to end up in the column. And to express them in such a way as to keep the readers' interest."

He tipped his head to the side. "I take it the newspaper is concerned about lawsuits."

"They most certainly are! To such a degree I wonder they have a gossip column at all. Mr. Mosley edited our first efforts into mere nothingness."

"Considering the note you received yesterday, we must assume you've attracted someone's attention. In fact, I'd be much more comfortable if you'd allow me to drop you at home and handle this task myself."

He gave me a hard stare, which I'm sure was meant to make me back down.

"I have no intention of going home. We've placed several suggestions in these columns which I cannot allow Mosley to edit out if our plan is to be successful. And I don't see how I'm in any danger with you at my side."

"Flattery will get you nowhere in this case, Frances. The

danger is if the writer of that note is also watching the buildings. I'm sure you don't want anyone to know you have anything to do with the newspaper business. And they will if someone sees you coming and going from there. I don't want the killer to know you are involved in any way."

"Nor do I, which is why I have a veil." I demonstrated by pulling the black netting down from the brim of my hat. "This should do well in protecting my anonymity."

"Ah, yes, I barely recognize you," he said, but made no further objection as we'd arrived at the newspaper office.

We opened the door to an angry growl, and it took a moment to realize it was not directed at us. Young Mr. Ryan manned his post at the front desk, but an older man stabbed his index finger at a sheet of paper in the typewriter. He shot a glare our way and turned to leave.

"You'll have to do it again," he shouted over his shoulder before disappearing through the doorway.

Mr. Ryan, red-faced, showed us directly to Mr. Mosley's office. No questions this time. George had a point. Perhaps I was disguised enough to go unnoticed, but the staff of the paper definitely recognized us. He might be worried about me, but I didn't want the killer connecting him to the newspaper either. Perhaps we needed to find another way to deliver the columns, while still keeping Mosley and the rest of the newspaper staff ignorant of my identity.

Mr. Mosley stood up at his desk as we entered his office, his posture defensive as he barked at the young man, "I thought we agreed you were to inform me first when someone is here to see me."

The assistant turned from Mosley to us and back. "But you said you were expecting them," the young man stammered.

"Yes, yes, of course." Mosley sighed and waved him away. I caught his arm before he could leave and pressed a paper-wrapped package into his hands.

"My housekeeper made these rolls this morning, and I managed to save a few for you," I whispered.

A grin nearly split his face in two. He uttered a hasty *thank you* before rushing back to his desk.

"Are you feeding random boys now?" George gave me a wink as Mosley ushered me into a chair. The second chair held a large stack of newspapers so George was required to stand.

"He's so thin. I'm inclined to believe he doesn't get enough to eat."

Mosley waved a hand. "Don't waste your concern, ma'am. And sorry for the confusion. We had an unwelcome visitor earlier today. Thus the new rules."

"I thought you agreed to adopt new security rules when we were last here." George folded his arms over his chest. "It took an intruder to make you see the sense of it?"

"All part of the business." Mosley shrugged his indifference. "Anything new on the case? I haven't heard a thing from the police since they took poor Mr. Norton's body and began the investigation."

"I'm afraid not," George replied. "Though we have plans to speak with Inspector Delaney later this afternoon."

The man shrugged and sat behind his desk. "Spent a lot of years chasing down stories from the police. Now I'm stuck in the office all the time. Oh well. Old habits and all. I suppose you've brought me the columns?"

Good heavens. Did nothing unsettle this man? "Yes, but what of your intruder? Was he here in relation to the column?"

"Oh, him. Don't know who he was, but he was angry about the Miss Information column, all right. Came in here spouting off about the filthy things this filthy rag chooses to print. Thought we were done with all this gossip, he says. Then it starts up again. Well, I ask him if he doesn't like it, why does he read it, eh?"

"Good point," George said. "He could only note its absence if he'd been a regular reader. Rather hypocritical, I'd say."

"Exactly," Mosley agreed. "People can complain about it all they want, but that column sells papers, so somebody's reading it."

"Did he have a more specific complaint?" I asked. "Perhaps to the hints of upcoming gossip? Did he by chance mention anyone in particular?"

"Naw, just wishing we'd shut it down. Stomped around the office a bit, shaking his fist. Then finished up with swearing to buy this rag if that's what it took to stop the spread of this vicious gossip. As if I hadn't heard that one before."

"What did he look like?" George asked.

Mosley was still shaking his head in wonder. "Eh? What did he look like?"

To our surprise, the man rumbled with laughter until his eyes shone with tears. "Like a toff disguised as an old-time highwayman, that's what. He came in here with a kerchief tied around his face."

We stared at the man as he leaned back in his chair. "You're joking," George said at last.

"Not me. I suppose the bloke thought if we recognized him, we'd write about his little antic in the paper. Not a bad idea at that," he added, poking a finger at me.

"Aside from his face, can you describe him?" George asked.

"About your size or a little bigger. Middle-aged, fair hair just turning to gray. Well dressed."

George turned to me. "Well, at least this time Charles has an alibi."

I frowned. That could describe quite a number of gentlemen. But it could also describe Gordon Archer. "Is that all that happened? He came in to your office, shouted, and left?"

"Well, he left after two of the gents from down the hall stepped in to see what the shouting was about. I thought he was riled enough to start throwing punches. Instead he just slithered out. Gave me a funny feeling."

"Yet you didn't contact the police?"

"What? Because some toff comes in and kicks up a fuss? Bah!" Mosley waved a dismissive hand.

"Well, I'm pleased you decided to establish the new rules," George said, "but for heaven's sake, never say you're relying on Mr. Ryan to keep intruders in the front office. Perhaps Delaney can post a constable here."

Mosley scoffed. "Never needed a guard before."

"I'm certain Mr. Norton would disagree with you. In addition, Mrs. er, Smith received a rather angry missive in the group of letters you gave me yesterday. Not threatening, but somewhat unnerving. We came here today, in part, to warn you."

"Sorry to hear that, ma'am." Mosley did indeed seem regretful. "It does tend to come along with the business though."

"Did Mrs. Archer receive angry or threatening letters?"

"I'd be surprised if she didn't. She might have mentioned them to Norton, but I never heard about them." He opened a drawer and pulled out a large envelope. "Here are today's responses." He handed the envelope to me.

"I think I should open them here. If you can spare us the time, that is," I said to Mosley. "We have been dropping some provocative hints in the columns. You should be aware of who may be barging in to your office tomorrow."

He made a sort of "go ahead" gesture with his hand. "I won't object to a word of warning."

Though it was clear a warning wouldn't necessarily spur him to action.

There were three letters. After reading each I passed them on to George. One was filled with praise for exposing the horrible acts of the upper class. Two were further pieces of gossip. I told Mr. Mosley what they contained in a general manner, without providing the details.

"It never occurred to me that Mrs. Archer obtained some of her information in this manner. Do you know if that's happened before?"

"Probably. But Norton would have urged her to confirm the stories before we used them."

"I'd say this means the hints you dropped in the first column are what brought forth the angry man," George said. "We should review those notes again to determine who Mary was talking about. Perhaps a tall, middle-aged man recognized himself."

Perhaps. But that still left us with the problem of determining if he was just a reader angry about a column, or if he was our killer.

Chapter 17

It was shortly after noon when George and I left the offices of the *Observer*. The sky threatened rain but for the moment we remained dry, and the clouds served to relieve the heat of the past few days. In fact, it was quite refreshing.

"There's one more task I'd like to accomplish before we meet with Delaney," George said as he assisted me into his carriage. "If you don't mind accompanying me, that is."

"I don't mind at all." I settled into the seat and busied myself with my veil. "But Lily and I have an appointment with the modiste this afternoon so I can't spare more than an hour or two."

He gave instructions to the driver and climbed in beside me. "That should be plenty of time and I doubt you'll want to miss this."

"Just where are we going?"

"You sound rather suspicious."

"That grin you're wearing is decidedly mischievous. I *am* suspicious."

The grin became a smirk. "I think it's time we took our investigation to Mr. Norton's home, don't you?"

"Are you joking?" I gestured to the window. "It's broad daylight."

"Ah, Frances." He placed a hand over his heart and heaved a theatrical sigh. "You don't wish to be seen with me."

"I don't wish to be seen breaking into someone's home, with or without you. How can you even consider it?"

"That doesn't say much for your sense of adventure, but as you wish." He reached into the pocket of his waistcoat and removed a latchkey.

"Norton's key, I presume?" I angled my head to scowl at him around the brim of my hat. "I suppose you think you're very clever."

"Well, I don't know if I'd say *very clever*. But more so than the average lout."

"How did you obtain it?"

"I discovered it when we inspected Norton's office the other day."

"But the office had been cleaned. There was nothing in his desk."

"Yes, but there was an overcoat hanging in the closet." He tossed the key in the air and caught it in an elegant motion. "This key was in the pocket."

My lips parted on a gasp. "Delaney missed it?"

"Delaney wasn't the inspector in charge, remember? Besides, the police wouldn't have needed this key to enter Norton's flat. They simply would have acquired one from the landlord."

"Then it's likely the police have already searched his flat."

He nodded. "But if they missed this key, one wonders what they might have missed at his home."

I gazed at him in admiration. "I'm beginning to think you are very clever. But what of this landlord you mentioned? Key or no key, won't he be curious about two strangers entering Norton's flat?"

He lifted his shoulders in a shrug. "I'm hoping he won't be in residence, but at any rate, we'll soon find out."

We must be near our destination then. I hadn't paid attention to our route. Curious, I glanced out the window. The area looked familiar. "Isn't that Portman Square?"

He stretched across me to see for himself, his hands on the window frame next to my head. "It is indeed."

"But aren't we going to Mr. Norton's home?" I tried, and failed, to push him back to his seat. Instead, he turned toward me, his devilish grin mere inches from my face. I laughed and pushed against his chest.

"For goodness' sake, sit down."

"Not until you tell me what you're thinking. I can see you've almost put it together."

"Very well. We are on Baker Street, are we not?"

He gave me a nod.

"Was Mr. Norton by chance a neighbor to Mary Archer?"

"Excellent detection, Lady Harleigh." He dropped a kiss on my nose and moved back to his seat.

"I'd been wondering how she'd come to work for him. If they were neighbors, they must have known each other casually at least. Though I'm surprised he lived in Mayfair."

"He didn't. He was at least a block north of Mrs. Archer's home, which places him in Marylebone. Does that better suit your aristocratic sensibilities?"

I threw him a dark glare. "I'm no snob, George, as you well know. Mayfair is an expensive area to live. I simply wondered how he could afford it. Since we'd previously suspected blackmail . . ." I lifted my shoulder, allowing the words to trail off.

A smile spread across his lips like a slow-moving stream. "Have I told you I love the way your mind works?"

Was he never serious? "How long have you known they were neighbors?"

His smile inched down on one side. "I'm ashamed to admit, only since this morning when I finally checked the direction Mosley had written for me."

The carriage stopped before a large, double-fronted house

and we climbed out. George told his driver to walk the horses then escorted me at a quick clip to the first door of the house, fitted the key in the lock, pushed the door open, and drew me inside. I barely had a chance to blink.

Far from the bachelor quarters I'd expected, the house was compact but cozy. The entry led into a parlor in one direction and a stairway in the other. We both moved to the small parlor. I glanced around while George turned up the gas on the fixture overhead. Two cozy armchairs sat in front of the hearth, a low table between them. Two matching chairs stood against the wall, ready to be pulled into service near the hearth if needed. A desk and writing table took up a considerable space under the window.

"What's your impression?" He moved beside me.

"It's incredibly tidy, wouldn't you say? I know Mr. Norton wasn't killed here, but wouldn't the police have come to search the house?"

His lips compressed to a thin line. "If they have, someone's clearly cleaned up after them. There may be no point in searching, but since we're here, we might just as well."

"Search for what, in particular?" I asked.

"Paperwork, I'd wager. Documents, perhaps even photographs. If they were going to expose someone, they had to keep the evidence somewhere."

"If the murderer doesn't already have it."

He shrugged. "That's always been a possibility." He waved a hand toward the desk. "Why don't you start here? I'll search the rest of the house for a safe or some other hiding place."

It seemed highly unlikely I'd find anything worthwhile in the desk. I heard George move through the dining room as I ran my gloved fingers over the writing table. Not so much as a speck of dust. With a shrug, I lowered the writing panel of the desk to reveal a clutter of paper and stuffed cubbyholes. Ah, perhaps I'd been too hasty in my judgment.

I pulled the chair over and began my search with the loose pages, scanning them and placing them upside down in a stack. Nothing. Nothing. Nothing. Cubbyholes next. Removing some rolled papers from the first one sent up a cloud of dust. I made a mental note to clean my own desk as I shook out the pages. How long did it take for so much dust to collect? A letter within the rolled pages was dated more than a year ago. Not likely to help.

My gaze landed on an envelope in one of the center cubbies, one not coated with dust. I pulled it out and saw Mr. Norton's name written across the front. My heart beat a little faster when I recognized Mary's writing. I pulled out the note inside and groaned. The same bloody note we'd found in Mary's file. The one we couldn't decipher. If she'd sent a copy to Norton, it must be important.

A scream tore through the silence, followed by a growl of pain.

George! I jumped to my feet and rushed toward the sound. It had come from the back of the house, probably the kitchen. Passing through the dining room, I swept up a large glass pitcher, then pushed through a swinging door into the kitchen.

Highly placed windows lined the back wall, allowing for abundant sunlight. But it was the room's occupants that made me blink. George leaned against the wall near the door, his teeth barred and his hand pressed against his head.

"Dammit, woman! That hurt."

He was not speaking to me. Backed up against a worktable stood a gray-haired, rather round woman. She wore a dark maid's uniform with a stained white apron and wielded a broom like a broadsword.

She lunged toward me and I held up the pitcher as if that would protect me. In one swipe, George grabbed the straw end of the broom and wrenched it from her hands.

"We aren't here to hurt you," I said. "Or to steal anything. We're completely harmless."

Without her weapon she appeared older and quite defenseless. Still, she fairly spat at me. "Then whotcher doin' 'ere?"

"We're investigating a murder." George's voice was thick with suspicion. "The question is, what are *you* doing here?"

"The landlord asked me to come an' give the place a clean." She straightened her spine and stretched herself up to a height that would place her barely at the top of my shoulder.

Still holding the broom, he stepped around the worktable and pushed open a door along the side of the room, revealing a cramped sleeping quarters. The sheets on the bed were tumbled. He raised a brow as he turned back to the woman. "Did he ask you to move in as well?"

She sniffed. "It's where I used to live afore Mr. Norton died and the landlord threw me out. Now I'm back in."

"You were his housekeeper?" She was the most unkempt housekeeper I'd ever seen.

"I cooked for 'em. Cleaned this 'ouse and others around 'ere." Her gaze took in the both of us. "You really investigatin' 'is murder?"

George closed the bedroom door and gestured to the dining room. "Perhaps we should sit down and have a chat."

Seated around the table, George explained our mission, which was of some interest to the woman, whose name, we learned, was Mrs. Wiggins. She told us of her own bustling, if exhausting, enterprise. In exchange for room and board, she cooked and cleaned for Mr. Norton, took in some light laundry, and cleaned five other houses in the neighborhood, including Mary Archer's.

"It was me wot introduced them," she said, with a sad shake of her head. "Not long after 'er 'usband passed, I could tell money was running low. She let all the servants go and put me on one day a week. I mentioned 'er situation to Mr. Norton and 'e got the idea to give 'er some work. Never dreamed it'd lead to such a bad end. But you think it's whot she wrote whot got 'em killed?"

"Do you know what she wrote?" I asked.

"Just gossip 'bout toffs, far as I know. She wasn't too keen on it at first. Took 'er to the market down the street a-ways, and we got into a good jaw-waggin' with some friends of mine. They started givin' her bits and bobs regular-like, so from there I left 'er on 'er own. Don't know whot she'd write that'd make someone kill 'er. Kill 'em both."

There was regret, and horror, in the woman's eyes. I reached across the table and squeezed her hand. "I don't think it was something she wrote, but something she planned to write. Something much bigger. And I think I know what it is."

I almost laughed at the expressions of astonishment on both their faces.

"Let me get it." I slipped in to the parlor and returned with the cryptic note, handing it to George. "Mary has one exactly like it except hers is older. She must have copied it for Norton."

Though he looked skeptical, I persisted. "It's the only one we haven't deciphered and the only one I found in Norton's desk. There was nothing else from Mary here. It must have something to do with the column they were about to publish."

His brows dipped downward as he stared at the note. "But what does it say?"

I sighed. "I have no idea."

The conversation with Mrs. Wiggins kept us longer than anticipated. We left her at Mr. Norton's house—the poor woman had nowhere else to go after all—and made it through the light traffic swiftly. Still, a cab was already waiting at my door when we pulled up.

Climbing out of George's carriage, I held up one finger to the cabman and slipped into the house where Lily awaited me in the hall, bouncing on her toes with excitement.

"Thank heavens, you made it," she said. "Are you ready?"

There was no time to change, but I supposed I was presentable. I took a glance in the wall mirror, to be sure. Straightening my hat, I turned and gave her a smile. "Let's be off."

There was just room for the two of us in the open cab. Lily closed the half door in front of us and once we were cozily settled and moving down the street, I caught some of her enthusiasm. "Have you considered the color and fabric for your dress? As it's your engagement party, all eyes will be on you."

Wisps of Lily's fair hair floated in the breeze. She pulled them away from her face and gave me a curious frown.

"What's wrong, dear?"

"Why is there a veil on your hat?"

I instinctively lifted my hand to my hat. The veil was still tucked neatly around the brim. "Oh, this? I didn't want to be recognized."

"Why not? Where on earth did Mr. Hazelton take you?" Indignation raised her voice an octave.

"To the office of the *Daily Observer*." I saw no need to mention the search of Mr. Norton's house. "I didn't want anyone to see me and suspect I was the new Miss Information."

"Ah, the investigation." She placed a gloved hand on my arm and leaned in. "For a moment I wondered if the two of you had just come from a clandestine rendezvous."

I chuckled. "There was no romance involved in our errand today, I assure you."

Lily tilted her head as she studied me. "Perhaps not today, but surely you have some sort of understanding?"

"We do not." I watched her expression to make sure she understood me. "I hope you haven't mentioned that to anyone else."

"Of course not." She caught her lower lip between her teeth. "Well, just Lottie and Aunt Hetty." She glanced nervously at my scowl. "And Mr. Evingdon."

"You've discussed this among you?" I turned to the window to hide my reddened cheeks. "Have the lot of you settled on a wedding date?"

"I thought spring would be nice."

"Lily!" I snapped my head back around.

She huffed. "I'm joking, Frances. But I truly don't know what you're waiting for. Neither of you grows any younger."

It was my turn to huff. "What makes you think he wants to marry me? I'm an aging widow, as you just pointed out, with a child and no fortune. I have nothing to offer a man like George. Mr. Hazelton, that is."

Lily turned on me with an expression of exaggerated patience. "I think he wants to marry you because he clearly admires you. I see how he looks at you, how he spends as much time as possible in your company, even to the point of sharing his work with you."

I opened my mouth to speak, but she cut me off with a wave of her hand.

"Mr. Hazelton isn't required to find a bride with an illustrious lineage or buckets of money. He's a third son. He can marry whom he chooses, and it's clear you are his choice. I just don't understand why he hasn't already asked you."

My fingers twined together as I gazed off at the passing traffic, the roof of the cab, anywhere but at my sister. "Ah, well . . ."

Lily's gasp nearly jolted me from my seat. I turned to see her clutching her chest as if in pain. "He *has* asked you!"

"Ah, um. Well."

"And you demurred." She shook her head in amazement. "What is wrong with you, Frances? Don't even consider trying to tell me you don't love him."

The cab jerked to a stop before I could form a response.

"Ah, here we are." Lily released a little squeal of excitement and clutched my arm. "I'm getting married, Frances. I only hope Leo and I will have the type of relationship you and Mr. Hazelton share."

Gathering her skirts in one hand, she pushed open the door and climbed out, then popped her head back into the cab, eyes wide, blond curls bouncing.

"Well?"

I collected myself and followed her out to the street. My sister was moving faster than me in more ways than one.

Madame Celeste was my favorite modiste. It made no difference if Lily stopped in for half a dozen new gowns, or if I brought in old gowns to be refurbished. She treated us each as if we were her favorite customer. The moment the bell jingled on the door, Madame took Lily into her care. She led us to a dressing room, positioned Lily before a full-length mirror, and began draping her in bright silks to see the effect of each color on her skin.

With Lily's hat in my custody, I took a seat off to the side of the small room where I could watch the proceedings and listen to their chatter, while indulging my thoughts. Lily had asked a very good question—what *was* wrong with me? When I married Reggie, I was a commodity on the marriage market. He enjoyed the revenues, but I held no other place in his life—just an investment he'd purchased with his title.

Lily was right. I had no evidence to believe George viewed me in that manner. The little evidence I did have indicated quite the opposite. A life with him would be completely different from my first marriage. Wouldn't it?

The bell on the door jangled again, causing Madame to jerk around in surprise.

"I'll be just a moment, *ma petite*," she said before swishing through the curtain separating this room from the front of the shop.

"How do you like this color?" Lily asked, as I heard Madame Celeste greet Lady Caroline Archer in the other room.

Lily drew a length of deep violet silk across her shoulders. I examined the effect in the mirror while straining to hear the exchange outside the curtain. "Perhaps the rose," I said, wishing they'd raise their voices just a bit. I couldn't hear a thing.

"No, I already have too much of that color. Maybe the blue?"

"I'm sure that would be lovely, dear. Excuse me a moment, won't you?"

Damn my curiosity. I parted the curtain and stepped out. "Caroline, I thought that was you." My polite smile faded with the coldness of her gaze.

She turned back to Madame Celeste. "So, tomorrow afternoon?"

"Yes, my lady. Everything should be ready by then."

"Excellent." She picked up her bag from the counter and flicked a quick glance my way. "Lady Harleigh, if you have a moment?"

Clearly relieved at the dismissal, Madame backed through the curtains where Lily waited for her. I turned to Caroline in confusion.

"Is something wrong?"

She looped her reticule over her wrist and adjusted her glove. "Well, if you consider bringing a murderer into my home wrong, then yes, something is wrong."

Heavens, where had this come from? "Are you referring to my cousin Charles?"

"Of course." She lifted stormy hazel eyes to mine, daring me to dispute her claim.

I most definitely dared.

"You've been misinformed, Caroline. I don't know who told you such a malicious lie, but I'll thank you not to spread it further."

She raised a brow. "Are you saying he was not arrested by the police?"

We'd moved closer to one another, our whispers like the hissing of cats.

"That is precisely what I'm saying. Because he was close to

Mary, the inspector in charge had questions he hoped Mr. Evingdon could answer. He was never arrested."

"I heard the only reason he was let go was because his brother pulled some strings. That doesn't negate his guilt." She gave me a glare of pure venom. "I know what the two of you are about. You're trying to find someone else to blame for dear Mary's death. That's why you visited me, hoping to learn of some disagreement between us."

Clenching my teeth, I barely held my temper in check. "You are wrong, Caroline. And if you spread this rumor any further, you will unfairly blacken my cousin's good name and make yourself an object of ridicule when the murderer is discovered."

She drew herself up and raised her chin. "The truth will out," she said. Pulling open the door, she stormed out to the street.

The truth will out if I had anything to say about it. And just when had her sister-in-law become "dear Mary"?

Chapter 18

$\iff$

M̲y head was already spinning with information by the time we returned to the house and I prepared for our meeting with Delaney, but I was still eager for his findings. As I made my way back downstairs with one of Lily's sketch pads, I met Mrs. Thompson on her way up to tell me she'd left the gentlemen in the drawing room. Perfect. I gave her instructions to bring tea and stepped in to greet them.

George was comfortably ensconced on the sofa, his arm draped across the back. Delaney perched on the edge of the chair next to him and Charles, looking very ill at ease, paced behind the sofa. Perhaps it wasn't the best idea to have him in a room with Delaney, but George had brought him, and he usually knew what he was doing. The two seated men stood until I joined George on the sofa, the sketch pad in my lap. I planned to document our information and try to make sense of this case.

"An excellent idea, Frances," George said. "Perhaps we'll see some connections." He turned to Delaney. "Since we both have information about Mrs. Archer's murder, would you prefer to discuss her case before we discuss Mr. Norton's investigation?"

Delaney nodded. "The coroner puts her time of death on Tuesday evening, no later than eight o'clock," he said. "We also know the man seen at her house could not have been Mr. Norton because he returned from picking up her columns at about seven."

"Crikey, please tell me you're not considering me a suspect once more." Charles's face was drawn in concern.

Delaney pursed his lips as if he'd rather not speak at all. "No," he said, finally spitting out the word. "As it turns out, one of the neighbors confirmed your story just last night."

George raised a brow. "You're still interviewing neighbors?"

"The gentleman who lives across the way from Mrs. Archer left to visit a relative Wednesday morning. The constable posted at the house saw him return yesterday and took his statement. He recognized your chaise when you drove past the house, having seen it a few times at Mrs. Archer's in the past weeks. Apparently, he admires your equipage."

"Ah! A good eye," Charles said with a bit of bluster.

"Yes, well, he confirmed you didn't stop that night, but just drove by."

"Did he see the other man?" I asked.

Delaney grimaced. "Not well, but he did see someone leave her house and climb into a carriage waiting around the corner."

"If the man was not the editor, nor Mr. Evingdon, do you assume he's the murderer?" So far, I'd written nothing on the sketch pad aside from the time of death.

"We do." Delaney gave me a firm nod. "Particularly because witnesses noticed a man fitting the same description near the *Daily Observer* offices at approximately half past eight that night. He emerged from the alley that runs to the back of the building. Mr. Norton was last seen in his office shortly after seven o'clock. As two of the clerks were leaving for the day, they walked past his office and bid him good evening. He told them to latch the front office door before they left through the back door, leaving it unlocked. They claim Norton was the last person in the building aside from the printers."

George leaned forward. "The printers were in the building when Norton was murdered and they neither saw nor heard anything?"

"Unfortunately, no. The printing operation is quite noisy so the machine room is isolated from the offices in another building across a small yard. Once the presses are operating, the workers would have no idea of the comings and goings in this building. But one of them stepped outside with his pipe about half past nine and noticed all the windows were dark. If Norton were alive and working, he'd have lit the lamp by then."

Mrs. Thompson knocked on the door just then and brought in the tea things. The interruption allowed me time to jot down the few things we'd covered. Once she left, and we were all served, I perused the notes.

"If Mary was murdered no later than eight o'clock, and the clerks saw Norton at seven, can we even tell which of them was murdered first?" I turned to Charles. "What time did you drive by Mary's house?"

"Between seven and half past."

"Half past seven? I thought you said it was dark."

He frowned. "It was dark. It was raining. Clouds overhead, mist settling in. That's why I couldn't see the other man clearly. If he was the killer, I'd say he got to her first."

"Would that give the murderer enough time to travel to the newspaper offices before eight?"

"He had a carriage nearby. At that time of night traffic into the city would be light. I think he could do it with ease," George said.

I went back to my writing. "All right, then. Mary was murdered around half past seven and Mr. Norton no more than an hour later. Other than the unknown man, I don't suppose your constables found any clues at either location?"

"Nothing other than the files at Mrs. Archer's house. And we don't yet know how helpful they'll be. Mr. Norton's office was chock-full of odds and ends." He pulled his notebook from his pocket and leafed through the pages. "The inspector from that case gave me a detailed inventory."

He handed the list to George. I moved behind the sofa to read over his shoulder. Just the usual things one would expect to find in an office.

George returned the list to Delaney. "Would have been helpful if he'd left a calling card."

Delaney tsked. "Criminals these days." He folded the page back into his notebook.

I bit my lip as a thought struck me. "Do you know what else is missing?"

All three men turned to me. "The column. Not that I would expect it to be part of the inspector's inventory, but we know it's missing because Mr. Mosley told us."

"Mosley told you something was missing from the office, but he didn't mention this to the police?" Delaney's bushy brows were drawn dangerously low.

I held up a finger. "He didn't exactly tell us it was missing." I paused to collect my thoughts, certain two of the men in this room thought I was wasting their time. Charles likely didn't care.

"I wrote two columns for Mr. Mosley. One was to be published on Wednesday and the other on Thursday. But when Mr. Hazelton delivered them, Mr. Mosley insisted I write one more. He wanted to keep to his regular schedule and Mrs. Archer always delivered three columns on Tuesdays—one each for Wednesday through Friday."

My announcement was met with blank stares.

"Mosley only ran a column on Wednesday and Thursday. He didn't have one for Friday because the killer took it."

Delaney scowled. "Isn't it just as likely she deviated from her schedule?"

"No," George said. "Lady Harleigh's correct. Mosley insisted I return with the additional column as they never deviated from the schedule."

"If the killer took it," I continued, "it suggests Mr. Hazelton's theory is correct. Mary and Norton were about to expose someone. He murdered them and took the evidence."

George shook his head. "He took the column. We still have the files so we may well have the evidence here."

"How are they sorted?" Delaney asked. "Did she keep the notes after she'd written the columns?"

"Yes, but what she wrote about in her regular column would hardly incite anyone to commit murder. I think we've found the note that's caused all the trouble. We just haven't determined what it means."

I stepped over to the card table to retrieve both copies of the note, remembering, belatedly, that we'd now have to explain where we found the second copy. I handed them both to Delaney and glanced expectantly at George as I settled in next to him. He pursed his lips and leaned forward.

"I suppose it's our turn to contribute information," he said. "One of those notes was in Mrs. Archer's files. The other we found at Norton's home."

Delaney brought his hand up to his face and massaged his jaw. "Just how did you get in there?"

"Housekeeper let us in." George gave him an innocent smile and relaxed back into the sofa.

"Housekeeper?"

"Mrs. Wiggins. A charming woman."

"The point is," I interrupted, "Mary made a copy of that note and gave it to Norton, which leads me to believe it's important. It was also one of the teasers we published Wednesday."

I explained to Delaney about including the hints of this scandalous material in the columns I wrote. "Only two of which have been published so far. I suspect this particular hint drew the attention of the man who visited Mr. Mosley at the *Observer* yesterday."

Delaney jerked his head up from his notebook. "What do you mean by 'visited'?"

"Someone made a surprise visit to the office and spoke to Mosley in a threatening manner," George said. "The man railed about the Miss Information column running again, and after creating quite a ruckus, he turned tail and ran when two other men from the office arrived at Mosley's door." He shrugged. "He did not provide his name, but he also fits the rather vague description of the man from the scene of both crimes."

Delaney frowned. "A name would have been most helpful. When did you say this happened?"

"Yesterday," I said. "So, it's possible he was alarmed by the publication of this note."

"Whose initials are these?" Delaney tapped the note with his finger.

"We weren't able to decipher this one."

He studied the note and narrowed his eyes. "This first group of initials could be businesses. *W-H & S*, for example. Hardly sounds like a person's name."

I leaned in to peer over his arm as he held the notes.

SSE, CTS, W-H & S, CACC. 6 March, 1898. LH, SH, LM, LR at least J.

"You're right. The first group of initials are unlikely to refer to individuals. I hadn't thought of businesses." Nor had I ever seen the notes side by side. "They're in two different hands. The newer one is Mary's writing, but I don't recognize the hand on the older note."

"I'll take these back with me and set my sergeant to searching for names of businesses that match these initials." I stopped him before he could tuck both notes into his book.

"May I keep the older one? I'd like to see if we have anything else from her files that matches the handwriting."

He handed over the note. "I'll station a constable at the newspaper office," he said.

"We warned Mosley this column might attract some unwanted attention. He was supposed to engage some type of security," George said.

Delaney gave a disgusted grunt. "Whether your column drew his attention or not, it's too much of a coincidence. His intruder fits the description of our murder suspect. Both victims were involved in writing a column for the *Observer*. And this man turns up at their office, throwing a fit about the column returning. He may be our man. I'll speak to Mosley tomorrow and see if he can give me a better description."

Delaney jotted some notes in his book and glanced up. "Is there anything else?"

"The three of us visited Mrs. Archer's house today." George held up his hand at Delaney's thunderous glare. "Mrs. Carr, Mary's sister, escorted us, as Mr. Evingdon might be interested in purchasing the house."

Delaney waved a dismissive hand. "Yes, yes. Of course he is. I assume you are confessing this only because you found something of interest there?"

"I'm not entirely certain. Did your men leave her study in disarray after their search?"

"They shouldn't have done." Delaney inched forward in his seat.

"That was the condition we found it in when we arrived, as though someone had upended all the drawers and spilled their contents onto the desk."

"I've had a constable stationed there since the murder."

"I saw him," George said. "Two nights ago, to be exact. He was removing Gordon Archer from the property."

"Yes, that was in Constable Evans's report. Archer said he was simply ensuring the place had been locked up."

"I don't mean to suggest Constable Evans was negligent in

his job, but is it possible Archer had already been inside the house when the constable found him?"

Delaney raised his brows. "You ask this because you found the house in disarray?"

"Only the study. If it wasn't your men, that means someone else was inside."

"Or someone managed to get in last night while your constable questioned the neighbor," Charles suggested.

"As much as I'd like to vouch for my men, I didn't see the room after they left. I'll check with Constable Evans though. Is there some reason you suspect Archer of entering the house other than the fact you saw him outside the property?"

"I have reason to suspect him," I said. "I spoke to both of the Archers briefly at the funeral and their attitude about Mary's murder was unsettling at the very least. They came very close to saying it was her own fault."

Delaney's brows drew together. "When I spoke to them they seemed quite distraught by the matter."

"At the funeral they claimed that by associating with a lower class of people and living on her own she was courting trouble. They were upset by her death, but still rather cold about it, especially Mr. Archer."

I held up a hand before he could reply. "Today I met up with Caroline Archer at the dressmaker. She was highly incensed that I brought Mr. Evingdon to her house two days ago because she understood he was a suspect in her dear sister-in-law's murder."

"Where did she hear such a thing?" Charles banged his fist on the back of the sofa, making George jump. He'd been so quiet I'd forgotten he was back there.

"I thought we'd managed to keep that quiet," he added.

"She didn't tell me where she heard it, but she was under the impression you'd actually been arrested, and I had the sense she'd find it very convenient if you were charged." I turned back to Delaney. "She accused me of visiting her with the hope of finding trouble between the Archers and Mary." I shrugged. "Of course, we were, but frankly her shift in attitude about Mary is suspicious, as is Mr. Archer's attempt to break into Mary's house."

I lifted my hands in a helpless gesture. "Can you question him about that?"

Much to my surprise, Delaney agreed. "I'd like to speak to him about the break-in at his sister-in-law's house, and I'd also like to find out how he learned we'd brought you in for questioning." He nodded to Charles. "We did keep that quiet."

Delaney's glance took each of us in. "Anything else?"

George chuckled. "No, I think that's about all we have."

We all came to our feet. "I'll continue to work on that note," I told Delaney as I walked him to the door. "Will you tell us what you learn from Mr. Archer? I realize I have no official capacity, but I'd like to know if you arrest him."

Delaney stopped, his hand on the doorknob. "Lady Harleigh, I've come to enjoy working with you in this unofficial capacity. But you know nothing about police work."

I bristled, but he held up a hand before I could speak.

"I'm going to talk to Archer about the break-in, but if he has any type of excuse, and I suspect he does, I have no cause to arrest him. We need a lot more evidence than we have now. So, unless I can lead him to a confession, you shouldn't expect to hear about an arrest."

He opened the door and stepped out. I made my way back to the drawing room where George and Charles were both seated on the sofa now.

"Delaney has no intention of arresting Gordon Archer," I said, dropping wearily into a chair.

"What? Not even for you?"

I looked up to see George grinning at me. I scowled back.

"There's not enough evidence, Frances, and you shouldn't put all your suspicion in one basket, as it were. Why are you so determined to see Archer as the culprit? There weren't any notes about him in her files."

"We haven't dug through the cache from our pillaging yet," Charles said with a glance toward George's document case.

"I think that's an excellent place to start." He rose to his feet. "Find some evidence that points to Archer, and Delaney may just accommodate you with an arrest."

"Wait, aren't you going to help us?"

He gave me a sheepish grin. "I've some work of my own to do but I have every confidence in the two of you. If there's something to find in that case of paperwork, I'm sure you'll find it." He smiled as he headed toward the door. "I do have one further suggestion, though. There's something important in that odd little note. Not only did both victims have a copy, but when it appeared in the column, it struck a nerve with someone. I'd try to find out what it says."

Chapter 19

With George gone, Charles and I had no choice but to return—albeit grudgingly—to work. He emptied the document case, filled with papers from Mary's desk, on to the card table. I returned to the sofa with the puzzling note. No matter how long I stared at it, it refused to solve itself. I was on the point of picking up a pencil to jot down names that could match the initials when a commotion in the hall drew my attention.

"For heaven's sake, don't drop her, Graham!"

Don't drop her? That was enough to break my fragile thread of concentration. I left the note on the table and opened the door.

Graham was indeed in the hall, accompanied by Hetty and Lottie, and carrying my daughter in his arms. A hundred horrifying scenes flashed through my mind in the blink of an eye. I stumbled to Graham's side on rubbery legs to touch Rose's warm cheek.

"What happened?"

They all spoke at once, creating a great deal of noise with no discernible explanation. Finally, Graham spoke above the din.

"She's fine, Frances. She fell off her pony and twisted her ankle. The doctor's already seen to her and it's neither broken nor sprained. Might I take her to her room while I still have the strength?"

He allowed Rose to droop in his arms, provoking a giggle from her and a sigh of relief from me. Leaving the others in the hall, Graham and I took Rose up to her room, fussed over her, and tucked her into bed. Little by little, the whole story came out.

"You tried to take Pierre over a hedge? What were you thinking?" Her face crumpled. She was seven. What was *I* thinking? Poor decisions should be expected.

"I called the doctor immediately when she and the boys came home," Graham assured me. "He's certain if she rests the ankle a day or two, she'll be fine."

"I'm sorry, Mummy."

I squeezed her hand. "I'm just glad you're all right, dearest. But we will talk about this later."

I gave instructions for Rose's dinner to be brought to her room tonight, and as her eyes drooped, headed downstairs with Graham.

"Thank heavens you were at home today, Graham."

He squeezed my shoulder, the aristocratic version of a warm hug, reminding me he did have a human side. "I should be returning there now," he said as we descended the stairs. "But may I offer a word of advice first?"

"Of course."

"It might be wise to distance ourselves from Cousin Charles, or at least not host him here so frequently." He slowed his steps so we lingered outside the drawing room. "I understand he is a suspect in Mrs. Archer's murder and we don't want such scandal touching the rest of us."

Bother, this story was spreading. "Where did you hear this?"

"Caroline Archer."

What was she up to? I took Graham by the arm and moved farther away from the drawing room. "Caroline is mistaken. Inspector Delaney has exonerated him of all suspicion, and in fact, he was never arrested in the first place."

Graham raised his brows. "Truly? Well, that's a relief. Always liked Cousin Charles. Would hate to think ill of him."

I drew a calming breath and reminded myself this man had just shown kindness to my child. Perhaps he wasn't beyond all hope. "If you hear this rumor from anyone else, I hope you'll put an end to it."

"I most certainly will." He squared his jaw and moved to the door. "Can't have anyone gossiping about the family."

I closed the door behind him and joined the others in the drawing room where Hetty served the tea. "I'm sorry to report, Charles, that Caroline Archer is still telling tales about you."

He dropped his head into his hands and groaned. I sat down next to Lottie on the sofa and told them what Graham had heard. I also informed Lottie and Hetty that Delaney had ceased to consider Charles a suspect.

"Yes, thanks to Hazelton and Lady Harleigh, I'm no longer a wanted man." He smiled at Lottie, who blushed, reached for her cup, and knocked over the sugar bowl. "I hope your afternoon's work has gone as well."

"We are not quite so deep in paperwork as the two of you seem to be," she said.

"Ah, this?" Charles said, indicating the new stack of papers on the card table. "Account books, receipts, and miscellaneous notes from Mrs. Archer's house."

"Would you like some help in sorting through it?"

"Lottie, my dear, you are indefatigable," Hetty said, filling a plate with a selection of treats from the tea tray.

I wasn't sure if that was the right word. She was definitely a helpful sort, but I daresay her offer had more to do with spending time with Charles. Well, she could certainly do worse.

"Yes, dear. If you're willing, please do assist Mr. Evingdon while I work on this note." *And enjoy a much-needed cup of tea.*

Charles stood and motioned for Lottie to precede him to the card table where our cache from Mary's house lay. She hesitated. He insisted. I rolled my eyes and turned away from the inevitable moment when they would both move at once and knock one another down. Instead I picked up Lily's sketchbook.

"It's a good thing Lily hasn't been sketching much lately," Hetty said. "It appears you are putting that pad to a more practical use."

I gave her a smile. It was Hetty's idea to use the pad and easel a few months ago during our last investigation, which was also my first. In the intervening months, I'd never once considered we'd need it again for such a similar purpose.

"Are you any closer to solving this one yet?"

"Not a whit. No witnesses, or rather witnesses who saw only a figure of a man, allowing for only a vague description."

Hetty frowned. "How vague?"

"Enough that it could be stretched to fit dozens of suspects. The man was seen nearby at the time of both murders. The only thing the two victims have in common is the column. So, we keep returning to them to search for our suspects."

"And the stacks and stacks of notes for potential columns," Lottie added. "Perhaps we should go through them all, identifying the subjects involved and set aside any who fit the description of the man seen at the crimes."

I watched her and Charles interact as I considered her suggestion. She'd watch him through lowered lashes until he turned her way. Then she'd quickly avert her gaze. He drew up a chair for her comfort, carefully stacking the papers before handing them off for her review. His gaze lingered on her from the side.

Well, at least something good might come of this investigation.

"Actually, Lottie, we may be beyond that now. We think one of the hints we published attracted the intruder to the *Daily Observer*."

"There was an intruder at the *Observer?*"

Charles brought her up to date on that point.

"Then is the intruder also the murderer?" she asked.

"Frances thinks it's Gordon Archer."

Hetty turned a sharp glance toward me. "Why do you view him as a suspect?"

I rubbed a spot between my eyebrows that was beginning to throb. "According to Mr. Hazelton and Inspector Delaney, we have no reason to believe he would do anything to harm Mrs. Archer or the editor." I shrugged. "And they're correct. But I can't quite drop him as a suspect in my mind. Particularly when his wife persists in condemning Charles. I have no evidence. I simply don't like his attitude about Mary, or that he tried to break into her house."

"He also has a habit of leading clients into risky investments," Hetty said.

"*Leading* might be overstating it," Charles said. "He advises them, but they asked him for that advice."

"He advised me to open an account in the five percents. Not much of a risk there." I looked up at Hetty. "What about Graham's investment—that shipping company? Did you ever manage to find out if they were insured?"

"They are most certainly not insured." Hetty's voice was filled with outrage. "In fact, I learned the company doesn't even exist."

"How do you mean, they don't exist?"

"It means there is no such company," Charles supplied in a helpful tone.

"I know what 'doesn't exist' means, Charles. What I don't understand is how it is possible that a company Graham invested in doesn't exist."

I held up a hand as he opened his mouth to answer. "Perhaps Aunt Hetty could explain it better."

The three of us turned our attention to her. "In a way, Mr. Evingdon got it right. I had a conversation with Mr. Kendrick before meeting with Graham this morning. He used his resources to investigate the name on the stock certificate Archer gave to Graham." She shook her head. "There is no such company registered in England or any other country who trades with Brazil."

I wasn't quite following her. "Does that mean the investment was fraudulent?"

"Exactly. While I suppose it's possible Archer was also defrauded, the fact that he passed on the stock certificates makes me wonder if he were in on the hoax. If not actually running it himself."

Stunned, I moved closer to Hetty, lowering myself into the chair facing her. "How exactly does this happen? How does someone perpetrate such a hoax as you call it?"

"Well, I've never actually been involved in this sort of thing before," she said. "But I understand the general idea. To gain one's confidence, someone like Archer offers sound investment advice. The fact that he's a principle at a bank gives him a certain gravitas, but since the board could have him removed, he must make some good investments. While doing so, he'll keep an eye out for clients he can dupe. Someone who doesn't pay much attention to his finances. Sooner or later, he'll contact those people and tell them about an amazing opportunity, something they shouldn't miss. A few may take him up on the offer and invest with him. At first, he may actually invest their money somewhere, and he'll return their investment after a time, with interest or dividends."

Hetty took a sip of tea and Lottie picked up the thread. "Once he has their trust, he then lets it drop that he's on to an amazing deal. A very exclusive private investment. The returns promise to be spectacular. Yes, of course, there are a few risks, but he considers them to be minor so he is putting as much of his own capital as possible into the deal." She shrugged as if imitating the swindler.

"Don't stop now." With a motion of her hand, Hetty encouraged her assistant to proceed with the explanation.

"The potential investor is so excited he begs to be let in on the deal. The swindler pulls back. This is a long-term investment, he cautions. You can't expect quick returns, you must be in for the long run, but it will be worth the wait."

"Heavens, Lottie! You are so compelling, I'm ready to force my money on you." And I clearly wasn't the only one entranced by her story. Though I didn't think Charles's mind was on money.

"That's exactly how it works," Hetty said. "The swindler paints an enticing picture, then pulls back just enough to make the investor pursue him."

"But eventually, he accepts the money, doesn't he?" I asked.

Hetty's eyes widened. "Of course, but he waits until just the moment before the investor is about to give up. Then over the course of time he can remind the investor that he begged to be involved in this deal. That's how he manages their expectations."

I was still a little lost. Fortunately, Charles voiced the question I was trying to form.

"But if there really is no company to invest in, what does he do with the money?"

"For the most part, it goes into his pocket," Hetty replied. "Here and there he may dole some out to one of his clients and call it a return on his investment. That way he can string them along a little while longer. At the same time, he tells another client or two that the project went bankrupt, or the shipment was lost at sea, or the company went under. And all their money was lost."

Lottie chimed in. "But remember, he did warn them about the risks."

Hetty let out a snort of disgust. "It's a devious trick. They were never going to get their money back."

"Are you telling me he's simply stealing from them? That's horrible."

"It goes far beyond horrible. I believe Archer perpetrated a fraud on Graham though it's going to take a great deal of convincing to make him realize it."

"He doesn't believe you?"

Hetty spread her hands. "Who wants to believe they were played for a fool? Especially to the tune of six thousand pounds."

"Goodness!" Lottie gasped. "I had no idea it was that much."

"It jolly well sounds like Archer's a criminal," Charles added.

"Actually, you're right." Hetty seemed surprised to be saying those words. "This is definitely a crime and should be reported to the police."

"Wait!" I shouted, as if one of them were off to alert the police at that moment. "It's not only a crime, it's also a motive."

Hetty frowned in confusion. "A motive for what, my dear?"

"A motive for murder."

Chapter 20

Waiting for George to return was out of the question. I slipped out the back of my house into his garden and tapped on the library window. Seated at his desk, he jumped at my tap and made a show of clutching his chest before rising from his desk and meeting me at the drawing room door. Honestly, one would think he'd be used to this by now.

"You have some new information?" he asked, leading me back to the library.

I seated myself in a guest chair at his desk and gave him a sly smile as he walked around to the other side.

"Ah, you look decidedly pleased about something." A smile crept across his lips and he watched me, his fingers steepled in front of him.

I caught myself. "Actually, it's terrible news and I've no right to be pleased." As I gave him a brief explanation of Archer's activities, at least as they pertained to Graham, his smile compressed to an angry line, his shoulders tensed. I knew I needn't go on.

"Hetty can explain the whole business to you if you like. I'm sure she'd do it better. But from what I understand of this, I find it hard to believe Graham is the only victim."

"No, he wouldn't be. If what you're telling me is true, and I don't mean to say I'm questioning your information," he quickly added upon seeing my scowl, "Archer wouldn't stop at one victim." He leaned back in his chair and stroked his chin, thinking.

"You see what this means, don't you? Archer now has a motive for murder."

He raised a hand to slow me down. "Now you're jumping to conclusions. I completely understand Archer would never want a breath of this to get out, but we have no reason to believe Mary was aware of his unsavory business dealings."

I slumped against the back of my chair. Oh, dear. He was right. "There was not one piece of gossip or scandal as inflammatory as this in her files. If she knew what Archer was doing, then he would be the most likely suspect. But I have no idea if she knew." How terribly disappointing. "What can we do?"

George was still lost in his thoughts. "Mrs. Wiggins said she took Mrs. Archer to the market near her home and introduced her to some friends," he mused. "That would mean maids and housekeepers."

I nodded. "If you think about it, they're the perfect source for this type of information. Servants are aware of everything that happens in a household, and we often confide a great deal of private information as well. When a master cheats them, as Graham did, or discharges them, or somehow treats them ill, what's to stop them from selling information, or gossip if you will, to a ready buyer?"

I leaned forward on the desk, my chin resting on my fist. "Her knowledge of Archer's exploits would explain why she chose to work for her living and refused to take any support from him. In her eyes, his money was tainted."

He raised his brows. "But that brings us back to the same question. How would she know?"

"Well, her husband was his brother." I frowned. "Was Jasper involved with the bank?"

"I completely forgot about that connection. He was employed there, but transactions of this sort would never have been sanctioned by the bank. Archer did this on his own. Unless his brother was in on the scheme, I doubt he would have known."

We both pondered this for a moment. "I have to disagree with you. They were brothers. They worked in the same building, lived in the same house. Even if Jasper wasn't involved in the scheme he might very well have found out, just considering the amount of time they spent together. Gordon Archer might have unconsciously mentioned it, or perhaps they argued about money." I spread my hands as I pled my case. "It's even possible someone who lost a lot of money complained to Jasper and he investigated the cause, thus finding his brother out."

"Are you assuming Jasper told Mary?"

I shook my head at the hopelessness of ever learning the truth. "We will never know."

He raised a finger. "I'm not so sure of that. It would certainly help to learn if there were other victims of Archer's scheme. If indeed it was his scheme. I can check at the clubs for others who lost large amounts of money with him. A little conversation might lead me to finding out if anyone mentioned it to Jasper."

That sounded like a good start. "Well, we already determined that servants know everything that goes on in a household. If we can learn who worked for Jasper—as a valet, perhaps—we can put some questions to him."

"What sort of questions could you ask without giving yourself away?"

"Arguments between Mary and Jasper about family funds? Or arguments between the brothers?" I shrugged. "Leading questions."

"And how do you find out who held that position? It's been well over a year since Jasper died."

"That part should be easy. The papers you brought from Mary's house included the household account books. Her payments to servants would be among them. I should have no problem finding a name. Finding where he is now"—I twisted my lips in a crooked smile—"that will be the problem."

When George left in pursuit of swindled investors, I returned home to find an empty drawing room. I alternately basked in the silence and wondered where everyone had gone as I crossed the room to the card table and dug into the stack of Mary's documents. It took only a moment to find an old account book, which included regular payments to her servants—one John Milton among them. Through process of elimination, and the comparison of wages, I determined him to be Jasper's valet. Though I was rather pleased at discovering this bit of information, I still had no idea how I was to locate the man. Then I realized I had a source at Mr. Norton's house.

I rang for Mrs. Thompson and penned a short note, stopping just before my signature. Heavens, what if Mrs. Wiggins couldn't read?

"Yes, my lady?"

Mrs. Thompson stood in the doorway. What to do? "Do you know if our kitchen boy is able to read, Mrs. Thompson?"

"Young Jamie?" She bobbed her head. "He reads some. Practices when he can."

"Excellent." I handed her the note. "I need him to deliver this tomorrow morning to the housekeeper at that address. Early, before she has a chance to leave. He may have to help her with the note, and the reply. Is he up to that?"

"I'm sure he is. I'll see he gets off early in the morning." Mrs. Thompson nodded and made as if to take her leave.

"Wait, Mrs. Thompson. When I left, I had a drawing room full of guests. Do you have any idea where everyone is?"

"They've all gone up to visit Lady Rose."

I raised my brows. "I think I will as well."

I thanked Mrs. Thompson and headed up to the nursery. Rose's room was across the schoolroom, next to Nanny's. A strip of light shone under both doors. Laughter greeted me as I opened Rose's door and stopped immediately upon my arrival. Hetty sat on the end of the bed, with Lottie, Charles, and even Lily gathered around. Each one wore a guilty expression. Poor Rose just looked pained.

"All right, I think Rose has had all the entertainment she can stand for one evening." I made a shooing motion to the adults. "Once her pain has subsided, she'll better appreciate your humor. For now, the doctor has asked her to be still and quiet."

Rose winced as Hetty leaned forward to kiss her cheek. To my surprise, they all departed without a word, though Hetty threw me a warning glare. I couldn't help smiling, pleased Rose had a champion in her aunt. When the door closed behind them, I pulled up a chair next to her bed. Folding my hands in my lap, I gazed down at her.

"It can be very difficult to entertain when one is in pain."

She gave me a wary glance. "It hurts."

I wanted to gather her into my arms and magically take all her pain away. Knowing I didn't have that power, I took her hand. If I couldn't protect her from hurt, I could at least arm her against it. But first I had to know why.

"Rose," I began.

"I'm sorry, Mummy." Her little face crumpled and tears squeezed out from her closed eyes. "I know you told me Pierre wasn't a jumper, but Eldon thought he'd do it and I wanted to be like the boys."

I shushed her and murmured comforting words. "I understand, dear."

Her tears stopped as if someone had turned off the tap. "Then you're not angry? I'm not in trouble?"

"Just because I understand does not mean I approve. You are

seven years old and I will be making decisions concerning your safety for the foreseeable future."

She sniffed and gazed up at me with watery eyes. "I'll be eight next month," she whispered.

"That's still too young to make such big decisions, but . . ." I paused, wondering how I should state this. I didn't want her to feel she was being rewarded. "I believe eight is old enough to take riding and perhaps jumping lessons."

She gasped and I had to suppress a chuckle.

"For your birthday I'll hire a professional instructor so you learn the proper technique for jumping."

"Really?"

"You are clearly a horsewoman, Rose. I won't take that away from you, but I insist you have proper instruction so you know what you're doing. And you will never do anything so reckless again. In fact, I may take those lessons with you. Would you like that?"

Her hand squeezed mine, and if she were able, I'm certain she would have jumped from her bed and danced a jig. Instead she wrapped her arms around my neck and squealed. The pain in her ankle made her settle down quickly.

"As for your punishment," I said, "I'd say you brought that on yourself with your injury. You will remain in bed until the doctor says you may leave it, and no riding without his approval as well. The only thing I will add is a letter to the boys' tutor. Because you were injured while in his care, the poor young man may be worried about keeping his position. So, when you see Uncle Graham, I expect you to explain the situation to him as well. Agreed?"

She nodded vigorously. "I'll tell him, Mummy. And thank you for the birthday gift."

I gave her a kiss and told her I'd send Nanny in to read to her. Perhaps the riding lessons would be a good thing for me, too. If I were a better rider, I might not worry so much about

Rose. I let out a small snort. And the sun might rise at midnight.

The next morning, I shared a lovely breakfast with Rose, eating off trays in her bed. Her lively spirits were due, I was sure, to the anticipation of the riding lessons rather than any diminution of pain. Each time I moved she winced until I finally realized I was jostling her and pulled up a chair.

I, too, was feeling a renewed enthusiasm for life in general, and our investigation in particular, as I gave Rose a kiss and headed downstairs. George had not come by with any news yesterday though that hope had been absurd. He couldn't possibly have gathered enough information yet, so I assumed he'd still be working on that aspect of the case today.

However, Mrs. Wiggins had proved quite helpful. Jamie had returned from his errand this morning with the name of John Milton's new employer. None other than Sir Hugo Ridley, of all people. I planned to pay a call on Lady Ridley this afternoon, and with Jenny's help I might find out what Mr. Milton knew about the Archer family business, and what Mary might have known about it.

Hetty, Lily, and Lottie were enjoying breakfast when I entered the dining room. "What are everyone's plans today?" I stepped over to the sideboard and poured a cup of coffee.

"I'm meeting with Leo's mother to discuss decorations for the engagement party." Lily's enthusiasm was bubbling over. "You'd be a welcome addition if you'd care to join us."

Oh, dear. I slipped into a chair next to Lottie. While I was happy to allow Patricia Kendrick to make all the arrangements regarding the party, I knew Lily would have some preferences and might not speak up to the woman she was trying so hard to please. What to do?

I needed to speak to Lady Ridley, or rather have Jenny speak to Milton, assuming I could arrange that. "At what time will you be leaving?" I asked.

"Almost immediately."

It was still too early for a formal call, so perhaps I could manage a decoration meeting in the morning and an interrogation by midday. I smiled at Lily. "Then yes. I'll be happy to accompany you, but I have to pay a call this afternoon, so if we haven't time to drop you off at home, you'll have to come with me. And we must take Jenny."

She raised her brows in inquiry, but before she could ask why I was pulling Jenny off her household duties, I turned to Hetty and Lottie. "Are the two of you occupied this morning?"

"I'm afraid we are," Hetty said in rather a rush. I'm sure the thought of discussing decorations for an hour or two was enough to make her devise any other distraction. She glanced at her assistant. "I could spare you if you'd like to go, dear, but we do have some further calculations to make today."

"I'm happy to stay and assist you," Lottie said. Clearly the call of engagement party decorations did not draw her in.

Hetty turned back to me. "I still need to know what to do regarding these fraudulent investments of Graham's."

"I understand, but I'd prefer you do nothing until we hear from Mr. Hazelton. He's trying to find others who may be in the same situation as Graham. If he can obtain any information about their investments, I'm certain he'll want to talk to you about it. Then, of course, we'll have to report to Delaney and find out how he means to proceed."

"Well, I hope you don't intend to mention any of this to Mrs. Kendrick," Lily said, waving the butter knife in my direction. "Can you imagine anyone else in Belgravia discussing the topics that come up around this table?"

"I've never had any conversations like this in New York either," Lottie said with a laugh. "They were all terribly boring and stuffy."

Well, this was an interesting turn of events—Lily taking me to task over my decorum. "I suppose this *is* rather unusual table talk."

"Far more interesting than discussing the weather or hunting," Lottie said.

"Or decorations," Lily added. "But I'm afraid that is exactly what we should be doing right now. Are you ready?" She popped the last bite of toast in her mouth.

With one more sip of coffee, I was. Jenny had been tending to our bedchambers and was delighted for the outing. Mrs. Kendrick had sent her carriage for us and it arrived just as we were ready to step outside. It appeared my morning was falling into place perfectly.

Fortunately, Mrs. Kendrick was an efficient planner, and very gracious regarding Lily's wishes. With a stab of guilt, I realized this event was a mere week away and I'd done nothing to assist with the preparations. She swept us right into the plans upon our arrival, presenting us with lists of options for decorations, music, and refreshments. She urged Lily to choose and only offered suggestions when Lily seemed unsure. I decided my sister would be very lucky indeed to have such a woman as her mother-in-law. Within two hours, everything had been decided and Lily and I were off.

As we took our leave of Patricia, I realized I could simply walk the few blocks down Park Lane to Curzon Street and the Ridley home. That would leave Jenny and me less than half a mile's walk back home on a lovely afternoon. I let Lily take the Kendricks' carriage, while Jenny and I proceeded to my next call.

"Have you any idea what you'll say to Mr. Milton?" I asked. We walked at a leisurely pace. The day was delightfully warm but it wouldn't do to have a glow on one's face when calling.

"I really don't, my lady. I suppose I'll just ask about his former post and see if I can lead him into a good coze."

"That sounds like an excellent plan. Don't push him if he seems reluctant to talk. I don't want to put you in an uncomfortable position and I'd rather not draw attention to our investigation."

Jenny chuckled. "Don't think I've ever met a man reluctant to talk about himself, my lady, but I'll be careful, don't you worry."

In no time at all, we arrived at the Ridleys' townhome. Jenny stepped down to the service area, and the butler guided me to a sitting room at the front of the house, then left to inform his mistress she had a caller. I walked around the room as I waited. It felt like a well-used family room, but with a nod to Hugo's wealth—silk upholstery, velvet draperies. The gilded frames on the paintings alone would wreak havoc on my budget. I'd just picked up some sheet music left on the piano when Miriam breezed into the room.

"Frances." She stretched out her hands as she glided toward me. "How lovely to see you."

"And you, dear." We kissed the air near each other's cheeks and settled ourselves on a nearby sofa. "I was just at the Kendricks' going over some details for Lily and Leo's engagement party, and I realized you were only a few doors down, so I thought a call was in order. I ran into Hugo the other day and realized I haven't seen you for simply ages."

"It has been some time, hasn't it?" Miriam returned my smile and her face took on a beatific glow. She was a lovely woman, blond and pink cheeked. Though a few years older than me, she would still be stunning at fifty, whenever that time should come. How Hugo, an agreeable, but rather irresponsible ne'er-do-well, ever won her, I'd never understand. Perhaps he had more charms than I could see. On the other hand, they may be quite obvious. This room for example. Such a large house in this neighborhood would come at a lofty price. He must be more careful with his finances than Graham.

"Hugo mentioned speaking to you. I think he said you were discussing investments." Her laugh tinkled like the sudden movement of a chandelier. "I was terribly impressed when he told me about it. I have absolutely no head for that sort of thing."

"I'm sure Hugo must have realized I am only just trying to understand it myself."

"He said you were talking about Gordon Archer."

"Yes, Graham has some investments with him." I hadn't expected the conversation to take this turn and blessed my good fortune, wondering how far I should take this falsehood. "Some of them profitable and some, completely abysmal. I wondered what Hugo's experience with Archer was. I'd love to make a good profit, but I must be careful."

"Then I must advise you to keep your money in the five percents, my lady."

We both turned as Hugo strode into the room, his pleasant smile bestowed on us equally. He lifted his wife's hand to his lips, and gave me a gracious bow before dropping into a chair across from us in a relaxed attitude. "As I told you the other day, every investment comes with some risk. It's very much like gambling."

"That is precisely what Archer told me." I feigned confusion. "I would have thought investing with a banker might contain the risk. That is, if I explained I was willing to take a slight risk, for reasonable profit." I wrinkled my nose. "Five percent is so meager a return."

Ridley stroked his chin as though he were considering my position. "You could certainly ask him to watch out for something for you. Like the earl, I've had both good and bad investment experience with Archer. He can't predict every outcome, but I trust his judgment. You might start with a small investment in something secure. Then if you realize some profit, take a little risk with that and don't touch your principle." He tipped his head to the side, trying to determine if I was following his logic. "Archer's not going anywhere and you are young. I suspect you want your income to last as long as you do."

Considering my suspicions about Archer, I wasn't so sure how long he'd be around, but I could agree with Hugo on one point. "You understand my intent completely. I want an income that will last into my old age."

"Which is many years away," Miriam said. "But your sister's wedding, it must be coming up very soon. I'd much rather hear about that."

"Ah, so the announcement's been made, has it?"

"Indeed. They won me over to their side."

Miriam smiled. "Young people are always in such a hurry. We received the invitation to the engagement party a few days ago. Is there a date for the wedding?"

We fell into discussion of weddings and whether a town ceremony is a better setting than one in the country. After another fifteen minutes I decided Jenny had had enough time to pry information from Mr. Milton and it would be safe to take my leave. For my part I'd learned very little. Ridley's investments with Archer seemed to be no more or less than he'd expect from any banker. Apparently, he hadn't suffered any great losses. I was hoping Jenny's inquiries had proved more fruitful than mine.

Chapter 21

After bidding the Ridleys a good afternoon, I collected Jenny at the door and managed to restrain myself until we reached the pavement. Finally, I turned the full weight of my curiosity upon her.

"Did you have an opportunity to speak to Mr. Milton? Was he at home?"

"He was, my lady, and I did. It was easier than I'd imagined as he's quite a talker, and happy to speak about Mr. Jasper, too. Real fond of him, he was. It doesn't sound like he and the missus disagreed about anything, leastways no more than any other couple might."

I considered her words. "I'd imagine if Jasper was involved in an unsavory financial scheme, and Mary found out about it, there would have been quite a row. Milton might not have known what it was about, but as Jasper's valet, I don't think he could have missed it altogether."

Another suspicion dashed. We turned into Hyde Park and took the Ring Road toward Belgravia. Even in my despair, I held one pathetic thread of hope. "Is it possible he simply didn't want to speak ill of his employer?"

Jenny shook her head in a decided negative. "Mr. Jasper is a former employer. Mr. Milton wouldn't worry about what he said. Since he doesn't work at that house anymore, his reputation and job aren't in danger." She shrugged. "He didn't hold back when he was talking about Sir Hugo, so I think he would have told me if there was anything bad to say about Mr. Jasper."

We approached Hyde Park Corner and paused for the traffic to clear. I gave Jenny a curious glance. "Did he say anything interesting about Ridley?"

She put a bounce in her step, warming to her story. "Well, when I was asking about the mister and missus arguing, he laughed a bit and told me the biggest argument he ever heard in that house was between Mr. Jasper and Sir Hugo. Said that was a real donnybrook."

"How very interesting. Did he say what they fought about?"

"I asked, of course, my lady, but he said he didn't know. He might have picked up a few words, but he didn't really remember them. He did remember when it happened though. It was just before Mr. Jasper quit working at the bank."

"Really, just before he resigned?" My heart added a little flutter to its usual beat. I had only just learned Jasper worked with his brother. I had no idea he'd resigned that position.

"Yes, ma'am. Right after the argument. The next couple of days he and the missus even talked about moving to Edinburgh as he thought he could find work there. He took a trip there soon after, and I suppose you heard what happened then."

I certainly did. The train ran off the tracks in the snow. Most of the passengers were fine, but a few, including Jasper, sustained fatal injuries. Poor Jasper. Poor Mary.

"So, they argued about something that caused Jasper to resign his position at the bank and plan a move to Edinburgh." I might be jumping to conclusions, but it sounded as though he not only wanted to stop working with his brother, but wanted to put several hundred miles between them. This was hardly proof—in fact it was complete conjecture—but it did sound as though Jasper had just discovered what his brother was up to. Didn't it? And could it be Ridley who told him?

"I got the feeling Mr. Milton isn't all that fond of Sir Hugo."

I turned a sharp eye on her. "Did he say how he came to be working for Ridley? Mrs. Wiggins told me he went there right after Jasper Archer's death."

"He said Sir Hugo talked to him at the funeral. Said Mr. Archer recommended him as a good valet and would he like a job? Considering he was about to be out on his ear, well, it wasn't like he could say no."

"Goodness, he must have been the valet from heaven if his employer's brother was aware of his skills." This sounded very strange indeed. Hugo and Jasper were friends. I could understand Hugo doing the kind thing. But I wondered why Archer involved himself in his brother's valet's welfare. "If I had a better opinion of Mr. Archer, I'd say he was simply trying to do a good deed. But for all that, Mr. Milton isn't happy in his employment?"

At this Jenny shrugged. "Can't always be picky, my lady. He was about to be out of a job and Sir Hugo is a respectable man to work for. It could be worse."

"Yes, I suppose that's true." By this time, we were back at home. Before Jenny returned below-stairs, I thanked her for a job well done. I knew she *could* afford to be picky in her employment. I didn't want to lose her.

I was surprised to find George in my drawing room with Hetty and Lottie. Even more surprising, my card table was now covered with papers and files, bound and unbound. I gaped at the mess as I removed my hat and left it on the table by the door.

"Aunt Hetty, was my library not large enough to contain your work?"

The trio glanced up as I moved toward them. "There you

are, dear." Hetty gave me a smile. "Apologies for causing this disorder to your drawing room. Mr. Hazelton came to me in need of information and I thought there'd be more space out here."

"There used to be," I said, taking a seat at the table and glancing at some of the documents. "Is this Graham's paperwork?"

George moved next to me. "Some of it. Henry Kendrick sent over some documents for your aunt today. Companies Archer's bank invests with."

"Really? What are you doing with them?"

"We are cross-referencing them with the list Mr. Hazelton brought," Lottie said.

At my raised brows, George explained further. "It took going around the clubs all night and most of today, but I found several gentlemen willing to speak to me about losses from some unfortunate investments they made with Archer." He shrugged. "Taking into consideration even legitimate companies can provide a poor or negative return, I thought it best to determine if those investments did indeed involve legitimate companies. Hetty was gracious enough to apply to Kendrick for the list."

"Impressive work," I said. "And?"

"Well, as I've only just gathered everything, I don't know yet." Hetty inspected the list in her hand. "I can tell you I found no reference to the first two companies on your list."

"And if the company name isn't on the bank's list, it is not a legitimate company?" This seemed far too easy. Somehow, I must be a step behind.

"Not necessarily," George said, as Lottie and Hetty started a search for the next name on the list. "The document Kendrick provided is a list of companies the bank has approved for their clients. If one of Archer's clients gave him some funds to invest, he should have chosen one of those companies. They've been vetted and given a risk factor. If the company name is not on the bank list that doesn't necessarily mean they don't exist, but it calls into question why Archer would choose to invest with them."

"How did Mr. Kendrick obtain the bank's list?"

Hetty turned and flashed me a grin. "He sits on the board of directors for the bank."

"Ah, that's certainly handy." I saw George's list held about eight names, which would take the ladies some time to re-search, so I drew him aside and told him what I'd learned from Jenny's conversation with Jasper Archer's former valet.

Lines of worry crisscrossed his forehead. "So, Jasper had an argument with Ridley and abruptly resigned his employment. I never thought to ask why he was going to Edinburgh in the first place. That does have to make one wonder what Ridley told him."

"If Ridley was angry about losing money with Archer, it seems to have left no lasting resentment. He's still investing with the man and seems to consider him a friend. He even hired Mr. Milton on Archer's recommendation."

We'd moved away from the card table and seated ourselves on the sofa. George palmed his eyes and I noted the dark circles under them. How long had it taken for him to travel from club to club to find the eight men willing to tell him of their losses?

He leaned back and gazed up at the ceiling. "If their argu-ment was about an investment, Ridley might have received some sort of satisfaction from Gordon Archer."

"Perhaps Jasper confronted his brother and made good on Ridley's loss," I suggested.

"How would he have explained how a loss turned into a gain?"

I pulled a face. "Insurance? Hetty was trying to find out if the shipping company Graham invested in was insured. If Rid-ley was angry enough to go to Jasper, he might start shouting about his loss to all and sundry. Even if the company didn't exist, it might be worth Archer's while to tell Ridley insurance would cover his losses just to keep him quiet. And offer him a lucrative investment to win back his trust."

He pursed his lips. "I don't suppose you know the name of the company Ridley was angry about?"

"I don't even know if that was the source of the argument. Mr. Milton couldn't hear what they said. He only knew that right after that visit from Ridley, Jasper resigned and planned to leave town. A rather drastic step for a man who needed to work for a living."

"That means we don't know if Mary Archer knew anything about her brother-in-law's fraud either."

"Her husband must have given her some reason for resigning, don't you think? And after his death, something made her turn away from her brother-in-law and refuse his support. I suspect Jasper found out about the fraud, and while he didn't want to ruin his brother, he couldn't be a party to it and so resigned. I can't believe he would take such a drastic step and not inform Mary of the reason."

"But can you explain why she kept quiet about this for over a year and suddenly"—he shrugged—"what, she threatened him with exposure?"

"Perhaps he agreed to stop and she recently learned that was not the case."

I sighed as he rubbed the back of his neck. "I know this is a lot of speculation about one argument, but it fits the situation so indulge me for a moment. Mary had to approach this cautiously. At the time of Jasper's death, she wasn't writing the gossip column. She had no forum to expose Archer's crime. Her only choice would have been to go to the police. She would have ruined the family, her husband's good name, and any chance her nieces had for a future. And that's if the police took her accusation seriously. If they didn't, Archer might have had her locked up as hysterical." I gave him a level look. "I suspect she confronted Gordon Archer and received his promise to stop."

"I agree you have a good theory, but we have no idea if any part of it is true."

George tipped his head back and blew out a breath. "We are speculating far too much. We must stick to facts and certainties."

"Sadly, those are few. Ridley argued with Jasper about something. Whatever it was made Jasper confront his brother then resign from the bank. After that, he left for Edinburgh and was killed in the train accident. Soon after, Ridley hired Jasper's unemployed valet." I wrinkled my nose in disgust. "Our facts and certainties are pathetically meager."

"Perhaps it would be helpful to talk with Ridley."

"You can hardly ask him what he argued with Jasper about. I've already inquired into his investments with Archer and he seems to swear by the man. I don't think you'd get him to admit, even to himself, that his losses with Archer had anything to do with trickery. Even Graham rejects the notion. And I think Ridley considers Archer a friend."

"Thus, any inquiry on my part might lead to a warning for Archer. It might be best to leave Ridley alone for now."

He drew a breath and released it in a half sigh, half growl. "What we really need is something that proves Mary Archer knew about Gordon Archer's fraudulent dealings, and that he knew she was writing a column."

"Why do we need to know that?"

"Because the editor was murdered as well as Mary. He had to know the editor could also expose him. Therefore, either Archer knew Mary was writing the column, or she threatened to go to the press, and somehow she must have implied that the editor already had the information or at least had access to it."

I had to agree. "For him to murder someone, to murder his

own sister-in-law, he had to know exposure was imminent. If it was Archer, Mary must have threatened him."

He tilted his head to the side. "All right, so she threatens him with exposure and he murders her." He raised a brow. "What about the editor?"

I sat back and tried to imagine a scene. "Mary and Gordon argue. She tells him he must stop his fraudulent practices. He refuses. The argument becomes heated. She threatens him with exposure unless he stops. Enraged, Archer attacks her, threatening to silence her forever. To save her life, she tells him she's just given the information to the editor in the form of her columns. If she dies, the story will be printed anyway. His hands tighten around her neck and she breathes her last."

He stared at me in fascination. I shrugged. "Then he goes after the editor."

"Ah, but there's a flaw to the picture you paint." He smiled as he shook a finger at me. "Unless she told him the name of the paper or of the column, how does he know who to go after? Many papers publish gossip."

I grimaced. "That is a rather large flaw."

We stared at one another for a moment, weighing all the possibilities. I could hear Hetty and Lottie murmuring at the table in the corner of the room. George finally broke the silence. "Do you recall if Mr. Mosley was taking care of all Mr. Norton's work?"

"He didn't say that precisely, but he seemed to be doing so."

"Did you ask him if he'd received anything from Mrs. Archer after the murders?"

"I never met the man without you by my side, but no, I don't recall asking. And how could that be possible? Mary couldn't send a letter after her death."

"No, but she could have put something in the post before her death."

I considered the idea. If Mary had taken such a precaution,

she must have known she was treading on dangerous ground. It would have been safer to go to the police—but then the family would be ruined.

"It's worth checking into," I said. "We shall have to go to the *Observer* and ask Mosley. But if he'd received something of that magnitude, wouldn't he have informed Delaney?"

He linked his fingers together in his lap. "He seemed to be rather snowed under with work, didn't you think? If something was delivered, he may not have gotten to it yet."

"Perhaps we should check with Delaney first. If he has nothing, then we can talk with Mr. Mosley." I let my head fall back against the sofa, remembering I was now a columnist. "I should take him another set of columns anyway."

"We should talk to Delaney." He threw me a warning look. "But remember this is a theory only. I realize you feel strongly about Archer as a suspect, but we have nothing that even resembles proof."

Before I could respond, Hetty called for our attention. "All right, you two. I think I can safely say none of these companies are sanctioned for investment by the bank."

We moved over to the table where Hetty and Lottie had been working. "Neither are any of them listed on any of the exchanges," she added.

"That could mean only that they are privately held," George said. "Not that they don't exist."

"Two of them don't exist." Hetty's tone was firm. "South Sea Equity and Central American Coffee Company were both part of Graham's portfolio. We've already verified them as fraudulent."

Hetty pointed to their names on the list. Something felt oddly familiar about them.

"There are three others on your list which follow the same pattern as the fake companies. They are not sanctioned by the bank, not listed on the exchange, and Archer sold shares just before the companies suffered a catastrophic loss." Hetty extended a finger for each point she mentioned. "The odds are very good that none of the five companies exists anywhere outside Archer's imagination."

I glanced at George. He appeared far less than pleased with the news. "I find her argument very compelling, don't you?"

He blew out a breath. "I must admit, I do. While we should continue our due diligence on the other three companies, I think it's time we took this information to Delaney. There should be enough here for the police to charge Archer with fraud." He held up a cautionary hand. "Not enough to prove murder, you understand. But it does give rise to suspicion. Delaney will likely question Archer about his sister-in-law, but I'm afraid that's all we can hope for."

Disappointment weighed heavily on me as he gathered the documents into a stack.

"Wait." Lottie stayed his hand. "If you plan to take these papers to the police, we should make a record of them for ourselves."

George gave her a curious glance. "For what purpose?"

"What if the police don't feel they have enough evidence to question Archer about the murders? It may be up to us to pursue this evidence until we find the murderer." She shrugged. "If we are to give away the original documents, we must at least have a record of them."

"She's right," I said. "It may be up to us. And the Kendricks will be at the Ridleys' soiree tomorrow. Hetty may be able to obtain more information about these companies from Mr. Kendrick so she'll need a list of the names."

I took a seat next to Lottie and we began recording all the documentation in a ledger. Within half an hour we had a list of the fraudulent companies and the gentlemen who had invested in them and lost everything. We made note of which companies we knew to be illegitimate, and those requiring further investigation. As I reviewed the list, I realized why some of the names sounded familiar.

"My heavens," I said, earning curious glances from my companions. "We already have this information. We've even written and published a column about them. The initials for these companies are all in that cryptic note." I waved my hand at Mary's files, stacked next to Lottie's elbow. "I believe we've deciphered it at last."

Lottie dug through the first file until she found the note and placed it at the center of the table. We all leaned forward to study it.

SSE, CTS, W-H & S, CACC. 6 March, 1898. LH, SH, LM, LR at least J.

"The first notation is South Seas Equity," she said. "And *CACC* is Central American Coffee Company."

One by one we found the four companies on Hetty's list, two of which she'd already determined were fraudulent. The other two were in the "Suspicious" column.

"The following sets of initials may well refer to people who invested in the fake companies," Lottie said. "That rather makes sense now. As of the sixth of March, 1898, those four people were duped into investing in those four companies." She wrinkled her nose. "But what does *at least J* mean?"

Hetty peered over my shoulder. "Perhaps it means at least those four people. And are you sure that's a "*J*"? There's a bit of a flourish to it."

I studied the letter. There was a flourish to it, and for good reason. "It's a signature," I said. "J for Jasper. He signed the note."

I fell back against the chair. Now that we understood the note, I don't know how it had eluded us for so long. "Jasper Archer wrote this note. That's why the paper is different and why the handwriting is as well. He either left it with Mary, or she found it in his belongings."

George read the note once more and gave me a smile. "Good work, Frances."

"I think this proves Mary knew what her brother-in-law was up to."

He tipped his head to the side and raised a brow. "It does seem to point that way, but the question remains; Did *he* know what *she* was up to?"

Chapter 22

∼

Our work took us well into the night, largely because George insisted we go through every single document and sheet of paper from Mary's collection.

"The note is enough to make Delaney open an investigation into Archer's dealings, but unless he confesses, it isn't near enough to convict him, even for the fraud charges," he said. "If Jasper, or Mary, had something in Archer's handwriting, or some solid proof he was deliberately swindling his clients, I'd feel more secure about our case."

We foraged through everything. And came up with nothing. We did, however, find two names from the list of swindled aristocrats that matched the initials on the note. And with our documents in hand, we set off to find Delaney the next afternoon.

We had no luck tracking him down at his division in Chelsea so we moved on to the *Daily Observer* to deliver my columns. For once I gave thanks for mourning clothing as I could carry off a veil without attracting attention. The day was growing warm as we stepped from the carriage and into the office.

Mr. Ryan was missing from his post at the front desk. George and I waited at the counter for a moment. We shared a glance and a shrug then pushed through the swinging gate that blocked the reception area from the offices.

"Seems the whole gang's here," Mosley said, when after a perfunctory knock, we stepped into the editor's office. Inspector Delaney and a constable were already there. Mosley waved us inside.

As George greeted Delaney, I sidled up to Mosley. "What has happened to Mr. Ryan? Never say you dismissed him?"

"Naw." Mosley gave an infinitesimal nod toward Delaney and the constable. "The lad makes himself scarce when certain people come to call."

Ah, that's right. Ryan's former life would not have made him friends with the police. I noted Mosley hadn't used his usual epithet for the boy. Perhaps the man had a heart after all.

"What brings the two of you here?" Delaney did not appear happy to see us.

"We have another column to deliver to Mr. Mosley," I said, holding up my envelope. "It is a boon that you happen to be here as we had hoped to speak with you as well. We have some information."

Delaney frowned at the editor who heaved a sigh, pushed his bulk up from the chair, and headed for the door. "I do have work to do today. Please keep your meeting brief." He pulled the door closed behind him. Delaney took the editor's chair behind the desk. George offered me a guest chair, and he and the constable remained standing.

"I'm afraid what we have to tell you is a little off topic," George began, "but if you bear with us, we can explain why it relates to the murders."

Delaney's brows drew together in a single bushy line, but he remained silent. Between the two of us, we laid out the details of Archer's fraudulent dealings. Explaining how we learned that at least two of the companies he sought investment for did not exist and that Archer simply put the money into his own pocket. We brought in the argument between Jasper Archer and Hugo Ridley that made him give up his job at the bank and seek employment in Edinburgh.

"The note I gave you details all of this." I placed my copy on the desk alongside a translated version. "I believe Mary knew what her brother-in-law was doing, and rather than blackmail him, she threatened him with exposure if he didn't stop."

Delaney did not appear to welcome this information. "And you supposed that rather than cease these alleged illegal activities, Archer murdered his own sister-in-law."

I took a breath. "My brother-in-law lost six thousand pounds in one of Archer's investments. It would be difficult to abandon such a lucrative operation, illegal or not. Someone murdered her. Archer had something to hide and I believe Mary threatened to expose it. He was also seen trying to enter her house a few days later, and he fits the description of the man seen fleeing her house on the night of the murder. Is that not enough for the police to question him?"

"More than enough," Delaney replied. "In fact, I finally convinced the man to meet with me this evening about the attempted entry of Mrs. Archer's house. I'd like to confirm this information first, but I doubt there will be time."

He picked up the notes we'd laid on the desk and gave George a quizzical glance. "These gentlemen all admitted that they were taken in by Archer?"

George shook his head. "Not at all. They still don't realize they were taken in. They believe they made a bad investment and lost. I never told them the companies they invested in don't exist. Wasn't even sure of that myself until last night."

Delaney stared at him in astonishment. "Are you telling me that this man"—he glanced down at the note—"this Mr. Peterson handed over two thousand pounds without knowing anything about the investment?" He leaned over the desk toward us. "And the Earl of Harleigh, six thousand?"

"They trusted their adviser." George shrugged and leaned his back against the wall. "Many find it easier that way."

Delaney tutted. "The day I trust anyone that fully . . ."

"Is the day you cease being an inspector." I smiled at the man. "It's not just your nature but your job to be suspicious of anything people tell you. The rest of us are more willing to trust the opinion of others. Particularly when an expert says he can turn your investment into a fortune."

"Does Archer know you've been checking up on him?"

George crossed his arms over his chest. "I certainly hope not. Most of what we learned came through casual conversation. None of those men, or perhaps you'd call them victims, should be suspicious of our conversations, but any one of them could drop a comment to Archer, alerting him unwittingly."

Delaney nodded. "I'll post a man near his home while we investigate. If we can arrest him for fraud, we can question him about the murders as well." He spared a glance for his constable, who scribbled notes in a book of his own, then turned a steady glare on us. "Nicely done," he muttered.

I glowed under his approval. I must say I was beginning to like this role of investigator. It was much like working a puzzle, though the stakes were much higher. I'd always been good at puzzles and I liked to think I was rather good at this.

"There's one more thing," George said. "We were hoping to learn if Mr. Mosley has received any correspondence from Mrs. Archer since her death."

His words brought me back to reality. So much for being a first-rate investigator. I'd forgotten why we even came here.

Delaney looked confused, so I explained further. "Since we think Mrs. Archer was planning to confront her brother-in-law with a threat to his livelihood, we thought she may have taken precautions to ensure her safety. Perhaps by providing another person with the details of Archer's fraud. Not just Jasper's note, but some documented proof. If she did, we assume that person

would be Mr. Norton. If she posted it, or asked someone to deliver it, it would have arrived after her death. We hoped to
check around his office for something in Mary's hand."

At this point the door opened and Mosley's head appeared in
the opening. "Are the three of you done yet? I really do have a
great deal of work to do before my day is over."

Delaney stood. "Actually, we just decided to have another
gander through Mr. Norton's files. I'm afraid your work will
have to wait unless you can do it elsewhere."

Mosley's jaw sagged. With a quelling glare from Delaney, he
snapped it shut. "Look here, I've been more than hospitable to
you, so why don't you tell me what it is you hope to find?" He
jabbed a pencil in Delaney's general direction. "After all, if you
find the evidence for the murder in my office, I should be the
one to break the story. It's only fair."

Delaney pursed his lips, staring at the man. "And what's to
stop you from breaking the story before we make an arrest?"

Mosley ground his teeth in impatience.

"Perhaps we can tell him what we want, just not how it signifies," George said.

"What good does that do me?"

I'd had enough. "Heavens, Mr. Mosley. If the inspector finds
the evidence here, I'll write your story myself. You'll have
more details than anyone else. Will that do?"

Mosley grumbled. "Guess it'll have to. Now, what do you
need?"

"Correspondence from Mrs. Archer."

"You have all that." He waved a dismissive hand. "You
blokes took everything with you right after Mr. Norton was
murdered."

"We're hoping to find correspondence delivered here after
the murders," I said. "Perhaps something hand delivered?"

Mosley lumbered around the desk, grumbling under his
breath. He pulled an open box off a shelf and plopped it on

the desk. "Don't know how you expect the woman to send something to her editor from beyond the grave, but feel free to look. This is everything that's come in since Mr. Norton was killed."

The three of us dug into the stack of papers in the box and sorted through all the correspondence. Nothing from Mary. "It's been over a week since the murders. If she had made any arrangements for something to be delivered, it would certainly have arrived by now."

"We have no way of knowing if she took such a precaution," George reminded me. "We were simply hopeful she had."

"Mary was a smart woman," I said. "I can't imagine her confronting Archer without some sort of security."

"Perhaps she trusted the man more than you would," Delaney said. "Archer did seem to instill trust in those around him."

"I suppose that's possible, yet Mary knew more than anyone else just how untrustworthy he was."

"She could hardly imagine he'd murder her."

"Well, since there's nothing new here, I'd best be going."

Delaney told us he'd begin the work of confirming the information we provided. If it proved true, the police could at least arrest Archer on charges of fraud. A far cry from murder, but it was a start. Perhaps Archer would confess under the pressure of police questioning. I was relieved that all this would be in Delaney's hands now.

He preceded us out the door and I turned back automatically to bid Mr. Ryan a good afternoon, but his desk still stood empty.

"Wait a moment." I placed a hand on George's arm. "There's someone else we should ask."

By the time I checked with Mr. Mosley and asked for some suggestions of where Ryan might be, the young man had returned to his desk and was chatting with George. I gave him a smile as I approached the counter in front of his desk.

"Mr. Ryan, I'm wondering if you can help me."

"Happy to help if I can, ma'am." He gave me a nervous smile.

George stepped aside as I leaned against the counter. "Mr. Hazelton and I are trying to find the man who murdered Mr. Norton and the woman who was Miss Information."

Ryan narrowed his eyes, watching me with caution. "You mean Mrs. Archer?"

I sighed. "You do know. Mr. Norton did trust you."

"He knew he could, ma'am. I also know you aren't Mrs. Archer's sister. You don't look nothing like her."

"No, I'm not her sister, but I was her friend and I want to find her killer. What I'm wondering is if a letter or package arrived for Mr. Norton since his death. Sent from Mrs. Archer."

The boy chewed on his lip and shook his head. I could understand his reluctance but I persisted. "Mr. Ryan, we are not the police. If you have anything, they needn't know it came from you."

"She didn't send anything to Mr. Norton," he said. "She sent it to me."

With that he reached down and opened a drawer in his desk. Pulling out a large stuffed envelope, he hesitated before handing it to me. "The police and me don't get along. I don't want to have to talk to them."

George stepped forward. "I assure you, we'll keep you out of this entirely."

Ryan nodded and handed me the package. I couldn't help but notice the name on the mailing label. I exchanged a glance with George. "It's from Mary."

"Yes, ma'am. She didn't send things often, but when she did, I usually just gave it to Mr. Norton. With him gone, I didn't know what to do."

"Thank you for trusting me, Mr. Ryan." I broke the seal on the envelope and pulled out a book.

"It's an account book." I placed it on the worn wood counter and opened it. With George at my side, we leafed through the pages of entries, wondering what to make of this discovery. "Why would Mary send this to Norton? The entries are over a year old."

He flipped to the last page of entries. "There!" He stabbed at one with his index finger. "South Sea Equity to Gerald Peterson. Two thousand pounds!" He closed the book and slapped his palm on the leather cover.

Both Ryan and I watched this exhibition with some confusion. Especially when George leaned over the counter to shake Ryan by the hand.

"What are you so excited about?" I asked.

"This!" He slapped the book once more, opened the cover, and turned it to me with a delighted grin. "See for yourself."

I stared stupidly at the page of entries until he placed his finger at the end of a row. The initials *G A* stood out. In fact, each entry was initialed *G A*. I drew in a breath as I glanced up at him. "Gordon Archer."

He grinned. "This isn't Mary's account book; it belongs to Archer. It's where he kept track of his nefarious deals. And it came from Mary Archer. This is what she was holding over his head. She had absolute proof of what he was up to."

"Heavens!" I prodded George to the door. "We must get this to Delaney."

Delaney and the constable had still been outside and if possible, he was even more delighted with this new bit of evidence than George had been. I doubt he even heard us when we told him we'd found it in a mail bin. His smile grew with each entry he read. "This should definitely speed up the process," he said.

Sir Hugo and Lady Ridley had no country home. Not that they couldn't afford one—they simply loved their city life. Hugo eschewed all sporting activities and Miriam busied herself with

several charitable organizations in town, and the constant refur-
bishment of their home. This would be society's first glimpse of
the Ridleys' new reception hall. They'd been working on it for
months and it was finally completed in time for the largest
event of the summer, the Glorious Twelfth reception.

We passed the small sitting room I'd visited just yesterday,
and through an arch at the end of a short hallway that opened
up to a two-story room. A gallery surrounded three-quarters
of the second floor. The gallery ended at a back wall of windows. Just below them the doors were thrown open and the
scent of roses from the garden wafted in. While guests mingled
in the theaterlike room, musicians serenaded us from a small
salon off to the side.

We quickly lost Lily as Leo came to claim her attention.
George and Hetty went in search of Mr. Kendrick to inquire as
to his knowledge of the remaining three potentially fraudulent
companies. That left me with Lottie, and as we had no greater
task than socializing, we set ourselves to do just that.

I felt rather carefree. We had turned over our information to
Delaney, and I was certain he'd be arresting Archer soon. I considered this a job well done.

"Lady Harleigh. Miss Deaver."

We turned to find Charles Evingdon heading our way, bear-
ing two glasses of wine. Lottie brightened immediately. I, too,
was pleased to see him. After the incident with Caroline Archer
he'd taken himself back to his home where he'd planned to stay
hidden away.

With a dramatic flourish, he handed each of us a glass. Lottie
blushed and spilled half the contents of her glass onto her hem
and shoe. I pretended not to notice and turned back to Charles.

"I'm delighted to see you out in society again."

His grin fairly beamed, dimples and eyes joining in. "Couldn't
believe my luck in receiving this invitation. Thought I was definitely persona non-something or other. But here I am."

"Society is very fickle. We all knew you could never do such a thing." My cheeks grew warm when I recalled that I had indeed wondered.

"That is excellent news indeed, Mr. Evingdon," Lottie said.

"Yes, I'm pleased I can once again show my face about town without frightening people." He gave her a charming smile. "Perhaps you'd like to listen to the music in the other room, Miss Deaver?"

The girl blushed furiously and accepted his arm. I declined, saying I wished to find our hostess. Once they left, I glanced around the room and instead saw George and Hetty in conversation with Mr. Kendrick. Yes, I know I was supposed to be done with this investigation, but that didn't put a stop to my curiosity.

Before I could join their group, Graham appeared at my side and after a rushed greeting, he leaned in and lowered his voice.

"You will be amazed to hear my news," he said. "Gordon Archer has been arrested this evening."

Amazement didn't begin to describe my feelings. Delaney had moved swiftly. "Do you know why?" I asked.

Graham shook his head. "My valet saw the police take him away less than an hour ago. Told me about it while I was dressing." He shrugged. "However, Hetty has been telling me that Archer has been operating a confidence scheme. Perhaps the police have found him out."

I conjured an expression of astonishment. "My goodness. If they have, it must give you some satisfaction to find he'll face charges. I wonder if you have any chance of getting your money back."

He brightened. "I hadn't thought of that. Though I'm not certain Hetty's right about my investment with Archer. I find it hard to believe fraud was involved."

I raised a brow. "Aunt Hetty's usually quite good at this. Why do you doubt her?"

"She claims the company doesn't even exist but I know others who invested in it and did very well. Ridley for one." He shrugged. "Perhaps my investment was just made at the wrong time."

"Really? Ridley invested in the same company and made a profit?"

"And a very good one at that. In fact, it was Ridley who encouraged me to invest."

Was it? How very interesting.

Chapter 23

It took a good thirty minutes to catch up with George again. I finally spotted him when I peeked into the music room. One of the younger Argyle girls was giving a creditable performance of Chopin's Waltz in E minor for an audience of a dozen or so. Though Lottie and Charles were clearly not attending. They were seated near the back, their heads together in whispered conversation, while George sat behind them, acting as chaperone.

I tapped him on the shoulder as I swept behind him, nodding to a door along the side of the room, before heading that way myself. Outside the door was a dark hallway, which I assumed led to the private family apartments. After a few moments, the door opened, music poured out, and he joined me.

"Had I known you wanted to get me alone in the dark, Frances, we could have arranged to send the others to this soiree on their own and had your house to ourselves." He waggled his brows.

"George, please."

"With pleasure." He leaned in and gave me a gentle, tantalizing kiss. Oh, my! I was lost for some moments before I realized my fingers were combing through his hair and I was very definitely kissing him back. "George," I whispered against his lips.

"Did you say more?"

"Yes. No." I pressed my hands against his chest to gain a bit of distance. "At least not now."

He took a step back, a wicked smile on his lips. "Ah, I thought it too good to be true. So, if not for this, why did you wish to meet me in this dark, secluded corner?"

If only I could remember. Oh, yes. Archer. "Graham is here. He came late to the party, but he came with some news. Delaney has arrested Archer."

His eyes widened. "Already."

"Not more than an hour ago."

He blew out a breath and leaned against the wall only to bounce forward as the door opened beside him and Hetty pushed her way through.

"There you are. What on earth are the two of you doing here in the dark?"

I pulled her to my side, allowing the door to close. "I was telling Mr. Hazelton that Archer has been arrested."

She raised a hand to her throat. "So quickly? But just on the fraud charges, I suppose."

"We don't know," I said. "Graham's valet saw the arrest and told him about it. He could hardly go out and ask Delaney. Since the police moved on this so quickly, I doubt they had time to build a murder case against Archer already, so I have to assume he was arrested for fraud."

"That makes the most sense," George agreed. "I'd like to go and see for myself. If he was arrested an hour ago, Delaney may be available to speak with me soon." He glanced from Hetty to me. "But I'll need the carriage to get there."

I waved away his concern. "Don't worry about us. I'll see if Charles can take us home."

"I'd be most pleased to take you ladies home."

Charles, with Lottie on his arm, appeared out of the darkness around the corner. Where on earth had they been? "Didn't we leave you two in the music room?"

"You did," she said. "We decided to return to the drawing room, but as we tried to get out of our row, I tripped over a gentleman's foot and tore my hem." She gazed up at Charles in awe. "Mr. Evingdon just spared me from sprawling headlong down the aisle."

I gave thanks for his quick reflexes.

"We were looking for the lady's retiring room, where I hoped to find a maid for a quick repair." She frowned. "But somehow we got turned around."

"When we heard your voices, we decided we must be on the right path." He gave me a brave smile as if he knew what I was thinking—how many dark corners did they hide in before making their way back here?

"Well, since you're here and you've agreed to take us home, perhaps Mr. Hazelton can go about his business and we can all rejoin the party."

"I certainly hope you all plan to rejoin the party."

As one we turned to see Sir Hugo at the end of the hall. Heavens, who next? "This tends to be a rather convenient spot for young couples," he said. "But I never expected to find a group of this size."

We proffered our apologies and made our way back to the reception rooms. Hetty broke away as soon as she caught sight of Mr. Kendrick. I suspected she wanted to bring him up to date on Archer's arrest. Charles and Lottie left in search of refreshments, and Hugo was pulled into a group to settle an argument. Fortunately, Miriam Ridley was headed my way.

"How lovely," she said as she came to my side. "I haven't seen you for ages and now twice in one week."

As we chatted, I saw Ridley listening to the gentlemen in his small grouping while watching his wife with an indulgent smile. How nice to have a husband simply content to watch his wife enjoy herself. She caught my wistful smile and pinkened. "I'll let you in on a secret. Ridley and I are tripping off for a little adventure tomorrow." Her brilliant smile told me she was delighted with the prospect of adventuring.

"Truly? Where will you be going?"

"We are to begin in Paris and from there, who knows?" Her smile faded as she linked her arm with mine and drew me in. "I'm sorry to miss the engagement party, but I thought Hugo needed a change of scene. He's been so downcast since Mary Archer's murder."

That came as a surprise. "I wasn't aware he considered Mary a friend."

Miriam lifted an elegant shoulder. "No, Mary was more of an acquaintance. His friendship was with Jasper, her husband. I think her murder brought the loss of his friend back to the fore. He's been distracted and keeping to himself. I thought it would be refreshing to get away. As much as he hates travel, I was surprised when he agreed to the plan and I decided we must leave immediately before he changes his mind. My maid is packing furiously at this moment." She chuckled as Ridley joined us. "You cannot back out now."

He looked rather pleased with himself. "I have no intention of backing out, my dear. Life is short. One should enjoy it while one can."

"I cannot argue with that," I said, noting that Miriam had turned to speak to someone behind her. "As you are to be off soon, I'm doubly glad I thought to drop by the other day. It sounds as if you'll be gone for some time."

His smile faded. "Yes, about your visit. Can you tell me why your maid was questioning my valet?"

My stomach churned though I allowed myself only a slight moue of distaste. "Questioning? Whatever would she question him about?"

"Oddly enough, about his time working for Jasper Archer. He thought she seemed very curious indeed. Do you know why?"

"I couldn't say. Jenny came with me on occasion to visit with Mary, both before and since her husband died. Perhaps she just saw that as common ground for starting a conversation with your valet." I smiled. "Is he by chance an attractive young man?"

His lips turned down, but he merely shrugged. "I hadn't thought of it in that light. When he mentioned it to me I gained the impression he thought your maid was seeking some titillating news about Mrs. Archer's murder."

I donned my most solemn expression. "If that was the case you can be sure I will take her to task. The details of someone's death are hardly fodder for gossip."

He leaned toward me. "Perhaps gossip was precisely what she was after. I'm sure you're aware of Mrs. Archer's vocation as a writer, Lady Harleigh, as you were such good friends."

I didn't have to feign surprise this time. How could he possibly know that? "Other than letters, I was not aware Mrs. Archer did any writing. Certainly not as a vocation."

"No? Then perhaps I have said too much."

"Perhaps, but now that you have said it, you must continue."

"I'm referring to the column she wrote for the *Daily Observer,* as I'm sure you know. Women can rarely keep such things to themselves."

Amazing. Why were men so eager to charge the entire opposite sex as hopeless gossips when he was clearly bursting to share this little tidbit with me? Since the man had knowledge of Mary's column there was no sense in denying mine. "How do you know this?"

He gave me a wry smile. "Her late husband's valet works for me now, remember? He mentioned how she would obtain gossipy information from other servants. In fact, I wondered if your maid was trying to find out if he knew who was writing the column now."

"Good God, Frances. Is that what all the paperwork is in your drawing room? Are you researching some writing project?" I turned to see Graham at my shoulder. While I faced away from Ridley, I gave him a significant glare, willing him to keep quiet.

I waved a hand in the air. "Just cleaning out some old records, Graham. Since Hetty is using my library, the drawing room was my only choice."

Ridley smiled. "So, you are not the new Miss Information?"

My cheeks grew heated. I hoped I could pass it off as a blush of modesty, but Graham's protest made the lie unnecessary. "I should say not. Frances has far too much integrity to spread gossip in such a way. I'll thank you never to suggest such a thing."

Ridley raised a hand as if to soothe Graham's wounded sensibilities. "Forgive me. There was no insult intended. It was foolish of me to imagine it."

Graham accepted the apology as if the comment had nothing to do with me, and Ridley made some excuse to move on. I watched his back recede into the crowd.

"He knows," I said, almost to myself.

"I should hope he knows," Graham replied. "No one insults a member of my family."

I'd nearly forgotten he was beside me. "Excuse me, Graham, but I must find Hetty."

It took a good quarter of an hour to find her and along the way I collected Charles and Lottie. Once I'd pulled all three aside, I explained my concerns about Hugo.

"Are you saying he was involved in the fraud with Archer?" Hetty asked.

I counted off each piece of evidence on my fingers. "He knows Mary wrote the Miss Information column. He tried to tell me Jasper's valet told him about it, but Mary wasn't writing the column when the valet was in her employ. Hugo was mentioned in the note Jasper wrote as one of the men duped in Archer's scheme over a year ago." I pictured the note I'd read so many times it was committed to memory. "Mary used initials for first name and surname, but this was Jasper's note and he used the men's titles instead. Thus, *S H* for Sir Hugo."

They all seemed to be following so I continued. "Those are the facts; the rest of this is conjecture. Hugo had an argument with Jasper. I suspect it was about his brother's fraudulent dealings. I further believe that since that time, rather than expose Archer, he's been encouraging others to invest with him."

"Like Graham," Hetty said, her forehead puckered in worry.

"Exactly," I said. "Rather than expose him, he joined Archer in his scheme, and probably made a good deal of money in the bargain."

"Money he'd lose if Mrs. Archer had exposed her brother-in-law," Lottie said.

"Giving him the same motive for murder as Archer."

Charles still looked confused. "But the police arrested Archer. If he didn't commit the murders, isn't he's likely to suggest his partner did? Then they'll come and arrest Ridley."

"Which brings me to my third bit of evidence," I said. "Ridley learned Jenny was questioning his valet about Jasper Archer and he's become suspicious. So much so, that the Ridleys, who never leave town on any account, are leaving tomorrow on an extended visit to the Continent."

This did not bring on the gasps of horror I'd imagined. "He's running away, possibly going into hiding."

"That sounds like a guilty man," Charles said.

"We can't be certain, of course, but this does make him just as likely a suspect as Archer. We need to get this information to Delaney so the police can question Ridley before he leaves the country and is out of their reach."

"I can go right now and tell him of your suspicions," Charles said.

I'm certain the expression on my face was as dubious as that of my companions.

Hetty took his arm. "I should go with you to help explain the more salient details." She turned back to me. "It might be wise to keep a watch on Ridley. Does he know Archer's been arrested?"

"I don't think so. Graham said it happened just this evening, so I don't know how Ridley would have heard of it. Lottie and I will keep an eye on him just the same."

Once Hetty and Charles left, Lottie and I did seek out Ridley. I hesitated to engage him in conversation for fear I'd give myself away, but we watched him from a distance for the better part of an hour. Weaving our way through the crowd we nodded and smiled at the other guests while avoiding all but the most superficial of conversations, leaving them each time Ridley moved on.

Then Graham came to Ridley's side.

Lottie relaxed her posture. "Perhaps the earl will keep him in one place for a few minutes at least."

The two men spoke quietly. Ridley's expression darkened, and he looked at Graham with a sharp focus. I squeezed Lottie's arm in my alarm.

"What is it?"

"Graham's telling him about Archer. I'm certain of it." I raised my eyes to heaven and huffed out a breath. "For all that men profess women gossip, I should have realized Graham could not have kept this news to himself. I should have made some attempt to keep them apart."

A servant broke into their conversation, handing Ridley a note. After a hasty glance at it, he excused himself from Graham.

"He's leaving." Lottie squeaked and nudged me with her elbow.

Indeed, he was, and at a brisk pace. He was halfway across the room already, past the entrance to the music room, and headed toward the family rooms of the house. I tugged on her arm. "We have to stop him."

A lady could never be seen running across a crowded room, but we moved as swiftly as propriety allowed. Still, he was nowhere to be seen by the time we rounded the corner and turned down a shadowed hallway. There were two doors along one side of the passage and a green baize door at the end that led to the servants' stairs. He might have left that way, but I couldn't imagine him escaping without any funds. One of the other doors must lead to an office or study.

I stopped in indecision and Lottie bumped against me. Somehow, we had to keep Ridley here until the police arrived, but we couldn't do that until we found him. I pulled her closer.

"Go through there," I said, pointing to the servants' door at the end of the hall. "If he went that way you should be able to hear him on the stairs."

As she passed by me, I turned back to the first door, pushed it open a crack, and peered into what appeared to be a library. I would have backed out again if not for a shuffling noise behind the door.

"What are you doing?"

I started at the sound of a female voice from within the room. Caroline Archer.

"Isn't it obvious? I'm making my escape. And if you're wise, you'll do the same."

"Didn't you hear me? Gordon's been arrested. You must help him."

Ridley released a grunt. "If I know your husband, he's helping himself, revealing everything to the police even as you're standing here, wasting my time."

Another rustling noise came from the room as I felt a tap on my shoulder. I smothered my gasp and turned to find Lottie behind me. I motioned for her to stay quiet and returned my ear to the space between the door and frame.

"Damn it, Ridley! You can't leave us to face this alone."

"Can and will, my dear. I fear Archer is telling the police all about me, and this party is about to come to an abrupt end. I prefer to be gone when that happens. But I have one more task for you before I go."

"Your tasks have not worked so far. Write a note to the columnist. Go threaten the editor. Stir up suspicion about Evingdon. None of it has helped, Hugo. We've had enough of your tasks."

"Fine, consider it a favor then. Take this."

Caroline let out a gasp. "If you're telling me to shoot myself, Ridley, I hardly count that as a favor."

Ridley tsked. "Do you honestly think me foolish enough to hand you a loaded pistol? It's Mary's. I invited Evingdon here tonight. Go hide it in his carriage and pay a groom to tip off the police. At least that way your husband won't be hanged for murder."

"He didn't kill them," Caroline said as footsteps sounded and approached the door.

"He's coming," I whispered, and took a step away from the door. At least I attempted to do so, but my foot landed on Lottie's loose hem. I staggered back, she lurched forward, and we both tumbled through the door in a heap.

Caroline shrieked. I struggled to return to my feet, assist Lottie to hers, and still keep an eye on Ridley, who rifled through his document case and pulled out—oh, dear, a gun.

Though I'm loath to admit it, Lottie and I cowered against one another as Ridley motioned us farther into the room, and we moved as one body toward the fireplace.

Ridley grumbled low in his throat, before exploding. "Gad, Lady Harleigh, one would think you're determined to make my life difficult. First you send your maid to question my valet, then you spy outside the door. Did no one ever tell you eavesdropping will bring you nothing but trouble?"

He waved his arm at the two of us while heaving a sigh. "Now I have to determine what to do with you."

Caroline looked on in horror, Mary's revolver dangling from her fingers. "Do? You can do nothing with them. Your only choice now is to go to the police and confess."

"Ha! I'll choose escape if you don't mind, and if you've any sense, you'll do the same." Ridley still pointed the gun toward us but cast a glance at Caroline. "Bring me the key from the desk. We'll lock them in here. That should give you enough time to find Evingdon's carriage and hide the revolver."

"And then what?" Caroline had obediently followed his orders, but squinted at him as she handed over the key. "What good is accusing Evingdon, when they are here to tell the police the truth?"

Ridley scoffed and dismissed her question with a wave of his hand. "The police won't believe them. Evingdon's her cousin." He jerked his head toward the door. "You leave now. I'll lock the door."

Caroline tossed a nervous glance our way and took a step toward the door. In that moment, I realized Ridley was lying. "He's going to shoot us, Caroline!" I called out.

She froze just as she passed Ridley, who gave me a narrowed-eye glare.

"Don't give him any ideas," Lottie whispered.

"It isn't my idea." I pushed the girl behind me and took a step forward. "You know he can't leave us alive. He's already murdered two people; what do another two lives matter at this point?" I stared into Ridley's cold eyes as I spoke, but just outside my focus, I could see Caroline, behind him, slowly turn around. Surely, if she looked at us, she wouldn't let Ridley commit two more murders.

"What's worse, Caroline, is that Ridley has his escape all planned, but he's leaving you and your husband to face the consequences of his actions." I tried to keep my voice steady, but even I could hear the desperation. "This is all Ridley's fault and he's going to get away. If you let him."

Caroline was watching me now, her lips compressed, eyes narrowed. Anger was quickly replacing fear. I had her attention, but Ridley was growing impatient.

"What's to become of you, Caroline? Even if your husband doesn't hang for murder, he'll go to prison. Your fortune will be confiscated. How will you live?"

"That's enough." Ridley turned to Caroline. "This is your last chance. Go now, or I swear I'll shoot you, too."

"You have a gun," Lottie said, her voice shaking. "Shoot him."

Caroline's expression twisted with rage as Ridley jerked back around to face us. "For God's sake, the revolver is empty. It's of no use to—"

Ridley's head twisted to the side as Caroline swung the revolver in an arc that connected with his skull. He collapsed to the floor.

Caroline stared down at him, her mouth gaping open in horror. The revolver slipped from her fingers and clattered to the floor.

I pulled away from Lottie, rushed toward Caroline, and threw an arm around her, drawing her away from Ridley and toward a chair. "Well done, my dear. Thank you."

She slumped into the wingback chair and leaned forward, dropping her head in her hands. "The selfish rotter." She turned her face to look at me, her eyes devoid of emotion. "He had it coming, don't you think?"

Indeed, I did.

Chapter 24

It became the scandal of the summer. The *Daily Observer* had their exclusive story, and as a columnist for that fine periodical, I had the honor of reporting it all. Well, not all, of course. I could hardly give a firsthand account of Ridley's capture without giving myself away. But everything that came after was fair game.

Caroline had struck Ridley with enough impact to render him unconscious. Lottie and I had only just secured him with the silk tiebacks from the draperies, when we heard the commotion coming from the reception rooms. I sent Lottie to see what had happened, and she returned with Delaney and two constables. Miriam Ridley followed on their heels and froze in the doorway as she took in the scene.

The constables pushed past her to lift the trussed, but now sputtering, Ridley to his feet. The man loudly professed his innocence as Delaney retrieved the pistol and document case from the floor. Miriam's face showed more dismay than surprise when Delaney told Ridley anything he said would be taken down as evidence.

"I'm going with you," Caroline announced, rising unsteadily to her feet. "That man couldn't tell the truth if his own life depended upon it."

Delaney took her arm and guided her through the door, where she exchanged a vicious glare with Miriam.

"For heaven's sake, take him out the back way," Miriam ordered, as the constables led Ridley away. She followed them all out as George and Charles pushed their way into the room.

"What the devil happened here?" In two strides, George reached my side, clutching my arms as he looked me up and down. "Are you well? He didn't harm you?"

I bobbed my head. "We are fine." Though now that he was here, I wanted to collapse in his arms.

Charles led Lottie to an overstuffed chair near the window and seated himself on the arm. "I say, you were only meant to watch the bounder, not capture him."

Delaney returned alone, took in the room with a glance, and headed to the desk to examine the papers Ridley had left scattered about. "To return to the first question," he said, "what happened here? And how did you determine Sir Hugo was our culprit?"

"I really only determined he was involved in Archer's scam." I gave Delaney an account of our evening from the time Charles and Hetty had left to retrieve him. "His plan to leave the country made me suspicious, but I didn't know he was the murderer until he produced the pistol."

"He told Caroline Archer to hide it in Mr. Evingdon's carriage," Lottie said. "They meant to implicate him in the murders."

"I wondered why I was invited," Charles muttered.

"Damn, I should have been here." George pulled me close and rested his cheek on my head. "I hate that you put yourself in danger."

"Just how did you stop him from leaving?" Delaney asked.

"Actually, Caroline Archer stopped him. Ridley thought an unloaded revolver wasn't a weapon and foolishly turned his back on her."

"But she would never have hit him, if you hadn't made her see the truth," Lottie added.

"How did you come to be in the room?"

Lottie explained how she and I had fallen through the doorway and I felt the rumble of laughter George tried to suppress.

"Now I wish even more I'd been here," he said.

"I'm just relieved you came so soon."

"Archer was already pointing a finger at Ridley by the time I caught up with Delaney," he said.

"Did he admit his own guilt in the fraud scheme?" As much as I enjoyed the comfort of George's arms, my curiosity demanded answers. I took a step away and turned my attention to Delaney.

"He denied everything until I showed him the account book and brought up the murder of his sister-in-law," the inspector said. "At that point he immediately owned up to the fraud charges and blamed Ridley for the murders. According to Archer, Ridley had been involved in his scam ever since Archer tried to cheat him."

"Ridley did reveal the scam to Jasper," George added. "But rather than expose Archer, he wanted a percentage of the spoils."

"I assumed as much," I said. "Do you know if Jasper ever told Mary?"

"He did," George said. "And left her the account book. She confronted Archer, and he agreed to stop."

"But he didn't."

"No, and as Mary dug up gossip for her column, she found out Archer was cheating his clients again so she renewed her threat. Archer claimed he wanted to stop, but Ridley threatened to expose him if he did. When he heard about her murder, Archer said he was on the verge of going to the police himself."

George waved a hand toward Charles. "That's just about the time Evingdon and Hetty arrived to tell us about Ridley, which only lent credence to Archer's story, so Delaney was quite eager to bring him in. I was all the more eager to return to the party when I learned the two of you were keeping watch over Ridley."

He gave me a smile, but I saw the strain still etched in his face. I regretted making him so worried, but was rather happy that he cared so much. "I didn't know at the time he was a murderer," I said. Under the weight of his steady gaze I gave him a rueful smile. "Though I admit I suspected."

"Why are you all hiding away back here?" Lily stood in the doorway with Leo just behind, her eyes alight with mischief. "It seems Sir Hugo's just been arrested." Her gaze landed on Delaney and she leaned against the door frame, crossing her arms. "I thought you were missing all the excitement, but it seems you may have been at the heart of it."

For my part, I was happy the excitement was over.

The day I'd been dreading finally arrived; well, the event I'd been dreading anyway—Lily and Leo's engagement party. While I'd come around to understanding that they were deeply in love and the two of them would likely be very happy, it was still hard to let my sister go. I'd only just reunited with her last spring.

"You'll still have her for a few months," Fiona said, as if she'd been reading my mind.

We were at the Kendricks' home, standing at the perimeter of the ballroom, watching Lily and Leo execute their first dance as an engaged couple. When more couples joined in the dancing, I turned back to my friend, pleased she'd made the trip back to town for this party. I'd missed her terribly while we'd worked on this case. She was the most skillful gossip ever born and could have written the Miss Information page without any additional aid from the London servants. But George had reminded me more than once that everything Mary wrote had to remain confidential. So, it was just as well Fiona had been absent. I would have hated to keep secrets from my dear friend.

Now that the case had been concluded, word was out, and all of society buzzed with the news. Archer had been arrested for fraud, Ridley, for two murders. Caroline had clearly known about her husband's misdeeds and had a hand in helping Ridley cast suspicion on Charles, but somehow, she managed to remain a free woman. Since she had saved my life and Lottie's, I was pleased with that conclusion.

I still didn't know whether Miriam had known about Hugo's crimes. He may have kept her in the dark about the murders, but I suspected she knew about the fraud. Oddly enough, she and Caroline remained friends. The two of them, along with the Archer children, quietly slipped away to the Continent a few days ago and were unavailable for comment.

Archer admitted he had Hugo employ Milton, the valet, to keep him close and ensure his silence, but as it turned out, Mr. Milton knew nothing of Archer's scheme.

But even in the midst of this scandal, all the gossip was about Mary Archer and her audacity in writing the Miss Information column—airing their secrets. Can you imagine?

Fiona had just echoed that sentiment, and as the music swelled, we stepped back into an alcove where we could watch the dancers, yet still hold a conversation. "You won't convince me you feel any sense of outrage at all, Fiona. Indeed, I think you wish you could be Miss Information."

She drew back and examined my face, compressing her lips in a pout as she realized I was teasing. "The position is open," I added with a smile.

"I do wish I could unburden myself of all the knowledge I carry with me—the tales, the scandals." She placed a hand on her chest and sighed. "But you know I only share that knowledge with my closest friends, and only when I'm certain they'll be discreet."

"Such a heavy responsibility," I said.

"Indeed. But though I have no wish to write about gossip, I am extremely jealous you were in possession of so much of it."

I could imagine she was. "Actually, I'm surprised George told you about that. Everything in Mary's files was supposed to remain confidential."

"He didn't tell me what was in the files. Only that he handed them over to you." Her lips twitched up in a smile. "I think he was rather proud of the way you handled yourself."

Fortunately, Fiona turned her gaze to the dance floor and didn't see my cheeks redden.

"It seems as though Mr. Evingdon has transferred his affections to your little protégée. He hasn't left her side all evening."

Following her gaze, I spotted them just as Lottie trod on Charles's foot. I doubted it was the first time this evening. I gave him high marks for courage in even attempting to dance with her, though I'd wager he'd be willing to accept any number of blows for the privilege of holding her in his arms. And rightfully so. Lottie may be lacking in grace, but she more than made up for it with wit, charm, and determination.

"She's become quite a favorite of mine," I said. "He'd be lucky to win her affections." Though by this time I was certain he'd already done so.

At Fiona's expression of surprise, I gave her a firm nod. "And I don't think he is actually transferring his affections. He and Mrs. Archer were not particularly compatible after all."

"No? Yet the poor man was arrested as a spurned lover turned murderer. What a shame if there was no love involved."

"He wasn't arrested, Fiona, but he might have been if not for George and Lottie." I gave a jaunty toss of my head. "And I suppose I played a small part myself."

"It appears he's over the experience now," Fiona said. "Ah, young love!" She gave me a sidelong glance. "And speaking of which, is there something happening between you and George?"

My faced burned again. Heavens, where had that question come from? "Between George and me? Certainly not young love. We are both far too old for such a thing."

A sly smile crept across her lips. "All right then, would I be far off the mark in calling it new love?"

I glowered at the woman. "You would be better to call it nothing at all; then I can be sure you aren't spreading rumors."

"I take exception to that, Frances. Have I ever spread a rumor about you?"

"No, Fiona, of course not." I was instantly contrite.

"And this would be the type of secret I'd treasure, you know. I'd be delighted to learn you and my brother had become close."

"Did I hear something about my sister spreading rumors?" I turned to see the subject of our conversation had joined us. Heavens, how long had he been standing there?

His eyes twinkled with mischief. "How could you suggest such a thing, Lady Harleigh?"

Fiona could barely contain her glee. "I'll leave it to you to explain your accusation to George."

With that parting comment she sauntered off, leaving me in this rather remote corner with George. I took a careful glance at his face only to see him grinning broadly. "Was she angling for the newly opened position of Miss Information?"

I waved a hand in her direction. "She was simply speculating about Lottie and Charles."

"Ah, I think their actions speak for themselves." His grin faded as he became more serious. "What will you do, Frances? Lily is about to be married and I doubt Miss Deaver will be far behind."

I tried for a casual shrug. "There are still some months before Lily's wedding. I hope Aunt Hetty will stay with me. And perhaps you and I will have another case to work on." I gave him a smile. "Partner."

"There is more than one type of partnership, Frances. If I

can't leave you alone for fear someone will shoot you, then I hesitate to leave you alone at all. Perhaps it's time we consider a more permanent form of partnership."

I met his gaze. "The revolver wasn't loaded, George, and if that's another marriage proposal, I think it might be worse than your first."

He shook his head in mock horror. "It couldn't be. The first one was abysmal. But you are giving me plenty of opportunity for practice."

His expression sobered. "I don't know the number, Frances, but I believe there is a limit to the times a man can bring himself to ask the same woman to marry him before finally accepting no for an answer."

My heart raced as the music in the ballroom swelled. I didn't want to say no, but neither would I tolerate another society marriage. I looked up into those lovely green eyes and smiled. "Perhaps I should ensure we don't exceed that limit by offering you a hint."

His brow quirked up. "I'm listening."

"When your reason for asking me to marry you is because you simply can't do without me, then I'll be prepared to say yes."

A devilish grin crossed his lips as he stepped back and took my hand. "Then, madam, prepare yourself to say yes."

In Dianne Freeman's charming Victorian-era mystery series, Frances Wynn, the American-born Countess of Harleigh, finds her sister's wedding threatened by a vow of vengeance.

London is known for its bustle and intrigues, but the sedate English countryside can host—or hide—any number of secrets. Frances, the widowed Countess of Harleigh, needs a venue for her sister Lily's imminent wedding, away from prying eyes. Risings, George Hazleton's family estate in Hampshire, is a perfect choice, and soon Frances, her beloved George, and other guests have gathered to enjoy the usual country pursuits—shooting, horse riding, and romantic interludes in secluded gardens.

But the bucolic setting harbors a menace, and it's not simply the arrival of Frances's socially ambitious mother. Above and below stairs, mysterious accidents befall guests and staff alike. Before long, Frances suspects these "accidents" are deliberate, and fears that the intended victim is Lily's fiancé, Leo. Frances's mother is unimpressed by Lily's groom-to-be and would much prefer that Lily find an aristocratic husband, just as Frances did. But now that Frances has found happiness with George—a man who loves her for much more than her dowry—she heartily approves of Lily's choice. If she can just keep the couple safe from villains *and* meddling mamas.

As Frances and George search for the culprit among the assembled family, friends, and servants, more victims fall prey to the mayhem. Mishaps become full-blooded murder, and it seems that no one is safe. And unless Frances can quickly flush out the culprit, the peal of wedding bells may give way to another funeral toll. . . .

Please turn the page for an exciting sneak peek of Dianne Freeman's next Countess of Farleigh mystery A LADY'S GUIDE TO MISCHIEF AND MURDER coming soon wherever print and e-books are sold!

Chapter 1

October 1899

Why does it always happen that just when I begin to feel life simply couldn't get any better, fate drops a disaster into my path to prove me right?

While I have no idea how common this phenomenon may be among people in general, it happens to me with rather exasperating frequency. For example, a little over ten years ago, when I was merely Miss Frances Price, I married the man of my mother's dreams and became Frances, Countess of Harleigh. A joyous occasion. I'd done my family proud. My husband was dashing and handsome. I learned too late he was also feckless and philandering. After making me miserable for nine years, he had the audacity to die in the bed of his lover. Once I'd emerged from mourning, I found myself similarly buoyant and optimistic. That period also ended in death, or more precisely, murder.

This cycle of highs and lows weighed on my mind because my life, at the moment, was purely idyllic and I couldn't help but wonder if disaster loomed right around the corner. Regardless, I carried on as usual, taking breakfast in the nursery with my eight-year-old daughter, Rose while we made plans for an upcoming visit to the country. When the time came for her lessons, I slipped downstairs to my library, where Mrs. Thompson, my housekeeper, had left a pot of coffee next to the morning mail on my desk, and waxwings trilled outside the window looking out over the garden. While enjoying my first sip, I learned that was the moment Fate would drop the other shoe.

My sister, Lily, and Aunt Hetty slipped into the room, both looking far too distressed for such a fine morning. Lily was soon to be married, and she'd been floating through the past two months as the happiest of brides-to-be. But with her blue eyes red-rimmed and watery, her complexion blotchy, and her golden hair spilling from its coiffure, she looked rather like a ghoulish version of her usual, sunny self.

The first twinges of apprehension tickled the back of my neck like icy fingers. "Dearest, is something amiss?"

She burst into tears.

Hetty wrapped her arms around Lily and threw a scowl my way. "Now look what you've done."

I must admit the exchange left me baffled. And concerned. I swept around the desk and leaned over my sister. "Lily, please, tell me what happened."

As her tears continued to flow, Hetty settled her in a chair and gave me the news. Lily was with child. I reeled back against the desk and uttered the first word that came to mind.

"Disaster!"

This brought on renewed wailing and a fresh bout of tears from Lily, and a peevish huff from Aunt Hetty.

"Honestly, Frances, you are no help at all. Lily turns to you with her troubles, and this is your reaction?"

I gave her a slow-burning glare, intended to make her cringe, or at least take her criticism elsewhere. It didn't work. Hetty was immune to glares, mine or anyone else's. As my father's sister, she shared his pragmatic nature, dark hair and eyes, and the uncanny ability to make money from anything. Hetty had survived the loss of a beloved husband, made and lost several fortunes, and held her own with businessmen and society matrons alike. She was not to be intimidated by the likes of me.

Instead, she sidled up to Lily and placed a protective arm around her shoulders. As if I were going to harm her in some way. For her part, Lily struggled to fight back her tears and mopped her eyes with a handkerchief.

"Of course I will help. You just took me by surprise." I glanced at my sister and sighed. "Your wedding is only eight weeks away, couldn't you have waited?"

Lily, with the face of an innocent babe, raised her handkerchief to her watery eyes. "That's exactly the point, Franny. We saw no reason to wait." As she waved the handkerchief dismissively, Hetty drew back and took her own seat. "After all, we'll be married so soon. I had no idea it could happen this quickly. You and Reggie were married for some time before Rose came along. And Aunt Hetty was married for years and never had children. How should I have known?"

How should I have known, was not likely to pass muster as an excuse for our mother. I could just imagine her reaction had I made such an announcement before my wedding. Though now that I think about it, it wasn't as if there'd been time. My mother had singled Reggie out as a possible husband for me before we even left New York. A mutual friend introduced us soon after we'd arrived in London. Reggie and I danced a few times, he and my mother came to terms, and we were married without ever having a chance to become acquainted.

Have I mentioned the marriage was a disaster? Is it any wonder I wanted Lily and Leo to have a long engagement period? To take some time and come to know one another?

Clearly, they came to know one another all too well. Now, what were we to do?

"Leo suggested we elope," Lily said, almost in a whisper.

Her words pulled me from my thoughts. "Oh, no, dear. That will never do."

She balled the handkerchief in her fist. "Well, we can't wait eight weeks as we'd planned. How on earth will I explain giving birth so soon? It would be less than six months."

"You wouldn't be the first, dear." Hetty patted her hand.

"No, you wouldn't but if it can be avoided, so much the better. However, an elopement is almost a proclamation that one is with child. I agree the original wedding date is out of the question, but an elopement is not a satisfactory alternative." So where did that leave us?

Since Lily seemed to have recovered herself, I ventured to ask another tricky question. "What does Leo's mother say?"

She gawked at me as if I'd just asked her to set herself on fire. "Mrs. Kendrick says nothing as she has absolutely no idea of our situation." Her voice had become a shriek. "You cannot seriously think I'd tell her? Frances, I'd die first." She stared and clutched at her throat as if choking. "I'd simply die."

"Well, we can't have that, but how do you intend to keep this from her?"

"That was the point of the elopement."

I was relieved to see Hetty narrow her eyes in confusion. "Were you planning to elope and stay away for nine months?" she asked.

Lily took a breath to speak, then stopped herself, sinking against the back of the chair. "Bother. I suppose we'd have to, wouldn't we?"

"Leo couldn't do that, dear, at least not without giving his father a very good reason. Unless he can come up with a plausible lie, you will still have to tell them the truth. Mr. Kendrick isn't likely to allow him a nine-month wedding trip."

Leo Kendrick was a businessman. In fact, he was a partner in his father's business. I wasn't entirely sure just what he did, except a portion of the business involved mining and part, manufacture. His grandfather had started the company, and his father expanded it and made it quite profitable. Enough to raise his daughters as gently bred ladies and send his son to the best schools and raise him as a gentleman. Though he planned for Leo to take over the running of their enterprise eventually, all four of the children were expected to make advantageous marriages.

Leo's oldest sister, Eliza, had done just that, and Leo's choice of Lily also met with his father's approval. Thank goodness, as the two were hopelessly in love. They'd have married months ago if I hadn't urged them to wait. I pulled my thoughts up short. I was not about to take responsibility for Lily's pregnancy.

But looking at her now, lost in her misery, I felt compelled to come up with a solution—as did Hetty, it seemed. Since she'd come in here to support Lily, she must have known about her condition at least a bit longer than I.

"Have you any ideas, Aunt Hetty?"

She shook her head. "I thought an elopement was their best option."

"It's not a horrible option, but it should be considered only as a last resort. Surely, we can think of something better."

"You're right." Hetty squared her jaw in determination. "We are three intelligent women. What would we do if we had every possible option to hand?"

"If Graham weren't selling Harleigh Manor, we could arrange a wedding there in under a week," I said. "Just have the closest family members in attendance. As long as we're not in town no one will feel snubbed if they aren't invited."

I sighed and leaned against the desk behind me. Selling the old family home was the best idea my brother-in-law ever had. The behemoth of a mansion had sucked several fortunes into its very walls, including mine. That fortune was the only reason Reggie had married me. Not that I didn't have other redeeming qualities. I was a consummate hostess, an intelligent conversationalist, and knew how to dress and act in society. While I was taller than the average woman, the rest of me was indeed average—fair skin, as society required, dark hair, blue eyes—nothing off-putting, but nothing to inspire my late husband to hold me in higher regard than my dowry.

Reggie's brother, Graham was now Earl of Harleigh, and he just couldn't afford to keep Harleigh Manor going. Fortunately, the house itself was built by his great grandfather on an un-entailed part of the property, and he was free to sell.

But it would be lovely to have use of that house now.

"A wedding in less than a week might be a bit too soon," Hetty said. "Your mother will only just be arriving, and Lily can't get married without her."

"Can't I?" Lily's lip trembled. I sympathized with her plight, but she could not marry before our mother arrived, then leave me to deal with her fits of temper. Not that she wouldn't be justified after traveling all the way from New York to attend her youngest daughter's wedding.

"No, dear, you can't." I turned to consult the calendar on my desk. "Her ship arrives on Tuesday. It would be wise to marry as soon as possible after her arrival so as to leave her less time to fuss about the change in plans."

"That's why the elopement was such an attractive idea," Lily said. "Leo's parents are away from town this week. Mother won't be here. We could marry and present them with a fait accompli."

In fact, they'd be presenting nothing. I'd be stuck with the dirty work. "That's not fair to Patricia Kendrick. Leo is her only son. She'd want to be at his wedding." I crossed my arms in front of me and gave her a long, hard look. "And the two of you will have to tell her about the baby at some point, don't you think?"

"Not until after the honeymoon. But you are right. I expect

her to be disappointed in us, but if we marry quickly, at least she'll see we took some action to mitigate the gossip." She gave me a pleading look. "That should help, don't you think?"

"Only if we find a country house in which to hold this small family wedding. So far, we only know what isn't available."

Hetty cocked her head as she turned to me. "Don't some families ever lease their homes?"

"Not for such short a time." Hetty and Lily had only been living in London since April when Lily made her debut. They still had much to learn about the ways of society. Aristocratic society, that is. One could lease one's manor out for a year or longer, and though everyone would know the family was having financial trouble, taking this step would seem like a sensible way out of those troubles. Renting one's family home out for a week, however, would give the appearance of running a hotel and would reek of middle-class business. It simply wasn't done.

"What of Leo's sister and her husband?" I ran through a mental list of distant acquaintance names. "The Durants, if I remember correctly? I know they keep a house in town, but where is Mr. Durant's family seat?"

Lily wrinkled her nose. "I'm not sure where they're from, but Leo would know better than I. Let me fetch him."

She rose and crossed the room as if Leo were waiting just outside in the hall. She opened the door and reached out.

Heavens, he was just outside in the hall.

I cast a glance at Hetty, who shrugged. "We all thought it better if he waited while Lily gave you her news."

Leo, usually friendly and gregarious, shuffled into the room, his head down. He darted nervous glances at me while Lily tugged him along behind her—a sight in itself. Leo was not a tall man, but he had a square, sturdy build, and Lily was so petite it looked as though she were guiding a repentant Goliath to a chair.

Good. He couldn't be any more uncomfortable than I, and

he'd been a party to bringing this situation upon us. I invited him to sit while I searched for the right words to begin.

Hetty had no such problem. "We've been discussing your situation, Mr. Kendrick, and Lady Harleigh seems to think an elopement might give rise to a great deal of gossip."

Leo chewed on his lip while he studied me, his warm brown eyes wary. "I rather think the gossip would be less vicious over an elopement than if we wait for the proper wedding date."

"Perhaps," I said. "But not by much. Since the wedding invitations have not yet gone out, is it possible for you and Lily to change your venue and date? Somewhere in the country in a week or so, with only family in attendance."

He contemplated the idea, then blew out a breath. "I can see the advantage to a quick, simple ceremony, but where exactly in the country did you intend the wedding to take place?"

"Would it be possible to hold it at Mr. Durant's family home?"

His eyes grew wide. "In Northumberland?"

I slumped back against the desk and let out a tsk. "That far away?"

He bobbed his head. "And I'm not sure they'd be agreeable to the idea. Durant's not very close to his family. Don't know if he'd be willing to ask them."

"Well, that settles it," Lily said. "We will have to elope." She perched on the arm of Leo's chair. "And we should do it quickly while your parents are away."

I hated the idea but before I could comment, a knock sounded at the door and Mrs. Thompson poked her gray head inside.

"Mr. Hazelton is here for you, my lady."

"Is he?" I couldn't stop the smile that slipped across my lips. No matter what problems bore down on me, just the thought of George Hazelton drove them from my mind.

"Must you see him now?" Lily flashed me a look of impatience.

I rose to my feet. "Yes, I must. He's on his way to Risings, so I'm sure he won't be here long, dear. Besides, you and Leo have a great deal of planning to do." I shot her a warning look as I followed Mrs. Thompson out. "Don't you dare leave before I return."

The second I stepped through the drawing room door, George pulled me into his arms. I made no protest. On the contrary, I thoroughly approved of his actions. George Hazelton and I were to be wed, though we kept that lovely secret to ourselves, so as not to steal Lily's thunder. Once she and Leo married, we could make our announcement.

I released a small sigh at the thought of Lily's wedding.

George pulled back and gave me a penetrating look. "That sounded nothing like a sigh of pleasure, Frances. Is something wrong?"

Dearest George. Still in his arms, I reached up to brush back a dark lock of hair. I loved that I had to tip my head back to look into his eyes, but was close enough to see the dark rim surrounding the paler green iris, so full of mystery. It could take years to unravel the mystery of this man, and I would treasure every one.

Slipping my hand into his, I led him over to the cozy conversation area of a large tea table surrounded by plump sofas and chairs, upholstered in a blue and white print. We settled into one of the sofas. "Just a little trouble with Lily and Leo's wedding plans. Nothing so terrible, I suppose."

He frowned, making two vertical lines appear between his brows. "Please tell me it won't keep you from joining me at my brother's home next week. A romantic rendezvous requires the presence of both parties. I can't do it without you, you know."

I placed a hand over my heart. "Ah, yes. You, me, and the dozen people who make up your shooting party. The ambiance leaves me breathless."

"I've only invited the Evingdons, my sister, and her husband. The rest are neighbors who won't be staying at the house so I believe I can arrange the ambiance you seek." His voice dropped to a low growl, sending shivers across my shoulders.

George was the youngest brother to the Earl of Hartfield, who was currently traveling on the continent with his wife, a second honeymoon of sorts. They set out on their trip a month ago and planned to continue their travels for another. As this was quite some time spent away from the estate, the earl had asked George to check on Risings, to ensure everything continued running smoothly. He agreed, of course, and would be leaving today for a stay of two weeks. And what would two autumn weeks in the country be without a shooting party?

The prospect of such an event left him as excited as a child with a new puppy. He'd asked me several times to join him, and I finally conceded. Though with Lily's wedding coming up, I thought I could only spare a week.

"Actually, this spot of trouble means I may be able to join you even sooner."

His brow smoothed as he grinned. "Have they decided to elope then? Wise choice."

I shrugged. "As it happens, it's their only choice."

"You're serious." He leaned back and took me in with a glance. "Truly? After all their plans they intend to elope?"

"They must marry soon." I gave him a meaningful look.

He responded with a blank stare. "They are marrying soon."

Clearly, I needed to work on my facial expressions. "No. I mean they must marry immediately."

His raised brows told me he finally understood. "Isn't your mother on her way as we speak? She'll be terribly disappointed if she misses the wedding."

"As will Leo's mother, but we couldn't think of another option. I suggested we put together a small family ceremony in the country, but Harleigh Manor is for sale, and so, unavailable." I shrugged. "As Leo's parents have no country home, there is nowhere to gather even a small family party."

"They could come to Risings. Plenty of room there."

"That's lovely of you to offer, but your brother is no relation to any of us. We cannot ask him to host a wedding, even a small one. It's far too much of an imposition."

"Correction." He held up his index finger. "You are soon to be my brother's sister, a very close relation indeed." A second finger joined the first. "He is not in residence, thus no imposition at all. And finally," his ring finger joined the others, "I am already hosting a shooting party as Hartfield has given me leave to entertain as I wish. Another dozen people or so will make no difference." He gave me a nudge with his shoulder. "Bring them to Risings."

I bit my lip, hardly believing my good fortune, or Lily's good fortune as it were. Perhaps this could work after all. Risings was in Hampshire. Not far at all. We could gather the immediate family quickly. My mother would arrive in just a few days, and both she and Patricia Kendrick could attend their children's wedding. This could work. A quick but proper wedding. No disappointed parents. Society none the wiser.

"If you are in earnest, and you really don't mind." I paused, giving him a chance to reconsider, but he merely cocked his head, awaiting my answer.

I leaned my head against his shoulder, relieved to have a solution. "Thank you, George. That would take care of everything."

"I am always happy to help you in any endeavor. And I'd also hate to exclude a mother from her child's wedding."

A grimace twisted my lips as I gazed up at him. "I confess the thought of telling my mother she missed the wedding is largely what motivates me." I shuddered at the thought.

He nodded. "Yes, I've met your mother. I would not want to be the bearer of bad news either."

"Well, now neither of us has that onerous task." I hugged his hand to my cheek. "Thank you, George. You always manage to have the solution to my problems."

"You offer the best rewards." He twined his fingers with mine and brought us both to our feet.

"I don't recall offering a reward."

"You'll be joining me at Risings at least a week before I expected you. I'd call that a reward."

He pulled his watch from his pocket, unaware he'd removed a letter at the same time. It fell to the floor while he checked the time.

"Do you leave right now?" I asked.

"Almost, I have a stop to make first, so I should be off."

As he headed toward the entry hall, I picked up his letter and trailed behind him. "Is your stop at Newgate prison?"

"What?" He snapped around so quickly I almost ran into him. "No. Why would you ask such a thing?"

I pulled back in surprise, the letter dangling from my fingers as I handed it to him. "This fell from your pocket." The lines of tension around his mouth faded as he relaxed his jaw. He took the envelope and shoved it back into his coat.

"I couldn't help noticing it came from Newgate. Are you corresponding with a prisoner?"

He let out a sharp laugh. "Hardly that, but it does relate to my errand. I'm taking it to the Home Office." He rested a finger against my lips. "Don't even ask. You know I can't tell you."

"I'm marrying a very mysterious man," I said, the words distorted by the pressure of his finger on my lips. With a smile, he replaced the finger with his own lips, and I was reminded how much I loved him.

A few minutes later, I'd seen him out the door and leaned back against it, considering the morning's events. I'd been presented with a somewhat sticky problem and, with George's help, managed to work through it. Holding the wedding at Risings was the perfect solution.

Fiona, George's sister and my best friend, would be there as her husband, Sir Robert, would be joining the shoot. She'd be a great help. Once I determined how to route my mother to the country when she arrived, this should be a relatively simple operation. One small wedding to plan. How difficult could that be? Perhaps I'd broken my cycle of highs and lows.